SAHARA DUST

A RANDA SOREL MYSTERY

Sahara Dust

Jim Ingraham

FIVE STAR
A part of Gale, Cengage Learning

GALE
CENGAGE Learning

Detroit • New York • San Francisco • New Haven, Conn • Waterville, Maine • London

GALE
CENGAGE Learning·

LIBRARY OF CONGRESS CATALOGING-IN-PUBLICATION DATA

Ingraham, Jim.
    Sahara dust : a Randa Sorel mystery / Jim Ingraham. — 1st ed.
        p. cm.
    ISBN-13: 978-1-4328-2508-9 (hardcover)
    ISBN-10: 1-4328-2508-9 (hardcover)
    1. Women detectives—Fiction. 2. Murder—Investigation—Fiction. 3. Police—Florida—Fiction. 4. United States. Federal Bureau of Investigation—Fiction. I. Title.
    PS3609.N467S35 2011
    813'.6—dc22   2011021898

First Edition. First Printing: September 2011.
Published in 2011 in conjunction with Tekno Books and Ed Gorman.

Printed in the United States of America
1 2 3 4 5 6 7 15 14 13 12 11

This book is for Slim, Pete, and Stefanie

CHAPTER ONE

Tyonek Horse was standing in shadows across the street from a café called "The Brig," watching people strolling along the brightly illuminated sidewalk, young and middle-aged couples walking hand in hand gazing into lighted shop windows. He was listening to waves crashing on the beach down the alley behind him. For more than a half hour he had been waiting for the arrival of Woodrow Barstow whom he intended to kill. This was in the late evening near a bridge on a barrier island off the gulf coast of Florida.

Because of the oppressively moist heat he knew he looked eccentric in his baseball cap and nylon windbreaker. He could have tossed the cap, but he had to wear the jacket, not only to hide the gun, but more importantly to hide the stainless steel prosthesis clamped to his right forearm. They would easily forget the man in a cap and jacket. They would never forget the man with the claw. He briefly considered that his Western boots, mostly hidden by his pant legs, might be remembered, but probably not—a lot of men wore Western-style boots. He wore them because they gave him an emotional connection to his Montana roots. He liked the two-inch heels. Although he had lived most of his life in the East, he was still at heart a Western Indian.

He hadn't seen Woody in months and had spoken to him only a few times during the investigation in D.C., but he'd have no trouble recognizing him. Years of training had given him a good memory for faces, and Woody's pock-marked face was unforgettable. That Woody had registered at the Sleepy Pelican Motel under an artificial name didn't necessarily indicate that he was here on a covert assignment or that he was still on the navy payroll. Even if he was, his death, if carefully managed, would go down as a simple murder. There'd be no reason for anyone to suspect it had anything to do with anything.

With cold predatory eyes he watched frolicking girls down the street in shorts and belly shirts screaming in playful laughter as they romped through puddles, pushing and splashing each other. He fixed his gaze on the tallest one, a blonde no more than seventeen. She had long tanned legs and an athletic grace he found attractive. He fixed the image of her indelibly in his mind for use later when he was alone in his motel room. Images of young girls and occasional prostitutes had become his only sexual companionship. Real women were repelled by his claw. The last real women he had spent any time with had vomited when he unstrapped the prosthesis in front of them.

It was while he was memorizing the image of the leaping girl that he saw Woody beyond her down the sidewalk. He watched him step into the street to avoid getting splashed. He looked different. His hair was long, pulled back from his face into a ponytail. He was in T-shirt and shorts and some kind of yellow shoes instead of the rumpled suits and brown wingtips he had worn in D.C., but he was the same sullen, insolent man he had dealt with up there.

We'll have a few drinks and talk about the investigation. If he came here in a car, I'll ask for a ride; if he walked here from his motel, I'll offer him a ride home. Either way I'll get him to an isolated spot. I'll make it clean. One bullet.

Reciting this to himself, he slipped his left hand into the slash pocket of his jacket and ran his knuckles over the grip of the subcompact pistol he had taken from the handbag of a prostitute in northern Virginia. He had personally run the ID numbers and learned that it was linked to a pimp in upstate New York. Eventually he would get rid of it, although he'd hate to—new, it would go for better than five hundred dollars. When he did get rid of it he'd make sure the police would find it. They'd trace it back to the pimp.

Tyonek crossed the street and followed Woody inside the café and, slightly repelled by the strong odor of whiskey on Woody's breath, he nudged him playfully with his elbow, careful to keep the prosthesis buried in the slash pocket of his jacket.

"Almost didn't recognize you in that hairdo."

Woody turned, glanced at Tyonek with indifference, said nothing and looked away. Tyonek took in the bulbous nose and pock-marked cheeks. Woody reminded him of an old cowboy actor—an unpleasant, squinty-eyed man with attitude.

"Want to sit outside where you can smoke, or get a table?" As the words came out he cringed from the subservience in his voice. He was grinning at Woody like a craven schoolboy, not that he felt inferior to him. It's just that Woody had a strong personality Tyonek could adjust to only by becoming belligerent, and right now that wouldn't be to his advantage.

Woody was paying no attention to him. In stale air and odors of whiskey, he was looking at heads and faces at the bar and at tables down the freight-car of a room, dimly lighted, fragments of conversations bouncing around it, flights of laughter. He made an affirmative grunt and headed past the tables, brushing arms and shoulders of seated people, ignoring their looks of protest. He found an empty table near the screened doorway that led to the outdoor smoking deck. He pulled out a chair, swung a leg over the back and sat down, resting both arms on the stained laminate, a man who seemed totally indifferent to the impression he was making upon others, a self-centered, self-satisfied, arrogant man who deserved to die.

9

"So where is he?" he said, fingering a cigarette from his shirt pocket.

"Don't smoke, please!" Tyonek said. "We don't want someone coming over. We don't need the attention."

A taunting smile simmered for a moment in Woody's eyes. He grunted—his way of acknowledgment—and tucked the cigarette behind his ear. "Then why meet here with all these people?"

"The heat," Tyonek said. "To escape the heat." Actually he had chosen this public place because asking Woody to meet him in some secluded spot would invite suspicion.

Woody looked at the windbreaker and was apparently amused by it. He grunted a kind of *harrumpf* through his nose and waved at a waitress. "Over here," he said, wiggling a finger, fully expecting the girl to rush right over to him, his tone demanding it. And she did. She even seemed apologetic for keeping him waiting. He had that kind of compelling personality—a dominating man Tyonek admitted he was afraid of. Not physically, although he was twice Tyonek's size. It was his relentless, unending inquiries Tyonek feared. Woody was a very clever investigator who could ruin everything.

Squinting at the girl, a tall kid with thin arms, Woody said, "A double scotch whiskey, and no ice."

The girl didn't look at Tyonek. She was about to leave when he said, "I'll have a beer, any brand."

"Oh," and she wrote something on her pad, apologetic for having slighted him.

Woody watched her move past customers crowded at the bar. "So, what do you want?" breathing whiskey fumes across the table. He didn't appear to be drunk, but, as Tyonek had learned in D.C., it was hard to tell.

"When I found out you were here—"

"Cut the shit, Tyonek. You knew damn well Frye would call

10

me. And you knew how I would respond. So why did you want me over here? Is Abu queering your game?"

"My game? I don't have a game. But that's not why I mentioned it to him. I didn't intend to use him." There was a pleading in his voice he couldn't suppress. Why pleading? He didn't give a damn whether this man liked him or despised him.

Woody slammed his palm on the table, drawing nervous glances. Tyonek jumped, startled wide-eyed. People around them stopped talking. Anxious eyes stared at them as Woody studied Tyonek with sullen disdain. "You called Frye knowing he would call me. You found out I booked in at the Sleepy Pelican. And it wasn't Abu Mosul you wanted me to find over here. He knows that you know where he is."

"I don't! I only saw him that once!"

"And you think I'm interested in him."

You're here, Tyonek confided smugly to himself. Aloud he said, "Colleagues on the East Coast told me you were asking about him."

"And Paris. Is she here?"

"Paris? No. Isn't she out west somewhere?"

Woody took in the look of surprise. It didn't fool him.

"I suppose you wonder why *I'm* here," Tyonek said.

Woody laughed. "If you were any more transparent, Tyonek, you'd be a window."

The waitress brought their drinks. Woody swirled his glass, tilted his head back and emptied the whiskey into his mouth. He smacked his lips and handed the girl a ten-dollar bill. She took the money and glanced, not at Tyonek, but at his nearly filled bottle.

Tyonek dismissed her with a flick of his fingers. "I wasn't using him to find you, if that's what you think. Why would I do that?"

"I've never figured out why you do anything," Woody said,

11

searching around as though for something more interesting to look at.

"You can pretend to be retired . . ."

"I am retired," Woody said.

"But you're still hunting. You were asking about Abu Mosul in Miami gunshops. And you know Raphael Cardozo is here."

"Who?"

"The arms dealer. You know who he is."

Woody leaned to one side and took out his wallet. He searched as though for something to write on, finally removed a small card. He waved at the waitress. When she came over, he asked for a pencil. She handed him a small pen and watched him write something on the card.

"There's been a convergence down here," Tyonek said, deciding that it didn't matter how much he revealed. Maybe by opening up a little, Woody might feel more comfortable with him, let his guard down.

"What kind of convergence?"

"A lot of people are here you've been interested in."

Woody gave the pen back to the girl, again watching her walk away.

"And that's why you wanted me here?"

"I don't know why you think that. It was just a casual conversation with the captain . . ."

"Bullshit," Woody said. He pushed his chair back. Without explanation, he got up and walked toward a sign that read REST ROOMS. There were at least four men down there apparently waiting to use the men's room. Tyonek watched Woody turn around and head for the front exit, making no sign to Tyonek that he was going outside. Tyonek hurried to the front door and watched Woody cross the street and go into an alley that led down to the beach.

A hot glow leaped to his chest.

Better than I had planned!

There would be no lights on the beach. This time of year it was darkened by law to protect the warming nests of sea turtles. Shades were drawn on every window that faced the Gulf of Mexico. When baby turtles emerged, it was lights on the horizon that were to guide them to the sea. Lighted cottage windows would distract them. If a hatchling emerged from the sand at night it stood a chance for survival. If it left the nest in daylight it would be picked up by a frigate bird and eaten.

No one will see it happen, and the crashing of waves on the sand will muffle the sound of the gun.

To avoid being seen following Woody down the alley to the beach, Tyonek hurried past three cottages and slipped between them, his feet crunching on dry sand. He could smell dead fish as he emerged through a tangle of sea oats and felt a salty breeze on his face. He could see nothing except lights on a distant causeway. He listened to waves spilling over the wet sand, anguishing that he couldn't see Woody when suddenly he saw a small flaring light less than a hundred feet from him. Woody had lighted a cigarette. Tyonek's pulse shot up as he removed the gun from his pocket and walked directly toward the tiny red glow of the cigarette. He could smell whiskey on Woody's breath as he walked up to him. While he pressed the gun into Woody's chest he felt something warm on his knee. He pulled the trigger. The gun jumped back at him as Woody collapsed without a sound. Tyonek bent over him and felt along his inert body to his jaw line. There was no throbbing in the moist neck. Not until then did he notice the smell of urine. Woody had been relieving himself. It was his urine that had spilled on his knee. He could feel the clammy moisture chafing his skin as he hurried across the sand and came out to the street a quarter of a mile south of the café. He looked at the wet spot on his leg and felt the chafing with disgust as he walked to the parking lot and got into his

Taurus. His heart was pounding and his hand shook nervously as he drove off.

He felt ecstatic! *I killed him and no one saw me!*

Following a habit he had acquired while stationed in Asia, he removed his boots inside the back entryway of his apartment, left them there and went inside. He put his soiled pants and socks into the washing machine in the bathroom. In the morning he would toss the pants into a dumpster. The thought of wearing them again repulsed him. He unharnessed the prosthesis and stood for a long time looking at the pistol. Although he hated the thought, he'd have to get rid of it. He had another gun, an old police special .38 revolver—clumsy, inaccurate, but what the hell. He couldn't keep the pistol. He tossed it onto his bed.

He got into the bathtub and turned on the shower. His heart was pounding, no longer from fear, now from elation!

No more interference from that son of a bitch! Woody Barstow is dead! I got away with it!

CHAPTER TWO

Detective Sergeant Randa Sorel moved her chair a few inches from the streak of sunlight that had been slowly creeping over the carpet. She was in Sheriff Chubleigh's office in Cherokee City, Florida, watching Olivia Mannheim of Naval Criminal Investigative Services lean forward in her chair and draw one leg under her, ready to leave, her expression over the past half hour having gradually changed from puzzled impatience to weary disgust.

A fragrance of roses drifted across the room whenever she moved. "Why are you being so difficult?" Olivia asked. "It was just a body on the beach. What's your interest in the case? You didn't even know the man."

Like Randa, she was sitting at floor level looking up at the sheriff who was in a squeaking chair on a platform behind a large oak desk, his head beneath the framed portrait of his hero, John Edgar Hoover, sunlight glinting on his dyed blond hair, his lips a stubborn slit under a puffy nose.

"You should be glad we want to take it off your hands, for God's sake," Olivia said. She had lifted a black handbag off the carpet and was searching through it, no longer interested in anything he might have to say. She had come here expecting easy compliance with a routine request and had been sandbagged.

"We're all interested in national security, Ms. Mannheim," Chubleigh said, picking at something on his cheek, "but you tell me this man"—he consulted a paper on his desk—"Woodrow Barstow . . . this Barstow retired from your agency five weeks ago. So what's his death to you now? He's a civilian. Was he working on something over here in my jurisdiction? He never cleared it with me?"

"It's pointless to argue with me, Sheriff. The FBI has already come in on this. If you interfere, they'll get an injunction against you." She sighed. "Isn't life difficult enough?" talking to herself, ignoring Randa who she probably thought agreed with Chubleigh.

It interested Randa that Mannheim had now twice avoided telling the sheriff whether Barstow had come to Cherokee City on official business.

"Let me explain my side of it," Chubleigh said, leaning forward, glancing at Randa as though to pin her to the chair. Although she was the primary investigator in this case, she had been brought here not to say anything but to be a witness, a precaution of a dedicated paranoid whose habitual manipulation of people convinced him that everyone he faced was trying to manipulate him.

"Our crime rate is sky high and people are screaming for results," Chubleigh said. "We've had burglaries and muggings and rapes and now this homicide, and you want me to just go out there and tell those reporters 'No comment'? I'm an elected official. You know what that means? I have to produce results. I have to demonstrate that I'm protecting this community."

"I'm only following orders."

"And I'm just trying to do my job. Goddamn it, I've been elected to protect the people in this county, and I deserve more than a hand in my face and orders to back off. Now you can tell me what this is all about or you can stand back and let me do my job. You come in here with your high-handed—"

"I've given you all the reasons I'm authorized to give," Olivia said, wearily adding, "You can take this up with Tyonek Horse. He's the agent they've assigned. Maybe you can work something out with him," getting slowly to her feet, a large woman with heavy legs, wide hips, and matronly bosom in a dark dress. "I'll need a ride to the morgue," she said to Randa, like dropping words on the floor for a servant to pick up.

"Horse, like in the animal?" Chubleigh said.

"He's a Native American."

Without a word the sheriff rose from his desk and walked to the window, his back turned while they left the room, hands in his pockets—his method of dismissing people he didn't feel obliged to please.

Outside under a hot sun in the parking lot Olivia said, "I don't envy you working for that man."

Randa waited until she was belted into the driver's seat of her minivan and was outside the compound before she even considered responding. She wanted to ask Olivia to roll down her window but decided to endure the fragrance, in itself not unpleasant, but too much of it in this confined space, her car baking hot from two hours under the Florida sun.

"What's he care about Woodrow Barstow?" Olivia asked.

Randa made a left turn onto Sierra Street. "Have no idea," waving at a trooper in a white and green patrol car coming toward the compound. She remembered him from an incident in the 'Glades last year; couldn't remember his name.

"It's a federal case," Olivia said. "We should respect that. I hope you don't intend to continue your investigation."

"Until I'm told otherwise, I have no choice," turning north onto Commerce Parkway.

Olivia asked, "Would he defy an injunction?"

"I have no idea." It was a lie. She suspected he might, for a variety of reasons not the least of which was his pleasure in giving people a hard time. Causing problems got him publicity,

17

and nothing seemed to please him more than justifying himself at press conferences. He loved the camera.

"Why does he want to hold onto this case? Or won't you tell me?"

"I work for the man," watching Olivia lift her skirt to allow cooled air to blow up her legs. Not a pretty sight.

"All this heat," Olivia said. "How do you stand it? You a native Floridian?"

"I've been here about eight years," Randa said.

"You have a slight accent."

"I was born in Egypt."

"You don't look Egyptian."

"I'm not. My parents were French and English."

"You came here as a child?"

"My mother brought me here when I was seven. I grew up in Rhode Island."

"Interesting." She flapped the skirt, gazed out the window, scratched her knee. "When do you expect Barstow's daughter?"

"If she started right after my phone call, maybe within the hour."

"Well, I hope I'm gone before she arrives."

"And why is that?"

"I'm getting too old to cope with these things."

"You've talked with her?"

"Briefly." Randa knew that Olivia had been alerted to Barstow's death by fingerprints Randa had sent north. And she knew that Olivia had flown from D.C. to Miami, then crossed the state by air. She hadn't been told that Olivia had stopped in Hampton. To offer condolences? How important was this Woodrow Barstow? Why was his death here in Cherokee City a matter of national concern?

"You went to her home?"

"Briefly," Olivia said.

"You knew her father?"

"Not personally."

They were stopped behind a pickup at a red light, a faint odor of car exhaust leaking through the vents. County Memorial was just beyond the intersection, a big white building over a screen of palms in a parking lot, lots of windows. It always made her think of sitting at bedside watching her lover, Charlie Hawkins, die—among the saddest hours of her life.

Olivia asked, "Have you met her?"

Randa smiled. The woman was probing. "I don't really have any information that can help you." Actually it was when Kirby Barstow contacted the Cherokee City office, alerted apparently by an FBI visit to her home, that Randa had learned that Barstow had a daughter.

Olivia smiled and patted Randa's hand on the steering wheel. "It would be helpful to know how far your investigation has gone, but I suppose you feel a certain loyalty. I do hope your sheriff isn't as obtuse as he appears. The FBI won't tolerate interference. You can be certain of that."

What I'm certain of, Randa thought, is that if Chubleigh defies your injunction, it will be for very different reasons from those he gave you. It will be personal. Everything Chubleigh does is personal. Getting re-elected is at the top of his list, and election day is up there in circles on the squadroom calendar. Randa laughed when she thought of it. She believed that everyone in the sheriff's department, including the cleaning lady, voted for someone other than Chubleigh.

After pulling into a slot in the shade of a live oak, Randa walked with Olivia in silence to the glass doors in the admissions lobby where they waited twenty minutes for the charge nurse to escort them to the room at the back of the hospital that served as a morgue.

Randa steeled herself against odors as she entered the autopsy room. She glanced only briefly at the body on the steel table—a face the color of dust. The body was covered, except for head and feet, by a stained cotton cloth. Because the body had been opened, the room smelled of death.

Olivia stepped right up to the table and leaned over the face. She took a photo from her handbag, studied it, then stared at the dead face. "I guess that's him," putting the photo back into her bag. "I'll need fingerprints."

Randa gave her a questioning look. "I sent them to you. I assume that's how you found out he had died."

"I have to verify that the prints were taken from this body in my presence. Just doing what I'm told."

Randa knew better than complain about bureaucratic redundancy: she dealt with it every day. But she was offended. Where the hell would she get Barstow's fingerprints except off his body? Maybe she thinks we took them off one of those bimbos on the beach he might have been handling—sweaty fingerprints, drunken fingerprints. Would a man stand drunk on the beach in the dark and allow someone to come right up to him and push the muzzle of a handgun into his chest if he was on official duty? Or had he come here to play? Questions Chubleigh had asked and Manheim had refused to answer.

She watched Olivia remove a small camera from her bag and hover over the corpse, taking several pictures of the face, designer panels of her dark dress trailing over the morgue sheet.

"When will the pathologist's report be completed?" she asked the lab tech.

"Have to ask Dr. Fouts."

The phone rang. The tech picked the handset off the wall, listened, gave it to Randa.

A voice from Admissions said, "A Kirby Barstow to see you."

Randa excused herself and walked up the long corridor to the lobby where she found a young woman in white shorts and blouse coming toward her.

"Kirby Barstow," the woman said. "Are you . . . ?"

"Sergeant Sorel," Randa said, feeling moisture in Kirby's small warm hand, interested that she carried her father's last name. No ring on the marriage finger, a woman maybe thirty years old, reasonably attractive.

Randa wished there were some way she could make the viewing easier, but the hospital didn't have a remote system. Kirby seemed strong enough or determined enough to handle the ordeal, her short legs moving briskly down the corridor, maybe forcing herself to get on with it.

She stopped. Olivia Mannheim had come out of the autopsy room.

Looking angrily up at Randa, Kirby said, "I won't talk with her."

"I don't think you'll have to," Randa said, watching Olivia go slowly down the corridor toward a distant seating area.

"Five o'clock this morning!" Kirby said. "She and two men pounding on my door! Took everything my father had at my house! Now she's here?" Eyes fixed on the retreating figure in the dark dress. "What do they want from him? The man's dead! Why can't they leave him alone?"

With head bowed, hands at her face, she went to the wall, leaned against it, sobbing.

Randa would have given a lot to know what was beneath the anger. As the daughter of a career government investigator, Kirby should not have been surprised that the FBI would pick up his personal things to look for classified leftovers. There had to be other reasons for this intensity of feeling.

Kirby was trembling when she stood over the body on the table. She stayed only a few minutes, sobbing openly. As they walked back to the front lobby, Randa remembered the day in Rhode Island when the doctor had left her alone in the hospital

21

room with her mother's dead body.

Looking down at that quiet face was not like saying goodbye to a statue. It was saying goodbye to the past. Although it had happened sixteen years ago, she vividly remembered being afraid because for the first time in her life she was alone—no parents, no brothers or sisters, just herself not even yet a citizen.

And with all that coursing through her, she had stood there like Kirby weeping over the mother she had loved. She wondered what contradictions were swirling through Kirby's head.

In the front lobby, after assuring Kirby that her father's body would be released within a few days, Randa managed to coax her into sitting for a while over coffee in the hospital cafeteria.

"It's a long and boring ride across Alligator Alley," she said as they carried plastic cups to a corner table where Randa sat with her back to the wall. "You said he had just moved in with you?"

"A little over a month ago," Kirby said, staring moodily into her cup, stirring coffee with a plastic spoon, a nick in the painted nail of her index finger. "His things," she said. "His car? When can I get that? And his watch. The other stuff—"

"We didn't find a watch," Randa said. "Just a pale band on his wrist indicating he'd been wearing one. It's why at first we thought it had been a mugging."

"Why'd they be down here if they thought so?" referring apparently to the feds.

"I have no idea," Randa said. "About all we know right now is that your father allowed an assailant to confront him, face to face. We don't know enough to even speculate."

"The watch is a Seiko with a brown leather strap," Kirby said. "My name's on the back." She removed her watch and showed Randa the word Woody etched into the stainless steel case. "His name on mine, my name on his." Tears floated over her eyes. "Christmas presents."

"We're looking for it," Randa said. "It could tag the assailant. They'll hold your father's things for a while. You'll be notified."

"Was there something about it in the local paper? Did it mention his name?"

"A brief notice," Randa said. "Yes, his name was mentioned." Why did she want to know that?

"I guess they didn't get here soon enough to stop it." What did that mean?

"We had his driver's license," Randa said, deciding not to mention that Kirby's father had registered at the motel as Nathaniel Hawthorne. "He had two hundred and eight-five dollars in cash, no credit cards. A motel cardkey. Oh, and a business card . . ." She paused, debated with herself, finally said, "There was a name scribbled on the back—Raphael Cardozo. That name mean anything to you?"

Kirby shook her head.

"Thought it might," Randa said. "It's odd. Most men carry things in their wallets—pictures, receipts, credit cards. The wallet contained none of that. And it was new."

Kirby shrugged, apparently not surprised. "Had he been drinking?"

It wasn't really a question. She knew the answer.

Randa said, "We traced his movements to a bar down at the beach. Because his car was in the motel parking lot, we assume he either walked to the bar or was given a ride. The bar's about a half mile from his motel and a hundred yards or so from where he was shot."

Kirby asked, "You have any idea . . . ?"

"All we know right now is that a witness saw him sitting with a man and saw the man follow him outside. As near as we can tell, your father was shot less than a half hour after he left the bar. He was seen going alone down a short path to the beach.

23

The man wasn't with him. They had been sitting together for only a short time, apparently arguing, two men who seemed to know each other. Did he ever speak of anyone here in Cherokee City?"

"Not to me." Kirby raised her cup and sipped at the coffee, staring across the nearly empty room. "He didn't talk much." She squared around to face Randa directly. "Do you think you can stay with this, the investigation? Will they let you?"

"I don't know. But until I'm told otherwise . . ."

"Why were they so disrespectful?" her eyes pleading with Randa. "They never said so, but it wasn't just that he dealt with classified stuff. It was different. He had his faults, but they didn't have to hate him." She dug into her bag for a tissue. She looked away and blew her nose.

"Why do you think they hated him?"

"They acted like he was a criminal. Things they said. They didn't show any respect for him! He gave his life!" staring hard at Randa, wanting the words to sink in. She got up and carried a soiled tissue to a wastebasket near the serving counter.

When she came back, Randa asked, "What was his specialty?"

"In the service? Naval ordnance. Most recently stuff they used in naval aircraft. He was an expert on high-tech stuff. That's why they transferred him to the NCIS."

"When was that?"

"Four years ago. Something out in Hawaii. I don't know. They brought him in off a cruiser. Some kind of scandal. He never talked about it, just said that's why they sent him there."

"Did those people this morning accuse him of anything?"

"They said things . . . not to me. But I heard them talking. That woman. I heard her say, 'It wouldn't be here,' like it was something specific they were looking for, like they thought he had hidden something."

"Like what?"

"Nothing! He wasn't hiding anything. I helped him unpack. Only his clothes and some papers. They took those. It was like the Gestapo! Dead-panned zombies poking everything, grabbing everything."

"Is it possible," Randa asked, "that your father was here on assignment?"

"He was retired! I do his taxes. He wasn't on their payroll." Randa had no idea how people on covert operations were paid, so that observation wasn't compelling. "That name I mentioned—Cardozo. You've never heard it?"

"No. Who is it?"

"A retired arms merchant. Lives out on Boliva Island."

That interested Kirby, but it didn't elicit a response. Randa watched her rub lip marks off the edge of her cup with her thumb, thinking about something. "The thing is," she said, "if he was working on something, he died a hero. He deserves respect. But they'll disown him. They'll say he was just a drunk somebody found on the beach." She put her hand over her mouth and looked away, staring with tear-filled troubled eyes across the room.

Randa wanted to say she would try to prevent that from happening, but she wouldn't make a promise she couldn't keep. It would depend on Chubleigh. He might not let the investigation go completely to the Feds. He might use media leaks to keep the story alive, but he wouldn't reveal anything the Feds wanted kept secret. He'd be interested in using the case only to get what he wanted. And, she was reasonably certain, what he wanted was the embarrassment of Raphael Cardozo.

That observation was confirmed the instant she got back to Chubleigh's office, having been stopped in the corridor outside the squadroom and told the sheriff was waiting for her.

"National Security, my ass!" Chubleigh roared, pointing Randa

25

toward the chair Olivia Mannheim had been sitting in. Major Buckley, head of CID, Randa's boss, was where Randa had sat. He was leaning back, fingers laced across the belly of his green uniform, a man in his forties, lean, athletic.

Looking at Randa, Chubleigh said, "I want to know why Cardozo's name was in the wallet of that dead man."

"I'm trying to locate the gun dealer whose card—"

"Do that later," Chubleigh said. "I want you in Cardozo's face before the FBI starts crowding us."

"I've heard this Tyonek Horse can be a pain in the ass," the major said.

In this office Randa thought of Buckley as the major. Everywhere else she thought of him as Buckles. In here he deferred to the overbearing personality of the sheriff. Everywhere else he was his own man, not someone you could get close to but easy to work with. Randa liked him. He was intelligent, and in police work intelligence was harder to come by than courage.

"Yeah, well so can I," Chubleigh said. "I don't care how many injunctions they get. This may be my last chance to discredit that bastard." Looking at Randa, he asked, "So what did you learn from the daughter? Is Mannheim gone?"

"I didn't wait to see," Randa said. "I got the impression her father was under suspicion."

"For what?"

"She thinks the FBI were at her place looking for something he was hiding. She has no idea what it is. By the way, he was an ordnance expert."

Chubleigh's eyes narrowed. "What kind?"

"Naval ordnance, I suppose."

"And Cardozo's an arms merchant." He glanced at the major, pleased with himself. "There's your connection."

He got up, planted both hands on the desk and leaned toward

26

Randa. "Go out there right now and put the fear of God into him."

"How do you suggest . . . ?"

She looked at Buckles, but he was no help. He was leaning back in his chair, face lowered, eyes heavy-lidded, studying something on the carpet.

Chubleigh yelled, "Make him think he's a suspect!"

"In the homicide?"

"What the hell else are we talking about?" like she was an idiot for asking.

He went to the window, fists jammed into his pockets. The major got up and led Randa to the door. Outside in the corridor she asked, "Any suggestions?"

Buckles laughed. He was still laughing when he went into his office and closed the door.

Randa knew very little about Raphael Cardozo. He was a retired arms merchant living in a waterfront estate on Boliva, a barrier island just off the coast. He was said to be active politically, mainly through supporting causes that favored minorities. From what Buckles told her, it was Cardozo's money that fueled a dump-Chubleigh movement. She had no idea why he disliked the sheriff. Maybe he didn't. Maybe he just wanted to get a friend into the office.

Apparently he had gone into retirement after being indicted for making an illegal sale to some insurgents in Africa. He was cleared of the charge because of an improper application of Treasury Department regulations. She didn't know the details except that it resulted in a forfeiture of his licenses. His daughter now ran the business.

Randa had never met Cardozo, and she believed as she drove in high sunshine across the causeway onto Boliva that she had never met his daughter.

CHAPTER THREE

Randa was on a ramp outside a seven-foot grilled gate waiting for an attendant to admit her to the waterfront estate. She had shut off the engine to keep the catalytic converter from overheating and was listening to a Mahler symphony, watching a big guy inside the gate in shorts and T-shirt, legs apart, a hand on his hip, a cellular at the side of his head, nodding. He had been nodding and talking for more than a minute.

As she looked above a thicket of trees at four brown pelicans sailing over the tiled roof of Cardozo's white mansion, she could smell the river odors that came into her bedroom through opened windows at night, reminding her of evenings on the Nile watching her friends in the reeds bathing their donkey and telling her to go home because she was a girl—big for her age and able to do what boys did but ridiculed when she tried to.

When the attendant lowered the phone and came to the vertical bars in the gate, she snapped off the cassette player and leaned out the window.

The man yelled. "He wants to know what you want!"

"I want to talk to him. Police business." She was in uniform in a state police cruiser. He knew what she wanted.

He turned his back, raised the phone, did a lot of nodding, lowered the phone.

"He says come back tomorrow."

"I'm not coming back tomorrow," Randa said. "It's now, here, or tomorrow in the sheriff's office with his lawyer"—a phony threat, but he didn't know it.

The man got back on the phone, talked a few seconds, then touched something on the inside of the wall. The grilled gate came slowly open. With a long sarcastic sweep of his arm, the man waved her in.

"Go around the right," he said. "Leave it in one of the spaces there. He's down the other side of the pool at the boat dock."

She made the big circle through a sheltering canyon of trees and nosed her car into a hedge outside a large swimming pool, no one at the tables, no one in the water, a breeze flapping little tassels hanging off table parasols. Two men in green uniforms were spreading mulch under hibiscus shrubs along a path that led through a mangrove basin to the Gulf. Sailboats were moving against a purplish haze out on the horizon.

She came out of the path onto a white beach in a shallow cove. Two young men were sitting on the fallen trunk of a palm tree, their backs to a tangle of mangroves. They were barefoot, both wearing baseball caps and swimming trunks. They were watching an older man, possibly Raphael Cardozo—a short, hairy man in boxer trunks on a catwalk yelling into the empty cockpit of a white fiberglass luxury cabin cruiser that probably cost five times Randa's annual salary.

No one looked at her. She scanned the area for a phone—if there was none, this wasn't Cardozo. But she saw a little box on a post at the catwalk, a wire running up to it out of the ground, probably a phone, installed before cell phones became popular.

"What the hell you hiding for?" the man was yelling. "Get your head out here so I can talk to you! You free-load off my daughter, but you don't own nothing here. These kids want to use her boat. When she ain't here, I tell them what they do, not you. Now get the hell out of there."

A tall man appeared in the companionway, embarrassed when he noticed Randa. It was Claude Lazard, an acquaintance of her boyfriend, Lee Fronzi. What was he doing here? She had met him a few times with a woman he lived with—Lucia Hodges. The name on the boat's transom was LUCIA'S FOLLY. Was Lucia Hodges Cardozo's daughter?

Cardozo turned and gave Randa a onceover. "You the cop?"

"Detective Sergeant Randa Sorel," she said, watching Lazard gathering clothes off the coaming, watching the two boys vaulting over the gunwale.

"Clean it up when you're through," Lazard told them, issuing an order maybe to repair his ego. "The owner'll be home in a day or so." He gave Randa a wave. "Nice to see you again," draping a towel over his shoulder, coming down the catwalk— good-looking man in his early forties, gray hair neatly combed, a small dark jungle on his chest.

Now and when she had met him months ago, she found him unattractively pretentious, vain, and self-centered. But, because he was Lee's friend, she greeted him warmly.

It seemed odd that Lee had never mentioned Cardozo in connection with Lucia Hodges. She and Lee had been lovers for almost a year and, Randa thought, shared everything. But he had never shared the knowledge that Lucia was Cardozo's daughter. Lucia was the sister of Lee's brother's wife, which made her family. And, as Randa reckoned things, it made Cardozo family. Why had Lee kept that from her?

"I have never said I owned anything, Raphael," Claude was saying.

"It ain't what you say. It's who you think you are," Cardozo said. "Big shot. You always gotta be a big shot," dismissing him, turning his attention to Randa. "You two know each other?"

"She's Lee's friend," Lazard said.

"Oh, yeah." Cardozo gave her a quick up and down. "He said it was a cop." His eyes reflected a small glint of approval as though judging Lee's taste in women, the kind of man perhaps to whom women were either trophies or servants.

When it became apparent to Lazard that he was not to be included in her conversation with Cardozo, he waved a brief goodbye and walked down the beach toward railed stairs that led through sea oats to a house she could see beyond the mangroves, a smaller version of Cardozo's mansion.

"So what you want with me?" Cardozo asked Randa, not bothering to introduce himself: she was a cop, a functionary. Why waste courtesy on a badge?

"Some information, hopefully," Randa said.

"I need my lawyer?"

"I don't think so. It's about the dead man we found on the beach."

He showed neither surprise nor interest. It was possible, she supposed, that he hadn't heard about the man, although it had been all over TV and was front page for two days in the local newspaper. It was also possible, and more likely, that he had suspected she was here to talk about Barstow and had cautioned himself to appear disinterested.

As she followed the shorter man over a wooden bridge through mangroves, she asked, "How long has Claude Lazard lived here?"

"I don't know—three, four years. Why? You want him? Take him, believe me. Good riddance."

Up at the pool enclosure he pulled out a chair for himself and sat down. "You want a drink—iced tea, lemonade, anything like that? You want booze?"

"Iced tea would be fine," she said, sitting opposite him, putting her bag near her feet on pink tiles. "Lucia Hodges is your daughter?"

"This about her?"

"No. I just wondered." She decided to save her questions

about Lazard and Lucia for Lee. She'd be meeting him in a few hours.

"Plastic," he said, tapping the tabletop. "I was gonna have glass—the look, you know, but they told me plastic was safer. People grabass around the pool." He was leaning back, arms folded, feet thrust under the table. "What are you five eight, five nine?" he asked, giving her chest a lot of attention.

He was pretending to be at ease, but she could see an undercurrent of wariness that told her she was not going to get much out of him. He's dealt with too many cops. Not a man she would readily trust, but he wasn't pretentious, and she liked that. She felt reasonably comfortable with him.

"My favorite tennis player is like you," he said. "I seen her at a restaurant on St. Armans—bigger than she looks, taller."

"Monica Seles."

He smiled. "You know her?"

"I've seen her play."

"Hell of a tennis player. Got stabbed. You know about that?"

"Yes," Randa said.

"Hell of a thing, and those Germans didn't give the guy nothing for it. Should've shot him. You play tennis?"

"Afraid not."

He turned and yelled at one of the gardeners. "Por favor, Pancho . . ." And a few words she didn't understand.

The man, whose name probably was not Pancho, took gloves off and walked across the lawn to the house.

"Iced tea, wasn't it?"

Randa nodded. "Tell me why we found your name scribbled on a card in the man's wallet."

The question didn't rattle him. "My name? Beats me. Who was he?"

"Your name was on the business card of a Miami gun dealer."

"So ask the gun dealer."

"I will," Randa said.

She was sure he knew the identity of Woodrow Barstow. She was sure he would tell her nothing. He seemed the type who would provide meaningless answers to amuse himself and hope to learn something from her. And, she thought, there's no way I'm going to put "the fear of God" in this man, laughing at the thought.

"I understand you're no longer in the arms business," she said.

"My daughter runs it now. You didn't know that?"

"Something about it," Randa said. "The guy on the beach, name's Woodrow Barstow. Did he try to contact you?"

"Why you asking me this?"

"It's a homicide, Mr. Cardozo. Innocently or not, you're linked to him. I have to follow up on that. If you really never heard of him, if you have no idea why your name was in his wallet, just tell me."

"You think I had him shot?"

She smiled. "You know he was shot?"

He shrugged. "Sure. It was in the paper. And his name. And somebody swiped his watch but left a couple of hundred bucks on him. And he was drunk. But it didn't say it was murder. That's different from mugged?"

"We don't think it was a mugging."

"You think I had a hand in it?"

"Did you?"

He sat back, again folding hairy arms across his chest. "If he was on his way to talk to me, he never got here and I didn't know it."

When the man brought the drinks, Cardozo thanked him. Randa thanked him.

She asked, "Did you know Barstow?"

"Know him? What makes you think I knew him?"

On the opening page of a beginner's textbook at John Jay College in New York she had read in bold print: *All Witnesses Lie.* Cardozo was lying, but challenging the lie was not in order. Going after heavy information without leverage wasn't good police work. She was here just gathering information.

"The name Woodrow Barstow mean anything?"

"Not to me."

"How about Nathaniel Hawthorne?"

"Him neither." He didn't recognize the name.

She took a few sips of iced tea, allowed him a few seconds to say something. He just sat there watching her, affecting indifference, but there was a lot going on behind the eyes.

"Did you ever have run-ins with Naval Intelligence?" she asked.

"No, I never did business with them. Army surplus a lot."

"How about Julia?"

"Have to ask her. I don't pay much attention. I'm retired." His expression challenged her to believe him. He sat back, maybe waiting to field some tough questions, maybe disappointed that she hadn't provided any. A retired man out of action for a while might welcome a chance to struggle with a cop. Maybe he actually was retired. Chubleigh didn't think so. Chubleigh thought his daughter was only fronting for him. Now was not the time to get into that.

She got a card from her handbag and slid it across the table. "When Julia gets home, would you have her give me a call? It's possible she knows something about the man."

He took the card, read it, left it on the table as she pushed her chair back.

"Thanks for your time," she said. "And for the iced tea. If you hear anything . . ."

"Why should I hear anything?"

She smiled at his obvious desire to keep this interview going while pretending to be disinterested. It probably didn't mean anything. He was a man, and men hate being disengaged.

She thought of the uncle who had brought her and her mother out of England to the United States. He had survived here less than a year, dying, her mother had said, of idleness and dislocation. But he had been poor. It's different when you're poor.

Cardozo followed her to the parking area and stood on the edge of the grass, hands in his pockets, a lot of questions on his face as he watched her drive off.

She had gained what she had come for: a glimpse into his involvement. She couldn't be sure whether he had been contacted by Barstow, but he knew who Barstow was. She had taken a risk by mentioning the NCIS, but it had paid off. Linking Julia to the navy had caused a leak in his composure. Something to follow up on, although being protective of his daughter probably didn't mean anything. People get that way with cops.

And another thing: she had gained a better understanding of why this man was driving Sheriff Chubleigh nuts. Cardozo lacked a few refinements, but he was miles ahead of the man in the squeaking chair—not a difficult accomplishment. She had long ago accepted the observation that people like Chubleigh, lacking in talent, work their way into positions of power not only to compensate for their inadequacies but to dominate the talented for revenge. She wondered which of the two men had started the feud.

She was home from headquarters and had just stepped out of the shower onto her new cotton rug when her front doorbell sounded. She sprayed cologne over her throat, put on a cotton robe and went to the door, peeked out through the sidelight, and saw Lee's convertible next to her SUV. She quickly opened the door.

Lee came into the room putting both hands through the opening of her robe, warm fingers sliding up her back drawing her to him.

"Brought the wrong keys," he mumbled into her mouth. They hugged, kissed again. With both hands on her belly, he followed her lockstep into the kitchen, the robe sliding off her shoulders.

"First we eat," she said, gently pulling away, raising the robe.

"We're not going out?"

"Don't want my casserole to spoil," she said. "I made it yesterday."

"So throw it out."

He owned a major construction company and had been rich all his life. He neither understood nor had patience with her little economies.

"I can't just throw out good food," she said.

"Starving children in China?" slapping her bottom. "Any white wine left?" heading for the refrigerator.

"I imagine so."

While he was looking for wine, she went into her bedroom and put on underwear, came out still wearing the robe. It was probably prudish of her, but she couldn't be comfortable sitting at the table scantily dressed—shadows of her mother.

For months now he had been coming here after work just like a husband. He had clothes in her closet, underwear in her bureau, shoes under her bed, toilet articles in her bathroom. He behaved like a husband, but she suspected he never intended to become one, and that troubled her: she wanted a family.

He had tried marriage and had run away from it. A son from that marriage had been killed in a car crash while Lee was in the navy. Maybe, as her girlfriend Gloria Schott said, he was incapable of commitment. And maybe it was something else.

Because she had only a few years left for childbearing, she worried about it, a lot. But right now, this evening, she had other things on her mind.

When they were on her lanai watching clouds across the river turning pink above distant palm trees, inhaling river odors, listening to vagrant sounds of motorcycles and cars on the causeway upstream where the river narrows into shadows of overhanging trees, she said, "Guess who I ran into out on Boliva."

"I heard," he said, surprising her.

"You heard? Who told you?" wondering which of the two men she had made nervous.

"Claude. He wanted to know why you were out there."

"He didn't know?"

"Apparently."

Which meant Cardozo hadn't told him. "Mr. Cardozo doesn't seem very fond of your friend."

"To put it mildly," Lee said. "And he's not a friend."

That surprised her. The few times she had seen him with Claude, they had acted like friends. Lee had expressed disapproval of Claude's womanizing, but otherwise . . .

"When you were in the navy, did he chase women a lot?"

"Still does."

"Is that why Mr. Cardozo doesn't like him?"

"Partly. Julia hired a detective to check on him. I think Raphael talked her into it. I'd like to see her dump him."

"I'd dump you."

He laughed, his eyes fixed on her, a lean, good-looking tennis pro is how she always thought of him, although he didn't play tennis. But he didn't look like a construction boss. She couldn't picture him in a hard hat and thick-soled shoes. She doubted he ever wore them.

"But Julia doesn't have your self-esteem," he said. "She's

always putting herself down, hanging back, like a second child."

"You're a second child," Randa said. "You're not—"

"But I did come here to run the family business when I didn't want to. The same thing she did."

"Some people think she's fronting for him."

"That's because she's a woman in a man's business. She's carrying it, believe me. And doing a good job." It did not escape her that he rose so ardently to Julia's defense. He had done it before.

She wanted to dig more deeply into his Pearl Harbor days with Claude Lazard, but that might spoil the evening.

That Woodrow Barstow had been sent by the NCIS to Hawaii to investigate a scandal at about the time Claude Lazard and Lee had retired from the navy at Pearl (and Lee with only sixteen years of service) was not a reason for suspicion, she told herself, even though she rarely believed in coincidence. He had explained to her several times that he had come home because of the death of his father. He had come home to run the Florida branch of the family business.

"So did those wonderful little muscles do their dance?" Gloria asked, fiddling with a wedge of celery that had slipped out of her omelet, her cheek glowing blue and red from the beer sign in the window.

They were in a corner booth in Slim's Dinette. It was ten-thirty next morning. Most of the booths were empty. A smell of fried eggs floated off the counter where two men were arguing about baseball.

"A spirited tango," Randa said.

"Bounced your ass right off the bed, right?"

Randa laughed, enjoying the humor in her friend's face, a pleasant face framed by crinkly hair like cascades of shredded wheat, blue eyes reflecting a lively intelligence.

They had been lunching and breakfasting together four or five times a week for more than two years, occasionally taking in a movie or a concert, occasionally on tired evenings sleeping over. Good friends.

Gloria worked out of the Federal Court Building, a case worker handling wards of the court. Like Randa she had never married. Unlike Randa she didn't want to, at least said she didn't.

They had met in the courthouse waiting room, sitting across from each other, bored by the magazines they had both leafed through, sharing a laugh when Gloria tossed a much-fingered copy of *The Perfect Housewife* into a wastebasket.

"You're still worried, aren't you," Gloria said, charging right into what was on her mind, always the social worker.

"About what?"

Gloria sat back, raising both palms. "If you don't—"

"No, that's okay," Randa said. "What am I supposed to be worried about?"

"Confronting Lee. You think it'll get easier?"

"Maybe it's not a problem," Randa said. "Maybe I don't really want children."

"But you are worried about something. Is it this new case?"

Randa spent a few seconds scraping cheese off her omelet. "Just running into a lot of coincidences."

Gloria watched her quietly. "You never get this distracted unless it's something personal."

Randa turned her gaze toward the window, stared at something in the parking lot, then devoted herself to picking little cubes of tomato out of her omelet.

"Okay, I'll stay out of it," Gloria said.

Randa looked up and smiled. "It's nothing, Gloria. Really, it's nothing."

After all, she had never told Lee about her family. Why should he talk about his? She had met his brother, his brother's wife, his brother's wife's sister. He had told her a lot about them. He just hadn't mentioned Cardozo.

What's my problem? Do I suspect something? Or do I just feel slighted?

Chapter Four

"I want you to call me Vicki," the woman said, "and please keep your voice down."

"Relax. The wind carries every word out to sea—Vicki." He grinned and looked past her at white clouds over choppy water slowly drifting toward the horizon—a gorgeous afternoon on the gulf, no rain expected for several days, everything working out perfectly.

They were on a wharf at least fifty feet from the only possible listener, an elderly man at a wooden table down near the restaurant apparently interested in a tern perched on the stub of a piling, certainly not listening to them.

"Nobody can hear us," Claude said. "That's why I brought you here."

A whiff of diesel exhaust came off the roaring stern of a launch pulling away. He pinched his nostrils and watched Vicki turn her head from the smell.

"Damn this place," she said.

"We'll soon be out of here. Relax."

She removed a pack of cigarettes from her handbag and fitted one to her rouged lips with long, thin, red-tipped fingers. She set it on fire with her gold lighter cupped in her hands and quickly looked up with startled eyes at a gull hovering over them, frantically raising both hands to ward it off.

"I hate those things. They shit on you."

"It's gone," Claude said. "For godsakes, relax. We've got only a few more days of this."

"Why is it taking so long?"

"Mainly because you've made it so damned complicated," Claude said. "You and your boat."

"*Your* boat," she said, fretting over an irritant on her lip. She got a tissue from her bag, wiped her lip, and studied the stain on the tissue. "So how do you know this so-called appraiser isn't one of them?"

"I've known him a long time."

"When you stole your girlfriend's jewels?"

"Very funny."

"So Hassim brings all the diamonds and you select two at random? Why not grab all of them right then?"

"Because they'd come after us. He's got a bodyguard, six-five or something, never goes anywhere without him. He carries a knife. When we get what we're here for, we want to be free."

"This field," she said, dragging on her cigarette, smoke streaming out her nostrils. "How can you be sure nobody will be there?"

"It hasn't been used since the Bay of Pigs. They trained Cuban soldiers there. Nobody uses it now."

"You're sure you can handle the demonstration?"

"You want to do it?"

"You made mistakes when you tried. Remember?"

"I can do it."

She looked away, dragged on her cigarette. "Does Lee know we're dealing with Arabs?"

"Are you crazy? He'd run to the FBI. I told him our customer's in South Africa."

"But he actually believes it's that Israeli stuff we're selling."

"You told him you picked it up as surplus. He bought it. He thinks what we're doing is legit. Don't worry about him. I can handle him."

"Then why's he still dogging us?"

"He doesn't like I'm using Julia's boat. I wish now I'd rented one, but the Coast Guard has seen me in it and waved me on. I can't change now."

"You think Lee's still in love with her? She's his sister-in-law."

"It isn't incest. I don't know, but he's afraid we'll hurt her reputation."

"Then he doesn't believe what we're doing is legitimate."

"He does, believe me," Claude said. "You saw it at the restaurant. It's just that the feds are always watching her father. They think he's still running the company."

She shrugged. "Does Abu know that Lee would turn us in?"

"He isn't worried about it. Abu isn't going after him. He isn't violent. I suppose he's capable of violence, but the last thing he wants is trouble. Stop worrying about that stuff."

"But Abu suspects he might."

Claude shrugged. "We discussed it."

"And he discussed it with the people in Marchland?"

"Why would he?"

"Because he's one of them, and I still think he killed Woody Barstow or had him killed. It couldn't be a coincidence they were both here, both near that same beach."

"Abu is too worried about his own neck to go around killing people. I don't care why Woody was here. He's dead. Some punk on the beach did us a favor."

"You don't know that. And I still think it was Woody I saw at the restaurant."

"It doesn't matter. So he came over here snooping around. He was out of the navy. Couldn't be anything official about it. I was in the navy, remember. I know how they operate. Once you're out, you're out. Stop inventing things to worry about. Relax."

43

"If you say 'relax' once more . . ."

"Okay, okay. Calm down," and he laughed.

The waitress brought their sandwiches and coffee. Claude ogled the girl's bosom. Vicki noticed it and said, "Grow up."

Claude thought the comment funny. He watched the girl walk down the planks to the restaurant. She had a cute little rump, he thought.

"Maybe I should be in a different motel," Vicki said.

"Why? Why do you keep making things more complicated? The boat. Me riding back and forth to Mangrove. It's crazy. Nobody wants to hurt you. They just want the goods."

"But you don't want me using cabs."

"It's only a precaution."

"But they know I'm here," she said fretfully.

"Hassim doesn't know where you are. Maybe Woody saw you, that's all. But he's dead."

She spent the next minute gazing out across the water at two pelicans paddling around a small boat. "Maybe using the boat was not the best idea," she said. "I just thought it would make Hassim think I'm someplace he can't go."

"I can stay down here and give him the address and the key or whatever else he'd need."

"But I want you to be there. I want you to go there first and explain to him where you are. I want you to see him get the crates. I want to be sure he has them."

"You can't explain where it is? You've never been there?"

"No. I did everything by phone. I have the address, but I've never been there."

"But it's in Mangrove Harbor?"

"Of course. Why else would I have you go there? And it's near the marina—that's all you have to know, for now."

"If you'll give me the address, I'll tell them were the stuff is, let them worry about finding it."

"I want you to see them pick the crates up. I want to be sure they have them."

"You're being paranoid."

"Why should I trust people like that—murderers, terrorists?"

"You don't know that," Claude said. "Abu says they're all right."

"You just don't want to admit how serious this is. It's an act of treason, for God's sake. How can we be too careful? Abu's a liar. And don't tell him where I've moved to. I won't be in Seacrest, remember?"

"Oh, yeah. The cottage on the beach."

She took a last drag on her cigarette and tossed it over the rail. "I still don't know why we're giving him half."

"Without Abu there'd be no sale. You know that."

She watched a man with a bucket leaning over the rail of a white ketch, a woman standing behind him yawning.

"Is it true Graham Greene lived for a while on Capri?" she said, after a moment.

"You're mispronouncing it. The accent is on the first syllable. It's CAP-ri, not ca-PRI. You're thinking of the song."

Her glance slid across his eyes like the blade of a knife. "You're a pain in the ass."

CHAPTER FIVE

Rain was pelting the window just to the left of the flag behind FBI Special Agent Anthony Sparzo's partially bald head. Every few seconds, wet fronds of a coconut palm brushed the glass, making a snapping noise that Sparzo paid no attention to. He was sitting back in his swivel chair, his shirt sleeves rolled to the elbow, arms folded across his chest, head tilted to the side. He was watching Tyonek with pained skepticism, not truly interested in anything Tyonek had told him but pretending to be—at least that was Tyonek's impression. When three men in the adjoining conference room started arguing, Sparzo asked Tyonek to close the door, not that he couldn't have done it himself. He just wanted to assert his authority, and that thought burned in Tyonek's brain all the way to the door. Instead of using his left hand, as he ordinarily might have, he pulled the door shut with his prosthesis, knowing that Sparzo cringed every time he saw it.

"They're just humoring me," Tyonek said, "giving me something to do until I retire. There's nothing going on up there."

"But there might be. Something that seems insignificant to you could have major importance. They didn't create the Strategic Information and Operations Center for nothing. It's the central gathering place for the kind of information they get from people like you. Believe me, they're not humoring you. I'm just sorry we're stretched so thin we can have only one man up there. Cherokee City's not big, but it's the kind of small port of entry these terrorists look for."

"The Coast Guard is better equipped . . ."

"Of course. No question. And I'm glad you're staying close to them. But the thing right now, Ty—is it okay if I call you Ty?"

Tyonek shrugged. He didn't care what they called him—except "Native American." He hated "Native American." It had no dignity. "Indian" had resonance. Indians were on horseback out on the plains. Indians were warriors.

"What we're working on right now is communication," Sparzo was saying. "That's why the RIOC was formed. They've got some eighty-six representatives of thirty-eight different agencies sitting in a room digesting all the intelligence guys like you provide. You're connected to the nerve center of Homeland Security. We live in different times, Ty. The old ways are gone. You and me and others like us will be replaced by a different breed of cat. These are embryonic days of the new order. And you're a vital part of the transition."

Tyonek sat there nodding, pretending to be impressed, pretending to be buoyed up by this patronizing bullshit. He probably knew more about the new security arrangements than Sparzo did.

"So what was Barstow working on?" Sparzo said, poking an inhaler up his left nostril, holding his right nostril closed with his finger.

"We didn't find anything at his daughter's place. I don't think he was working on anything. Getting drunk and chasing women is all. He was retired."

"Why book himself into that motel as 'Nathaniel Hawthorne'?"

"Insolence. He got his rocks off doing stuff like that. But I think he was over here for the same reason a lot of people are—

fresh fields for hunting lonely women. Maybe didn't want to do it where his daughter lives. He was a chaser. And the killing? I don't think it had to do with anything. He was on the beach taking a piss and got shot by some asshole who got scared off before he could steal anything."

"The paper said his watch was missing."

"Yeah, I guess the perp got that."

"Would a professional get up that close to him?"

"Maybe it was a hooker—down on the beach, you know."

"Yeah. Was Barstow in touch with Abu Mosul?"

"Not that I know of."

"He came here, you know. Gave us some bullshit about doing business with Cardozo's daughter."

"Yeah, she's in Brussels, supposed to be on her way back."

"You trust him?"

Tyonek laughed. "I don't think he'd do anything foolish. He just wants to get back into business is how I see it. But I'll keep an eye on him."

Sparzo noticed someone passing outside the glass doors. He excused himself and went outside. Tyonek watched him talking with a woman. He couldn't hear what they were saying. They were laughing.

It can't be important, like I'm not important, and he smiled. One thing about Sparzo he had noticed—the man worried about what people at headquarters thought of him. It made him easy to manipulate.

When Sparzo sailed back into the office, he said, as though there had been no breach in their conversation. "As you say," sliding into his chair. "Abu Mosul may be here for perfectly legit reasons. The Company freed him, and arms sales *is* big business in this country. Maybe, like they told you, he's just trying to earn a living. But if they assigned you to this, they must have some suspicions. And on that other thing, I agree—we're best off leaving that homicide to the sheriff up there. We don't have time or manpower for that. If they turn up anything, we'll move in. Just stay tight with them, keep your eyes open, and keep me informed."

He sat back and picked a tissue out of the lower drawer of his desk and spent a half minute cleaning his nose. He tossed the tissue into his wastebasket. "So what's the story with this task force, this woman Sorel. What's she like?"

"Typical sheriff's deputy. Nothing special. Lived in Egypt for a while as a kid, but I don't think that has anything to do with it. She's their lead detective. Supposed to be pretty bright."

"Nothing to do with what? You mean because something with the Arabs might be brewing up there?"

Tyonek's blood froze. He tried covering the mistake with a sheepish laugh. "No. I don't know what I meant. She's a . . . competent, I suppose. Not bad to look at."

Sparzo, as though only half listening, gazed absently past him for a moment, then asked, "This sheriff treating you okay? I've heard he's a ball buster."

"He's okay with me. As I said in my report, we get along fine."

"The Coast Guard people?"

"Yeah. Everybody up there. Very cooperative."

"What do they say about Cardozo?"

"They believe he's turned everything over to his daughter."

"Well, I guess the Patriot Act lets us keep an eye on that. Those two guys from the Hawaii thing are there. That mean anything?"

"No, that's been put to bed. One of them's living with Cardozo's daughter—a free loader. The other one's running a branch of the family business. His brother is married to Cardozo's other daughter. It's just family stuff. They both have acceptable reasons for being there. Nothing to be concerned about."

"But it's why you came to Cherokee City, isn't it?" Sparzo fingered papers in an open file jacket on his desk. "I haven't had a chance to look through all of this, especially what the navy turned over. Barstow probably had access to the same information, and that's probably why he was in Cherokee City."

"Could be," Tyonek said. "I came to Cherokee City because I needed a reason for not getting cashiered, as the Brits say."

"And Abu Mosul is in Cherokee City. That's a pretty hefty combination of coincidence, isn't it?"

"It could be that's what Barstow thought. I don't really see it that way. Fronzi and Lazard have been cleared. Their connections to Cardozo's daughters go way back. It's not surprising they came here when they left the navy. And Abu Mosul knew both of them from that submarine ride and the inquiries in Hawaii. He may have contacted one of them to get next to Cardozo for perfectly legitimate reasons, as he told you. As you say, it's the business he's in. I'm staying close to him. The Coast Guard knows about him and, of course, knows about Raphael Cardozo. Not much is going to slip past them."

"But it might," Sparzo said. "That's why your assignment is important. It's where we don't expect things to happen that we're most vulnerable."

"You're right," Tyonek said. "You're absolutely right."

"Just keep the reports coming." Sparzo closed the file jacket, giving Tyonek a bland smile. He clearly intended that the meeting was over.

Tyonek waited a few seconds, then got up and left the office, convinced that Sparzo would not be sending anyone north to keep tabs on him.

As he drove north on I-75 to his single-bedroom apartment in

Stonewall, he listened to music on the radio, country music. Johnnie Cash and Boxcar Willie were his favorites. He had been listening to country that evening in D.C. when he got that phone call from Albert Swanson telling him to go outside and wait on the corner. He didn't ask questions. He put on his jacket, laced up his boots and headed out. All the way across the line into Virginia, he sat behind Albert and tried to figure out what was going on by listening to what Albert was telling Marjorie. She was the driver that night. Someone from ATF&E was apparently supposed to be with them, but Albert hadn't been able to locate him.

It was almost three in the morning when they pulled into Lee City. They prowled around some back streets and finally stopped in front of a liquor store that had a steel grill covering the windows, old newspaper pages, a crushed beer can, and broken glass on the sidewalk. The house they were raiding was on the next street behind the store. Tyonek was told there'd be three men in the house he had to watch out for.

"So don't use your weapon unless you absolutely have to," Albert said. "Just wait behind the house and watch they don't come out. We don't want any tracks or fingerprints left here or slugs that can be traced back to us."

Tyonek had no more than stationed himself next to a fruit tree when a back window exploded right in front of him and a man came flying out. He rushed at the man who plowed into him, knocking him down. Before he could get up, a second man kicked him in the face. He caught the man's leg and was dragged to a fence when something struck his hand. There was no pain, just a bewildering sense of something wrong. He put his hand to his head and his hand went right through where his head was and, crazed by shock, he started screaming that his head had been blown off. He crashed into something in the dark and that was all he remembered. Glimpses of what had happened popped in and out of his mind as he came awake two days later in a hospital room in Bethesda. The memories jumped at him in pieces while he stared at the puffy bandage on his right forearm, feeling his hand, but because his arm was so short, he knew his hand was gone. For a long time, alone in the room, he lay there crying, no longer the perfect man he had been. For the rest of his life he'd be a cripple.

It was Albert told him about running around in the dark screaming his head had been blown off. Albert was at the door of his hospital room waiting for the woman from personnel to leave before he sat on the bed and told Tyonek to forget everything that had happened. They were never in Lee City, he said.

"You got these injuries in a car accident. Your car went down a banking outside of Germantown in Maryland. It was the accident crushed your hand and put those bruises on your face. We never went to Lee City. Burn that on your brain. You were alone that night. You never saw me or Marjorie that night."

He never found out why Albert had brought him to that house or why he lied about having gone there. He received a check for six thousand two hundred dollars for his car, which his insurance company said was totaled. When a woman from Internal Affairs questioned him about the "accident," he said he couldn't remember anything.

"I don't even remember being outside in my car," he said, and watched her write that down. She didn't probe him for details. She said she was pleased to learn that he hadn't been drinking that night. He must have somehow been crowded off the road, she said. For a while all he saw on people's faces was pity. The doctors, the nurses, the therapists, everyone in the office who used to kid him about being an Indian, now just looked at him with expressions of pity.

The agent who handed him papers that explained the benefits

of disability and retirement said a dozen times how sorry she was that Tyonek would have to leave after eighteen good years.

"There would be a commendation if you had suffered this loss in the line of duty," she told him. "But as it is . . ." She shrugged and said how sorry she was.

When he asked to see Albert Swanson or Marjorie, he was told they had been transferred to the West Coast and were on covert assignment. When he went to the special agent in charge of his old unit, he was told there had never been a raid in Lee City.

"You were delirious there for several days, Tyonek. You probably dreamed it. If it had happened, there'd be a record, and there is none."

"I didn't dream it!"

"Well, it's not going to do you any good accusing Albert Swanson of a coverup. He's got a flawless record. And Marjorie? I've known her for years. She's straight arrow." And using that expression made him laugh. "Sorry," he said in a limping apology.

Resentment gradually replaced old feelings of pride in being an FBI agent. During the long months of therapy he saw looks of pity supplanted by indifference. After returning to the field on a prolonged surveillance assignment, he was given a job in the records section. He remained an agent and received the pay of an agent, but in actuality he had become a clerk. He was told he could go out on permanent disability or could hang around the office and complete his twenty years and retire.

He refused both. He insisted on going back to the field. They said no. He accused them of discrimination and pulled the race card. It had lurked in his mind all along that he was being discriminated against because he was not a white man.

After a closed-door conference in the director's office, they changed their minds and gave him his choice of assignments.

He chose Cherokee City, Florida.

This was funny because someone at the Florida office told him that, because Tyonek had been given this assignment, Sparzo believed he must have a solid friend in a high place at headquarters. Agents were told to treat him with deference.

CHAPTER SIX

Randa was drinking from the fountain outside Major Buckley's office when the dark voice of Fog Rudenski startled her.

"How many crawling baby turtles did we catch in the crime scene?" Fog wanted to know, flickers of merriment in his eyes, a tall, friendly man recently made her regular assistant. Because of a wound to his throat, he spoke in a rasping voice that was hard to get used to.

Wiping moisture off her lip, Randa headed up the corridor.

"None," she said. "Those Save-the-Sea-Turtles were out there all night, in shifts, complaining."

"A wonder they didn't punch the lights out."

"They tried," she said, holding the door open for Fog to squeeze past her into the conference room. Agents Beatrice Kim and Harold Kaplan were waiting down the table, file envelopes in front of them. Usually Randa worked alone or with Fog, but Chubleigh, wanting to make the most of whatever time he'd have on this case, had given her additional help. To make it harder for the FBI to shut him out and with both eyes on the upcoming election, he had announced on television the formation of a special task force with Randa in charge.

"Our beaches are the life of our community," he had said, "and nothing will stop me from keeping them safe. I will spare no resources . . ." He looked resplendent in his white dress uniform, his hair shiny orange under the studio lights.

For nearly a year Randa had refused to accept a replacement

for Skip Morrow, her assistant who was killed last year by drug dealers in Georgia. But when working alone had become burdensome, she accepted Fog as her regular assistant. Like Skip he was intelligent and congenial, although nothing like Skip in appearance—a lot older, a bit taller, slightly stoop-shouldered, a little squinty-eyed, laughed a lot.

You could picture him driving a semi or a payloader, although he said he'd never had an appetite for hard outdoor work. Always wanted to be a cop. Attended Florida State for three semesters on a football scholarship and dropped out when he broke his leg in a motorcycle accident. Sometimes you could see the limp. Unlike Skip who was a rookie, Fog had been a detective for more than ten years, a trooper-deputy before that. Never married.

Randa settled into a chair at the end of the table. "So who wants to go first?" she said.

Bea Kim raised her hand. "I haven't found anyone except the waitress who remembers the man she says was with Barstow. She says she had never seen him before that night. She couldn't pick him out in a lineup, she says. Didn't pay much attention to his face. It was the other guy, Barstow, who was paying."

"Anyone else see Barstow go down that beach path?"

"Just the one I told you about. And now he says his back was turned and he was puking."

"He was drunk?"

"Ate a bad chicken sandwich is what he said. Only I didn't see chicken in the spill. Could be a dog got there before I did. Martinez sampled it for alcohol." And that brought laughter around the table, probably picturing Big Al on his hands and knees.

"Let's hope Al doesn't find any," Randa said. "The puking man could be our only witness. How about the beach patrol?"

"Until they found him dead, they didn't see him. But you know there's lots of ways to get to the beach, not just that access path. Stores and cottages along there, just go between them. No fences. Somebody wanted to catch a loner on the beach could just slip down there unseen."

"But Barstow let the person come right up to him. We know he'd been drinking, but he wasn't naïve."

"Because of the turtle thing it was really dark out there," Fog said. "Maybe he didn't see."

"But why was he out there?" She turned to Bea. "What did you . . . ? What's the name of that motel, the Sleepy Pelican? What'd you learn there?"

"They picked up a lot of latents. Not sure what good they are. Nobody saw Barstow after he checked in."

"And that was Tuesday around noon? That'd mean he was here two days before he was shot. And the beach patrol found him, what was it, ten-thirty Thursday evening?"

"There's another waitress might know something," Bea said. "I haven't caught up with her yet, works part time."

"Was he with a woman?"

"Nobody saw one. He just sat at the table with that guy talking. The way they looked, it was something serious."

"Even though Barstow was drunk?"

"Only according to the blood report. Nobody said he acted drunk, just noisy. Habitual boozers sometimes . . ."

"And maybe the talks came first and the booze later," Randa said. "His daughter wasn't surprised he'd been drinking."

"Oh," Bea said. "Remember we wondered why Barstow's shorts weren't unzipped if he was urinating when he got shot?"

"Doesn't prove anything," Kappy said. "Some men just lift one leg of their shorts."

"Yeah, okay," Randa said, not really interested in whether Barstow was shot while he was urinating or after he'd zipped up. There was urine in the sand. So maybe that's the only reason he was out there.

"What'd you find out in Miami?" she asked him.

He had some kind of creamy ointment on the tips of his ears, probably protection against sunburn. Made him look funny.

"Barstow wasn't there to buy a gun," Kappy said. "He was looking for a guy named Abu Mosul. And Raphael Cardozo's name didn't come up, not from Barstow or the gun dealer."

"You believe him?"

"Seemed to be telling the truth. He said Barstow took his card but didn't write anything on it and he himself didn't."

"Check the handwriting on Barstow's motel register against the scribble on the gun-dealer's card. Better take it down to Irene in forensics. If it's Barstow's handwriting on the card, maybe he had to write it down to remember it, although it's hard to believe an NCIS agent wouldn't have heard of Cardozo. That other name, Abu Mosul? Sounds contrived. Abu's okay, but Mosul could be a mnemonic. It's a city in Iraq. Maybe the guy came from there. Did you run the name?"

"Which?"

"Mosul."

"Not yet."

Probably never intended to. "When you get a chance. What about the gun dealer?"

"Local police cleared him. He just deals in small arms, local sales, nothing criminal they know about. He's properly licensed."

"Does he know this Abu Mosul?"

"Never heard of him. And couldn't figure out why Barstow came there looking for him."

"Did Barstow identify himself as a federal agent?"

"No. Just walked in the shop, looked at a couple of pistols, maybe stalling until a customer left. Then he asked the owner about Mosul, just like, you know, out of the blue. He took a business card off the counter and walked out."

"Abu Mosul," Fog said. "Sounds familiar."

"We can assume he's connected to firearms," Randa said, "like everything else in this case. But why would Barstow go to that particular shop to locate Mosul? Call up a couple of other gun dealers in Dade. Find out whether Barstow made inquiries with them. Maybe this guy you talked to was lying."

Bea raised her hand like a schoolgirl. "Why did Barstow register as Nathaniel Hawthorne? If he was here on some kind of covert assignment, would he use such a laughable alias? And if he was on assignment, wouldn't the Feds have provided him a driver's license that matched the phony name?"

"Maybe we'll find out," Randa said. "But if you saw that name on a motel register, you wouldn't think it belonged to a federal agent."

She closed the meeting after asking Kappy to stay local and help Bea search for witnesses. She told Fog she was going to Hampton to talk with Barstow's daughter. "In the meantime, get the best description you can of this Abu Mosul and put a bulletin out."

"You want me to do it?" Kappy asked. "Go back over there?"

She laughed. "You got something lined up? Use a telephone."

"Why do people call you Fog?" Bea asked, getting up—a husky woman, blonde, part Swedish, pretty face, married to a Korean airline pilot.

"Because I'm horny," Fog said.

Randa gave an involuntary glance at the scar on Fog's throat where he had been shot by a ten-year-old boy. Bea's asking him about his nickname seemed insensitive—everyone knew his voice was likened to a fog horn—but apparently Fog wasn't offended. When Randa had heard about the shooting from Buckles, he had said, "You've got to admire the guy. After the surgery, he went to the state attorney's office to plead for the kid. Said the boy was just trying to protect his mother."

"Where'd the kid get the gun?" Randa had asked.

"That's another story."

Randa was working on the question of names while entering a summary into her PC, following up on Bea's questions. If Barstow had come to Cherokee City on assignment from a federal agency, would he have allowed himself to get drunk? If he had come here just for drunken entertainment, would the NCIS and the FBI have told the sheriff not to investigate?

And why was his death a matter of national security?

Randa devoted the tedious ride across the four-lane highway through the Everglades to violin concertos by Wolfgang Amadeus, practically memorizing them by the time she stopped in front of the small white house on Siesta Court. Kirby Barstow lived in a gated complex of two- and three-bedroom cement-block houses circling a holding pond about the size of a henyard. In Florida it was called a lake. Because Kirby was expecting her, Randa had to spend only a few seconds on a hot front step pressing the doorbell. She looked around at a lot of palm trees, a lot of stucco, a lot of small lawns and closed garage doors.

For the next half hour she sat with Kirby on a screened lanai watching two gawky women across the way behind a chain-link fence lunging at a tennis ball.

"Fun in the sun," Kirby said, offering Randa a mint. "Got hooked on these things when I was quitting smoking."

She seemed calmer than when she had been at the hospital but no less despondent, no less resentful of the disrespect shown her father by people she thought should have honored him.

Randa's fingers got sticky getting the wrapper off the candy. Kirby went into her kitchen and came back and handed her a moistened paper towel. "Sorry about that." She waited for Randa to clean her hands, then took the crumpled paper back into the kitchen.

Randa was saying, "If they were just making sure he hadn't inadvertently kept among his personal things something classified—"

Getting back into her chair, Kirby said, "I thought at first that's what it was. I didn't even listen when she read all that stuff on the warrant."

"What changed your mind?"

"It wasn't just his things they went through. My books over there, my dresser drawers, even under my mattress! They took down everything on my closet shelf. Even looked in the air vents. They knew what they were looking for. I asked Mannheim, 'You think he took something?' 'Just doing our job,' she said. They stripped his bedroom of everything—his computer, all the discs, two file cabinets, boxes of stuff he brought down from D.C. He wanted to write a book."

"You think he might have gone to Cherokee City for material?"

"I don't know. He said the navy knew about it and would have to clear it. But nobody asked me about a book."

"I just wonder whether he was in Cherokee City for something more than recreation."

"All I'm sure of is he was no longer getting paid by the navy. He didn't talk about his book, and I had no idea he had gone to Cherokee City. Just left a note saying he'd be back." And the irony brought tears to her eyes.

She took Randa into a small office and showed her a space near her desk where her disc cabinet had been. "They took it, all my files! My clients' tax records! Everything! Now I gotta get a lawyer, and how can I pay for that?" searching Randa's eyes. "They hated him! He gave his whole life to the navy, and they treated him like shit!"

Later, out on the lanai, Randa asked, "You say it was after a month on sick leave your father retired? Had he planned to retire?"

"He'd talked about it. I never knew. He was one of those guys married to his job, even when my mother was alive. I never thought he'd quit. The drinking picked up . . . I guess living alone, you know?"

"You think he was forced out?"

"I don't know. There's a friend, a retired captain, lives over your side near Beauregard. Name's Frye, Captain Ernest Frye. He came over when my father moved down here. I didn't listen to them talking, but I know the captain thought my father got a raw deal. I asked Woody, but he wouldn't talk about it. I knew he felt betrayed."

"This captain a close friend?"

"They talked all the time."

Driving west on I-75, wishing she had brought something more than Mozart and Mahler, Randa wondered why the NCIS and the FBI were so intensely interested in what Woodrow Barstow had been doing in Cherokee City. She had to believe it was related to this Abu Mosul Barstow had been looking for. It was entirely possible that the man with Barstow in the bar on the beach road was Mosul. He could be someone connected to Raphael Cardozo. She could imagine Barstow writing Cardozo's name on a card to show in a crowded place rather than say the name out loud. Or maybe he had run into someone hard of hearing. But why not write on a napkin? Why take a card out of your wallet to write on? Maybe he was showing someone the front of the card.

She got a call in the morning from Lee, who had gone to Atlanta for a business conference with his brother Dominic. He'd be gone for a couple of days, he said, promising to take her to a barrier-island restaurant when he got back. They kidded for more than twenty minutes about what they would do when he returned to Cherokee City. Then, apropos of nothing, he mentioned that Rita, Dominic's wife, had told him that her sister Julia was flying home from Brussels and would be home probably tomorrow.

That puzzled her. He wouldn't normally tell her that. Why mention it now? Why did he think she cared what Julia was doing and when she would be coming home?

In her last conversation with Lee, they had talked about Julia but not about her being overseas. And Randa certainly hadn't mentioned wanting to question Julia in connection with her investigation. Lee said he had learned about Randa's visit to Cardozo only from Claude Lazard, who hadn't heard Julia's name mentioned. So how did Lazard know that she had asked Cardozo about Julia? And how did Lee get in on that? She could conclude only that her visit to Cardozo's estate had caused a conference.

Why?

Knowledge of Randa's interest in Julia could have come only from Cardozo. Lee had left her place early in the morning and gone straight to Georgia. Unless Claude or Cardozo had tracked him down, Lee must have made the call to Boliva. Why would he do that? If his call was innocent of intrigue, why would he think Randa might care when Julia was coming home?

"Hello?" Lee said, as though from a distant planet. "You still there?"

"Right here," Randa said. "Got something in my eye. Sorry."

What is Lee mixed up in?

They talked a few more minutes. He said he had to go. She said she missed him. She felt a wave of sadness when she hung up. She had never lied to him before.

She was in the kitchen pondering all of this when she got a return call from Captain Frye in Beauregard.

"Was out fishing," he said, in the clear, commanding voice of a navy captain. "Just got your message. In fact, I got another message saying you'd call. If it's about Woody, let's hear it."

Kirby apparently had phoned him.

"I'd like to meet with you," Randa said.

"No problem with that."

"Soon?"

"One hour soon enough?"

"Fine. But Beauregard's more than an hour—"

"Not here," he said so abruptly she had to believe he did not want a cop on his doorstep. Didn't have to mean anything: neighbors talk.

He named an exit halfway to Beauregard. "A little family restaurant there, forgot the name of it, just off the ramp going west, right-hand side."

"How will I know you?"

"I guess Kirby didn't tell you. I'll probably be the only one in there with a seeing-eye dog and a chauffeur. Otherwise, just look for a white-haired old gent in dark glasses."

That Kirby had not mentioned the captain's affliction cranked her up a few notches in Randa's esteem. She admired forbearance. She considered it a sure sign of intelligence, and of class, which she defined as having an advantage over someone and not taking it.

"I'm on my way," she said.

CHAPTER SEVEN

It was a pleasant ride up the interstate past grazing cattle in open pastures and thickets of pine and palmetto. Randa missed hills but loved the flat fields with grass poking up through standing water. She suspected her admiration of rain and greenery reflected an early childhood spent in a desert. Up north she used to borrow a friend's car to take her mother for rides in the country. Her mother loved the green fields and the trees. They reminded her of England.

The restaurant was exactly where the captain said it would be, and she had no trouble spotting him—white hair, dark glasses, navy blue jacket over a white shirt. He was patting the dog, perhaps letting it know that the approaching woman was not a threat. The dog's name, he told her, was Debbie. She was a large, classic tan and black Alsatian.

As Randa sat down she got a smile from a man sitting at an adjacent table, a young man in jeans and polo shirt, probably the chauffeur. There were no others at that end of the restaurant.

"A beautiful dog," Randa said.

The captain smiled. "So people tell me. Mind describing yourself? I like to see who I'm talking to."

Randa settled herself on the padded bench, laughing. "I'm a slightly overweight cop in her middle thirties. I'm wearing gray slacks and a cream-colored blouse."

"Are you good-looking?"

"Incredibly beautiful," she said, getting a smile from the man at the table.

The captain smiled. "Are you married?"

"Not yet."

"You're engaged?"

Randa laughed. "Not yet," imagining he was buying time while getting a sense of who she was. After all, he had only a voice in front of him. Couldn't be easy talking just to a voice, especially when you might be asked to reveal confidential information.

She noticed a large ring on his right hand. She touched his fingers. "That a class ring?"

"A football trophy. I was a linebacker at Michigan. You a football fan?"

"Any kind of sports, but only as a spectator."

"Don't play golf? I used to love playing golf. You a Tiger Woods fan?"

"Love him," Randa said. And she did, watched him every chance she got. Loved his smile.

The captain seemed to muse over that, clearing his throat, scratching his cheek, reaching a finger under the right lens of his glasses. "So, what are we here to talk about?"

"Your friend, Woody Barstow. I know how he died. I'd like to know why he retired."

"They forced him out."

The abrupt candor surprised and pleased her. "Why?"

"They thought he wasn't doing his job."

"Kirby seems to think . . ."

"Yes, I know. And she may be right, although I've seen no evidence of it. No question they were putting pressure on him, and that led to his drinking problems. It was a doctor at Bethesda who persuaded him to retire."

"Why all the pressure?"

"Impatience, maybe. They thought he should a long time ago have wrapped up the thing he was working on. They said he was boondoggling."

"Meaning . . . ?"

"They said he was dragging out the case just to keep a girlfriend on his payroll."

That was interesting. "A girlfriend?"

"Paris something, like the city. Courtland I believe her last name was. She was some kind of high-tech consultant. They said she was less informed about modern weapons than he, although he denied that."

"Any idea how I might get in touch with her?"

"None at all. NCIS might be able to help you."

"Right now they're not doing much talking. Did they suspect him of anything worse than that? Of stealing something? Anything like that?"

"I'm surprised Kirby would tell you that."

"She didn't. She was very protective of her father."

While giving that some thought, he leaned to the side and asked the man at the table to get him a glass of water. "You want something?" he asked Randa.

"I'm fine," she said.

The man to whom Randa had not been introduced brought a large glass of water from the counter and set it on a napkin in front of the captain. With his back to the counter, he took a small flask from his inside jacket pocket, unscrewed a silver cap and poured about two ounces of clear liquid into the water. An odor of gin drifted across the table as the man lifted the glass and swirled it a few times, then set it down so that the edge of the glass touched the side of the captain's hand.

"Thank you, Ben," the captain said, fingering the outside of the glass. "Oh, Detective Sorel, this is my friend Ben Jefferson."

A motorcycle roared past the restaurant, and he had to repeat the name.

Randa gave Ben a smile.

"I don't know," the captain said, "whether they thought Woody guilty of some more serious wrongdoing, but I do think they used his relationship with Paris Courtland just to pressure him, like something they held in their cheek waiting for the best time to spit it out, not in itself anything to get alarmed over: hell, half the men I knew in the service had mistresses."

"The way they ransacked Kirby's apartment . . ."

"I agree. That implies something, or seems to, doesn't it."

"Is it possible, or maybe even likely, that he was still working on that investigation?"

"If he was doing it on his own, I suppose, yes. It could be why he went to Cherokee City."

He took a drink from the glass, held it in his mouth for several seconds savoring it.

Randa said, "The woman from NCIS said her investigation into Barstow's death was a matter of national security."

"Everything they do is. What the hell else do we have a navy for?"

"Have you been in touch with Olivia Mannheim?"

"No, I've had no contact with that woman. My connection in this—what little there was—came from the FBI."

"All along or just recently?"

"Since Woody retired we've kept in touch. But they called me last Tuesday. Wanted to know the same thing you just did: was Woody working on something. I said I had no idea. They spotted someone down your way . . ."

"A him or a her?"

"A man called Abu Mosul."

He apparently heard her gasp.

"I guess you know the name," he said.

"I heard it only recently. I know nothing about him."

"As I understand it, he was a gift from the Israelis, some kind of arrangement with the CIA. He was in the defense ministry of Iraq and provided us with inside stuff about Near-East defense systems. I guess the CIA turned him loose when they got what they wanted. Anyway, he was spotted by the FBI right down there on Cherokee City Beach."

"How was Barstow connected to him?"

"They didn't say, but I guess he must have been; otherwise, why would he have gone over there? A coincidence?"

"You warned Woody the FBI had called?"

"He had a right to know."

"Why'd the FBI call you? Why not call him?"

"There was a lot of friction there. I guess they've been at each other off and on. It wasn't the first time I got a call like that."

"Anyone over there in particular?"

"Tyonek Horse. Maybe you know him."

She had understood Olivia Mannheim to say Tyonek Horse had only recently come in on the case. "I've heard the name," she said. "How long has Horse been talking to you about Mr. Barstow?"

"First time was several months ago, but it's only this past month or so he's called, I think, three times."

"Since Barstow retired."

"Maybe something to do with that."

"He must have known you'd mention the calls to your friend."

"I'm sure he did, but I hate to think it's the reason he made them."

"What happened to Woody is not your fault, Captain."

"Nevertheless," he said, his hand trembling on the sweating glass, sadness in lines on his face.

She watched him take a long drink, set the glass down, and

run his thumb and fingers up the outside of the glass as though he enjoyed the feel of the hard, wet surface.

After a while he said, "I don't know the substance of what he'd been working on. It's the only case they ever gave him, far as I know. It's why they transferred him off my ship. He visited me in the hospital at Bethesda after the accident that took my sight. He complained about a lot of things but didn't talk about the case. He was kind of an odd character. Gave people the impression he didn't give a damn about anything, but, underneath all of that, he was an honest man."

"When did he leave your command?"

"About four years ago. I saw him at the hospital maybe two years after that."

"Four years ago? I understand there was a scandal—"

"Back in Pearl, you mean? No. A scandal implies notoriety. There was no publicity about it. Something happened that made the navy bring Woody over there, that's true. But there was nothing in the news about it. They kept it inside. And so did he."

"Did he give you any hints you can tell me about?"

"Only that it was top secret, nothing of the substance of it. What little I know came from other people, and that isn't much. And maybe what I know isn't connected to it, although I suspect now that it might be. There are two common denominators: Woody Barstow and Abu Mosul. Abu was brought to Pearl on a submarine at about that time."

"A submarine?"

"That's what I understand. He was transferred ship to ship somewhere off the coast of Somalia. As I said, a gift from the Israelis. How much, if anything, it had to do with Woody's case, I have no idea except that Woody said he'd talked to him at the base in Hawaii."

She saw no reason to mention Mannheim's threats. Until her

orders changed, she was investigating a murder. But she had to be circumspect. Captain Frye was a friend of the victim, but he was also a loyal career naval officer.

"Can you share more of that with me?"

"Not much to share. Woody just said he'd talked to him, nothing about what was discussed. Whether this has anything to do with Woody's death, I have no idea. Could be his being on that beach was just bad luck. I think he might have been just relieving himself. He had an enlarged prostate, taking some kind of medicine for it."

"But he had just been at a bar. Wouldn't he have . . . ?"

"Maybe. But the need came of a sudden. It was a constant problem, I guess. Can't think of any other reason he'd go down to that beach. And now he's dead." And that brought on a lingering expression of sadness.

"Do you think the FBI were tracking this Abu Mosul?"

"I'm sure Horse wanted me to think they just happened to spot him, but I don't believe it. After all, he had been an active member of Saddam's regime. It's a wonder they let him roam around. Must be a reason."

"You think you were used?"

"Let's say the thought has crossed my mind."

And that brought an end to the substantive portions of her interview. He asked Ben to get him another glass of water. Ben got one and flavored it with gin. He said he'd be happy to answer any more questions she might have. But she decided to let it go for now.

As she was getting up, she said, "Is it okay if I pat Debbie?"

"Let her smell your hand first. If she doesn't growl, you can pat her."

Debbie didn't growl.

It was a long ride south on I-75. She and her windshield wipers

71

fought a heavy downpour all the way to Cherokee City. She had
to wait on the highway while a wrecker dragged a van out of the
cruising lane. The delay distressed her, not because she would
miss Gloria at the diner but because she had an urgent need to
relieve herself. It was a half hour of severe discomfort before
she got into a toilet booth in Slim's Dinette. She had no sooner
lowered herself onto the seat when she heard Gloria outside the
little door telling her that Bill White was waiting for her in a
booth at the end of the diner.

"You're lying," Randa said.

"He stopped dying his hair."

"You're lying."

"He says he's got some information about the man you found
on the beach."

"You're lying. He isn't even a cop anymore. He retired."

"You know you want to see him."

"Maybe on his back with his arms folded across his chest."

When she came out of the cubicle, Gloria was still laughing.

"Is he really out there?"

"And that isn't the worst part," Gloria said. "The worst part
is I can't stay here and watch."

"Like hell!"

"Truly. One of my charges has run off."

"Then I'm leaving with you."

But she couldn't. She had to go out there. Bill White was an
idiot, but he was a good detective. He wouldn't be here unless
he had something important to tell her. As she washed her
hands and gazed into the image of her eyes, she told herself she
could put up with the whining if that's what he came here to
do.

Chapter Eight

"Bill, how's it going?" Randa said, sliding onto the wooden bench across from the man she had not seen since he stood in the squadroom doorway several months ago waving goodbye to her and whoever else was in the room.

"Great," he said, reaching across the table to shake hands.

She casually tapped curled fingers against his hand on her way to picking up a menu, slighting him but only mildly.

"You're looking fine," he said, making a comedy of examining his hand, looking for flaws, grinning, probably disappointed that she didn't grin back.

He looked different. His hair was gray and he was sporting a mustache in an attempt, she imagined, to make himself look distinguished. It didn't. He still looked like an assistant manager of a shoe store.

"The PI look," he said. "At night I wear a felt hat and trench coat."

She gave that a nod. "Gloria says you've got something for me."

"I don't know how important it is," he said, looking up at the waitress.

"I'll have the turkey club on whole wheat," Randa said. "Coffee with regular milk, not those little half and half things."

"Just coffee," Bill said.

"And regular milk?"

"You got it," he said, getting a cigarette out of a pack from his jacket pocket. He fingered it nervously, then tucked it into a fold of hair above his ear. "Old habits."

He was nervous. Why? "I understand you've opened up an office in the Edison Building."

"That's right. William White, Private Eye. Right up there on pebbled glass. Let 'em know who you are in plain English is how I'm doing it. And doing well. Wanted to do it fast while the right people still know me. It's great being out, Randa. My own boss, don't have to take shit from nobody. And a pension to fall back on."

"Lucky you," Randa said, glancing out the window at a girl out there leaning on the tailgate of a pickup truck, one of those western shirts, bright red, looked good on her.

"I like to stay in touch," Bill added.

She didn't catch that, but said, "I see what you mean."

He was the rebound target Randa had turned to when Charlie Hawkins, the man she had been living with, was killed. She had been in love with Charlie and had hoped to marry him, hoped to have children with him; although, as she now admitted, it was more hope than expectation. Like Lee Fronzi, Charlie had never shown any enthusiasm for marriage.

The thing with Bill had been wrong from the beginning, and she was ashamed to have indulged in it. It ended when she found his ex-wife's panties in his dryer. It surprised her that she didn't get angry. She didn't care. If anything, she was relieved. It made her realize he had never been anything more to her than a cushion to fall down on, and that made her want to apologize to him, although she didn't.

For weeks after she dropped him, he trailed after her, begging her to come back, making a nuisance of himself. She tried to talk him out of it, but he wouldn't listen. He was in love, he said. For a while she felt sorry for him but shortly became irritated by his persistent attentiveness. Soon she began to loathe him.

Now as she looked at the face across the table, she was embarrassed that she had ever let him touch her.

"So what can you tell me about the body on the beach?" she said.

"I'd like to work with you on this. And look," shaking his head, "I've outgrown that other stuff."

"Good. What do you mean work with me?"

"You help me, I'll help you."

She didn't know what that was about, but it didn't sound healthy. "Doing what?"

"I know about the visit from the navy. And I know you may get enjoined to turn the case over to the FBI."

She might have asked how he knew that, but she wouldn't get the truth. What she said was,

"And . . . ?"

"I don't think you'll want to," He sat back and snicked a few wisps of air through the gap in his front teeth, confident that he had touched the right button. Smugness did not become him.

But he was right. He had provoked her interest. "Okay, what's it about?" exaggerating the impatience she was beginning to feel. He was trying to creep in, and that angered her. If he had legitimate business to discuss, then let's have it.

"This Barstow," he said. "I'm on a case. He just happened in. He wasn't the subject. It's just I found him with a friend of yours."

"Who?"

"Claude Lazard. He's got a new girlfriend. They were at the bar in a restaurant on Gill's Island."

She immediately recalled what Lee had told her about Julia's having hired a private detective. Bill was one of only three in the county. She took the risk.

"You're working for Julia Hodges."

It surprised and temporarily deflated him. "She told you?"

"Who's the girlfriend?"

"Can we get together on this? I mean, I shouldn't . . ."

"You came to me, Bill."

"As a courtesy. I'm still a cop. In my heart, you know."

"How does Mr. Barstow fit into this?"

"He followed the woman into the restaurant and sat at a corner table watching her. Doing what I was doing, I suppose. He had his subject, I had mine."

"He told you his name?"

"No. I didn't talk to him."

"But you knew who he was? There was no picture of him in the news. How did you connect . . . ?"

They stopped talking when the waitress brought her food.

She asked, "You've eaten?"

"With Gloria. She said she wasn't expecting you, but it was like the old days. She's a bad liar. I knew if I waited . . ."

When the waitress was gone, Randa said, "How did you connect the man in the restaurant with the body on the beach if you didn't talk to him or get his name?"

"How many guys you know wear alligator shoes? The reporter mentioned them—a white man in his late fifties wearing alligator shoes. I saw them on him. For the hell of it I drove down to the crime scene."

"And someone there gave you a name?"

"And I visited the morgue."

"Who gave you the name?"

"Come on, Randa. I know a lot of people."

And if you get anyone into trouble, nobody will know you next time. She let it go. "What can you tell me about the woman? She the one Julia's worried about?"

"All's I know is she was registered at the Beach Inn as Vicki

Bryant of Denver, Colorado. And she's no longer there. She checked out and paid cash."

"Before or after Barstow was shot?"

"The same day. That morning. I checked all the car rental agencies. No record of her. Couldn't find a cabbie who might've taken her to the airport. Nothing there. Nobody remembers seeing her. No record of a Vicki Bryant at the airport. She's vanished."

"She signed the register 'Vicky' or 'Victoria'?"

"Vicki with an i."

"She came in a cab?"

"To the restaurant? I don't know. She left with Lazard."

"She knew you were checking on her?"

"I hope not."

"And I suppose you didn't swap stories with Barstow?"

"Like I said, I sat way behind him at the restaurant and watched the group at the bar. I didn't contact him."

"A group?"

"There were three of them."

A stab in the gut told her this was why he had called her. The sandwich was at her lip when she paused and cautiously asked, "Who else?"

"Lee Fronzi."

He had saved that, knowing it would jolt her. And it did. It frightened her.

She lowered the sandwich. She could feel her arteries tightening. What a contemptible little prick!

"He joined Lazard there and was with Lazard when the woman came in. They all knew each other. Lazard didn't have to introduce him. I was pretty surprised."

And obviously elated. "Is this the woman Claude has been seeing?"

He nodded. But he wanted to talk about Lee. "I was really

surprised that Lee would be in on it."

"In on what?"

"Whatever's going on. He wasn't just a guy sitting with another guy's girlfriend. They were leaning into each other, all three of them head to head, not just small talk."

"You heard some of it?"

"Too far away. But you could tell it was serious stuff."

"And Barstow . . . ?"

"Like me, he was just sitting back watching."

She hated him for having brought this to her, but it was compelling and she had to hear more.

She took a deep breath, averted her face, and stared out the window. The woman in the red shirt was gone. There was a black SUV where the pickup had been.

"I can help," Bill said. "If the Feds enjoin you . . ."

"Stay out of it. What I want to know is why you were so interested in Barstow."

"He was following Vicki Bryant."

Not an adequate answer. Checking Barstow's identity at the morgue wouldn't tell him anything about Vicki Bryant, but he didn't go there to look at the face.

"You went through his things?"

"I just wanted to know who he was."

"What'd you find out?"

"Nothing. No ID. A Lee City, Virginia, label on his suit. That's near D.C., isn't it?"

"They think you were still a cop?"

"Come on, Randa. I'm just trying to—"

"Stay out of it. I mean it. I don't want to get nasty." Chubleigh would assume she had asked Bill for help. She didn't need that. "Just stay out of it."

She took a deep breath, gazed down the aisle at a man bent over a crying child. A woman squirmed out of a booth and lifted the child, and the three of them moved slowly toward the cashier.

"When was the first time you saw this Vicki Bryant?" she said.

"Just once before. He picked her up at her motel."

"And when you went through her things in her room, what did you find?"

"Come on. I don't want to lose my license."

"What'd you find?"

"Okay, there was nothing personal in her room except one of those canvas bags. It was locked."

"Nothing you could get fingerprints from?"

"The maid came in." He laughed self-consciously. His manner offended her not because he had acted illegally but because he took for granted that she wouldn't object. She felt like turning him in, but it would be a waste of time.

"That was when?" she said.

"Monday, last week."

"And you had been following Lazard for how long?"

"Two days. I was parked down the street when you were at Cardozo's. He left just after you did, played a round of golf at Chesterfield. Does he have private money? My impression is he lives off Julia."

"When do you report to her?"

"Tomorrow if she's home. I haven't written it up yet."

"Who did you follow from the restaurant?"

"Nobody. Barstow would have seen me. But I checked the motel. Lazard's wagon was there, so I took off."

"What exactly did Julia want to know? Just the sex stuff?"

"More or less, like was he cheating on her, you know."

"Then why chase down Barstow?"

"Old habits."

"Not 'old habits,' Bill. Stay out of it. You'll just get yourself into trouble."

She hailed the waitress and asked for a take-out box. She knew Bill was unsinkable and wasn't surprised when he asked, "Why is this a matter of national security?"

"I have no idea."

When the waitress brought the box, Bill tried to pick up her check. She took it from him, handed the girl two dollars, and went alone to the cashier, paid the check, went out, and got into her car and drove home. Whether Bill followed her outside she didn't know. She didn't look for him.

In her apartment, she turned down the thermostat, got into pajamas, and sat in her darkened living room staring at the TV wondering why Barstow was following Vicki Bryant if he had come to Cherokee City to find Abu Mosul . . . if that's why he had come here.

She didn't want to think about why Lee was involved in this. She deliberately set it aside. He was at the restaurant with Claude Lazard and the woman Claude was fooling around with. So what? Bill wanted to find something sinister in it. She didn't.

She fed two aspirins to her headache and went to bed.

Next day was the first of three days off. Lee didn't call, and she didn't go to headquarters. She washed the kitchen floor, laundered bedclothes, and worked up a sweat on the bike path down by the river. Getting back to her apartment, as she rounded a hibiscus clump at the edge of her parking lot, she found a man in a gray business suit leaning on the wall outside her door.

He was in his early fifties, a small, tightly made man who looked like Chi Chi Rodriguez only without the smile or the warmth. He spoke to her without stepping from the wall, which she interpreted as hostile.

"I recognize you from your picture," he said, his thin, bluish lips barely moving. He kept his right hand in his jacket pocket, affecting an attitude you associate with someone who sucks toothpicks.

"And who are you?" she said, reaching for her keys. She noticed a black sedan parked near an olive tree, no front license plate.

With his left hand, he got a folder from his inside jacket pocket, flipped it open, flashed it at her, then put it back. "Tyonek Horse," he said. "Federal Bureau of Investigation. They told me at the sheriff's office I'd find you here."

No. It wouldn't happen. "And just who at the sheriff's office told you that?" Nobody at headquarters would send an FBI agent to her home. She decided then and there not to invite him inside no matter how friendly he might try to become. An FBI man? How many had she ever seen who wore tooled-leather cowboy boots with a business suit?

"Just thought we might go over a few things," he said, moving from the wall, taking his right hand from his pocket. Only it wasn't a hand. It was an old-fashioned stainless steel prosthesis—two opposable claws.

He held it out and she took it without hesitation. He seemed pleased that she hadn't flinched. Maybe it's how he tested people.

"I'm afraid I can't talk to you, not here, not—"

"If Chubleigh doesn't mind, why should you?"

"I'd have to get that from him," she said, taking out her keys.

He was standing between her and the door. He didn't move. "We can save a lot of time," he said.

"If we talk about anything, it'll be in the presence of either the sheriff or Major Buckley."

He seemed amused. "Because it's your day off? You expect me to wait two more days? I've got to build a foundation here. Catching up to do."

"If you call the sheriff's office in the morning, there'll be a message for you."

"Come on, Sergeant. There's a lot I have to find out."

She regarded him with cold impatience, waiting for him to get out of her way.

"Why can't we just go inside and talk?" he said. "As you've probably been told, I'm taking over the case."

Like Mannheim, he apparently wanted to establish that he was new to the investigation. She was tempted to point out the lie but decided to save it. She wished he would move. She didn't want this to get awkward.

"Do you mind?" she said, jangling her keys.

He grinned. His teeth were stained and too big for his face, but they looked real.

"I want to go inside, Mr. Horse. Will you please get out of my way?"

"Why are you giving me a hard time?"

After she stared at him for several seconds, he stepped aside. "We have a lot of talking to do," with a flair in his voice that said: why be so foolish? You'll do it my way sooner or later.

Avoiding his gaze, she stepped past him, unlocked her door and went inside, her face flushed with anger. She locked the door.

In her bedroom she lowered herself onto her bare mattress, took off her shoes, and kneaded the soles of her feet, her head working through images of indignation. She went to the laundry closet and got sheets and pillowcases from the dryer. She made her bed, carefully tucking in all the corners, smoothing out the spread. Thoughts about herself out in the yard made her start laughing. She fell across the bed and lay there grinning into the odors of laundry detergent. She had no idea whether it was his boorishness or her stubbornness that had caused the impasse, and she didn't care. He was a man, and he was a pain in the ass.

After a lonely supper watching the evening news, half hoping, half dreading Lee would phone, she called the duty officer at headquarters. There was no record on his log of a visitor from the FBI. The sheriff had been in Chicago all day and Major Buckley had been at home since noon.

"I'd know it if the FBI had been here," the officer said.

She caught the major at home.

"No, of course not," he said. "You know I'd've called you."

"Who would have told him where I live?"

"Probably nobody. Easy to find out. Don't worry about it. Glad you didn't talk to him. I heard he's a ball buster."

"Mine are intact," Randa said. "You on board in the morning?"

"You want to come in?"

"If he shows, yes. When's Chubleigh getting back?"

"No idea. I don't even know why he's up there."

"But you're sure this man was not given clearance to talk with me."

"He probably doesn't think he needs it. You know how those guys are."

She didn't, but let it go. Tyonek Horse, she told herself, wasn't important. Derek or Buckles could deal with him. But Lee was important, and she lay in bed half the night worrying about what he might be mixed up in. In soberer times, she criticized herself for wanting love too much, for trusting too much. A hopeless adolescent. But isn't it the child in you that loves?

"Aw, you broke into a beautiful dream," Gloria said.

"Anyone in bed with you?"

"I wish. What time is it?"

"I don't know. I can't sleep."

"Wait a minute."

While Gloria was away from the phone, Randa snapped off the kitchen light and wiggled into a more comfortable position on the stool, forearms on the cool plastic counter, the handset pressed to her ear.

"Okay," Gloria said. "I would've had to get up anyway. It's three o'clock. So what's bothering you?"

"Nothing."

"Yuh, right."

"Is it possible I'm exaggerating things? I mean, if I'm worrying about Lee, for example, could it be that other thing? Unconsciously, you know, like an underlying force?"

"Are you pregnant?"

"No, of course not."

"What's he done?"

"I don't know, but he's into something. I'm worried."

"About what?"

"He and that guy I told you about, Claude Lazard. Something happened in Hawaii. Remember I said it was funny they both retired at the same time?"

"He had to take over the family business, you said."

"I don't think so any more. I mean, not the deciding reason."

"So ask him."

"But do you think the thing about wanting children is making me exaggerate the importance of this? Maybe it's nothing."

"It's not nothing or you wouldn't be worried. Make him face it. Does he want a family or just to fool around? Get it out in the open."

"I don't want to lose him."

"You're not eighteen, Randa. You want a family. And if he doesn't, then that's it. Be your own best friend."

"You think I'm an idiot, don't you?"

"Yes, now go back to bed."

84

CHAPTER NINE

Detective Bill White had turned his head and was picking an irritant out of his nostril. It clung to his thumbnail like a scale of a dead fish. He studied it a second, then flicked it onto the ground and gave Tyonek an apologetic grin. They were sitting in the shade of a large banyan tree on a bench in a downtown riverside park not far from Bill's office. An occasional breeze brought pale odors of decay floating in from the river.

"Only because I have a professional obligation to my client," Bill said. "But maybe I can tell you something about the other ones."

"But exactly who are you interested in? You were following Lazard. Is he your subject?"

"Primarily," Bill said. "Yeah, but I couldn't help getting curious about this other stuff. Something is definitely going on here. I don't mean to crowd whatever you're doing, of course. It's just that these . . . well, you know. I can't help noticing things."

"Like this Abu Mosul?"

"You're sure that's the name? He's registered as Douglas Trent."

"I know. So how'd you run into him?"

"He was with Lazard out on a slip at that marina. In these times, especially, how could you help noticing him? He's obviously not American. And that name. He's got to be a fucking Arab. So what's he doing here?" looking for an answer but not

85

confident he would get one.

With feigned impatience, Tyonek said, "Why were they at that marina?"

"On the beach road? I don't know. Just looking around."

"And the other one you mentioned—Fronzi. Was he with them?"

"Not there. It was before that. I saw him bring Lazard over to this Mosul's motel room."

"You watched the room?"

"Yeah, but they couldn't see me. Even if they came out. I was in the woods." All of this with a tentative smile. He obviously wanted to move into Tyonek's good graces but was pretty sure he couldn't.

And Tyonek was taking it all in, smiling as though impressed by Bill's acumen. *This man is not only stupid, he's dangerous.*

"You're sure Abu Mosul was in there?" Tyonek said.

"Somebody was. Somebody opened the door from inside."

"And you went to the office to find out who was registered in that room?"

"There was a boy at the desk. It didn't set off alarms. Look, I been doing this for a lot of years."

"And you're giving all this information to Sorel?"

"Oh, no. She told me to stay out of it. She's pretty straight with stuff like that. Old Chubleigh wouldn't want her leaning on a civilian private eye."

"But you're pretty close to her, aren't you?"

"Used to be closer," said with a sneaky laugh. "A lot closer, if you know what I mean. She's a great piece of ass."

"She dumped you?"

"I dumped her. Caught her with that rich fucking guinea."

"Fronzi."

"And you better believe he's involved in whatever you're here investigating."

It was clear that rancor was motivating this man. *He's jealous. He wants to bring Fronzi down. But it's more than that. He wants a big score.*

"What kind of a name is 'Chubleigh,' anyway?" Tyonek asked.

"What I heard is his father came to this country from England and gave his name as Chol-mon-de-ley, pronouncing it 'chumley.' But he had a cold and the guy wrote Chubleigh on the entrance papers."

"That's funny," Tyonek said, without smiling. "You get along well with him?"

"Nobody does."

A black bird with a long upright tail fluttered to the sidewalk and ambled on skinny legs to a candy wrapper, took a few pecks at it, then flew off.

"So what do you make of Barstow's death?" Tyonek said.

"I'm sure you know why he was killed better than I do," saying it like they were buddies. The only thing missing was the wink.

"And what is it you think I know?" Tyonek said.

Bill gave that a helpless shrug. "You . . . the NCIS . . . this Abu guy. I mean . . . hey, I'm not stupid."

You're very stupid.

"And," Bill said, "The woman Barstow followed into the restaurant knew him. When she turned his way he didn't melt into the woodwork like you would if you're shadowing a stranger. He ducked outside and ran to his car, afraid she'd see him. She knew him. I'm sure she's connected to what he came over here to find out. And Lazard and Fronzi and Abu Mosul . . . they're all in on it."

"Sounds like you've gone pretty deep into this."

"Like I said, I'm still a cop," grinning.

Tyonek nodded as though impressed. "You know where she is right now?"

Bill glanced at his watch. "In about fifteen minutes she'll be getting out from under the dryer. I'll be right behind her when she leaves the hairdresser."

A boy with a bag on his back rode past them on a red bicycle, the tires making a ripping sound on the cement walk.

"Raphael Cardozo. How's he fit into this?" Tyonek asked.

"He's a guy with big connections—him and his daughter."

Tyonek moved the steel claw from his thigh, stood up, and thrust it into his jacket pocket.

"I hope we can work together on this," Bill said, looking up at him.

"Let's see what develops. You plan to stay on the woman?"

"I think she's a key player."

"You're really convinced, aren't you, that something big is going on."

"I'm not stupid," Bill said.

"Well, you've got my cell number."

"If she gets together with some of those people, I'll let you know."

As Tyonek watched Bill walk up the path to his car, he imagined blood leaking from a hole at the base of Bill's skull.

CHAPTER TEN

Randa was at the slider in her kitchen checking the darkening sky, hoping the rain would let up before she went to the market. She needed laundry detergent, bleach, and ingredients for making spaghetti sauce. Also aspirin.

The phone rang. Maybe it was Lee.

It wasn't. It was a woman's voice. "Randa? Julia Hodges."

"Julia. Glad you called. When'd you get back?"

"My father said you wanted to talk to me, something about a guy that got shot."

"When can we get together?"

"Do I have to come in there? They said you weren't on duty. I'm exhausted."

"Your place is okay. When?"

"Anytime."

"Two o'clock?"

"If it isn't raining I'll be at the pool. I guess you know how to get here. My driveway's just up the road from my father's."

Two o'clock would give Randa time to market and make the sauce, hold the interview and get back in time to shower and prepare for a sitdown with Lee—if, as promised, he was back from Georgia.

You couldn't tell with Lee. Sometimes his brother Dominic would ask him to stay, for business reasons or just to play golf. Now that Lee's parents were dead, Dominic was the only blood relative Lee had here in the States. Unlike Randa, Lee was born here, but his ties to people overseas gave them a common perspective.

She didn't know why he resisted marriage. He said he loved her and enjoyed being with her. He had never come right out and said he didn't want to get married, but it was there. And it wasn't just the usual male reluctance.

Only she didn't know whether the resistance came entirely from him. The only two guys she had ever truly loved were both chronic bachelors. What did that say?

The rain stopped just as she reached the bridge that led to Boliva—sunlight breaking over the road like a Joycean epiphany, tossing her mind back to college, remembering how impressed she had been with the short stories and how disappointed with his later stuff. Yeats was the only other Irish writer she liked . . . no, there was also Edna O'Brien . . . thoughts floating through her as she watched seagulls gliding across the road ahead of her, terns studying the water from the railings, blue water glinting in sunlight beyond palm trees that stood like soldiers alongside the road.

She found Julia Hodges in a white, one-piece bathing suit on pastel cushions under a parasol, a towel over her legs, a drink in her hand. She was artificially blonde, a bony woman in her thirties, not at all what you'd expect a gun dealer to look like. She had a shallow voice that seemed to come out through her nose. Her smile was no deeper than the lip rouge.

Randa never understood what she and Claude saw in each other. But who knows about other people?

As Randa came onto the deck, Julia lowered dark glasses to the tip of her nose and waved Randa to a chair separated from herself by a small table. Two yellow hibiscus petals had blown onto the chair from a hedge that surrounded the pool. Randa placed them next to a glass that was upside down on a napkin, put there probably in anticipation of her arrival. A sign of welcome? Gloria might say a symptom of control. And Gloria could be right: there was a nervousness about Julia that kept you at a distance, reminded Randa of her mother—all smiles and friendliness until she got to know you.

"Lime water," Julia said, moving a pitcher from the shade of a potted palm. Randa reached for it, a half dozen wedges of lime floating in the ice cubes, their fragrance comforting her face. "They're from my father's tree," Julia said. "He had it brought up here from the Keys, for some reason," and she laughed, a throwaway comment undoubtedly intended to make an impression.

"So how was your trip?" Randa asked, watching ice cubes tumbling into her glass.

"Boring. How'd you know I knew that man?"

"Actually I just thought you might."

"I hadn't seen him since that time in Hawaii. I guess you know about that."

"Four years ago," Randa said, hoping to anchor the notion that she was well acquainted with "that."

"Is this connected to what happened out there?"

"Possibly, although . . ."

"My father didn't have anything to do with it. I want you to know that. He didn't even know about it. But they kept hounding him. Maybe that's why . . ."

"What didn't he know?"

"Nothing! They never said what was stolen, only that's why I was out there. Only it wasn't. Lee called me, said they were advertising surplus small-arms stuff. It's what I dealt in then . . . still do, a little. I wanted to see what they had, but they accused me of coming there to meet up with this guy they brought in the sub or something, I don't know. It was crazy. I never even saw him."

"This guy, he have a name?"

"Something weird, Abu or Booboo. I don't know what the hell it was. To this day I don't know what they wanted. A little half-pint bald-headed guy, Lee said."

Abu Mosul, the man Captain Frye had called a gift from the Israelis, was brought to Hawaii in Lee's submarine? This is a direct connection, isn't it? She let that slowly sink in.

"By 'they' you mean Barstow?" Randa said.

"He never said what was stolen, never said anything was stolen. It was what you got after listening to him. It was some kind of secret. Claude and Lee didn't know what he was talking about, just something was missing, and I was supposed to know about it because I came there to see Lee is all it was as far as I can figure out. So four years later he shows up? Why?"

"Maybe you can tell me."

"Because that guy is here?"

"What guy?"

"Booboo, the passenger on the submarine."

How did she know Abu was here? Her father? How did he know?

"Have you talked with Claude since you got back?"

"No." And she seemed offended by the suggestion.

But she had talked with her father and possibly had learned about Abu's presence in Cherokee City from Bill White. But if Bill knew about Abu, why would he mention him to Julia who was supposedly interested only in Claude Lazard's philandering?

"Claude hasn't been home?"

"This isn't his home, never was," Julia said with clear indignation. "He just slept here." Past tense.

Then somebody's been lying to me about that. It couldn't be the philandering Julia's worried about: according to Lee she

92

had known about it for a long time. So what had produced the anger?

"What can you tell me about Vicki Bryant?"

Julia's face froze. Her glasses slid down her nose and puzzled eyes stared at Randa. "Jesus! She involved?"

"I don't know."

"Aw, shit," Julia said, resting the glass on her belly, looking aside, discouragement wounding her face. "She involved in this?" Couldn't believe it.

Involved in what? What are you hiding? "What can you tell me about her?"

"Nothing. He's been screwing her. That's all I know. How'd you find out about her?"

"Just stumbled into it."

"Jesus, it figures, and I never thought of it. She was out there. He knew her before, said she was stalking him. Yeah, like my ass is green. He got her the motel room! He probably paid to bring her down here, and with my money, the son of a bitch!"

"Down here? From where?"

"I don't know. Up north somewhere."

Apparently Bill White had made his report, identifying the woman Claude was seeing but hadn't told her that Woody Barstow had been following Vicki Bryant, or else she would have known that Vicki was connected to Barstow's investigation.

What kind of game is Bill playing? "Claude has known her a long time?"

"He was shacking up with her outside the base at Pearl before they went on that voyage. I only heard about it from Lee. Claude said he broke up with her, said he was sick of her, that lying bastard."

"You met her out there?"

"I've never seen her. It was before I went there, like a year before, something like that."

"Before Claude and Lee went on that voyage?"

She mumbled an answer Randa couldn't make out. She was drifting away from this, possibly getting worried.

Randa asked, "Did you know that Barstow was following her? Why would he if she was here just to be with Claude?"

"I have no idea," as though resenting the question. She leaned down to pick something off her toe, turned her head, glanced toward the house. Looking for escape?

Randa asked, "This man Abu Mosul. You ever meet him?"

Julia glanced at her watch. She lifted the towel off her legs and sat up. "I just remembered something. No, all this happened while I was gone." The pretense to friendliness had disappeared.

"All what, Julia?"

"I don't know. People coming here. I thought it was just Claude screwing around, taking someone out on my boat at night. I just wanted to know who it was. I didn't know anything about this other stuff."

You did, Randa wanted to say, but you thought you could ignore it. Now you know you can't.

Julia dropped her feet to the deck and sat with her back to Randa, mumbling something Randa couldn't make out.

Talking to the sagging shoulders and the bumps on Julia's spine, inhaling the fragrance of sunblock, Randa said, "I have to find out why Mr. Barstow was murdered. I know this isn't easy."

"Maybe it was just some creep wanted his watch," Julia said, putting sandals on.

And if you know about the missing watch, you have obviously discussed this at length with your father. "That's altogether possible," Randa said. "But there has to be a reason why Barstow came here, and why he was following Vicki Bryant. What's Claude involved in?"

Julia stood up, took off her glasses and looked across the

mangrove trees. "I don't know that he's involved in anything. I do know my father had nothing to do with what went on in Hawaii and nothing to do with that man on the beach. We aren't involved in anything criminal if that's what you're getting at."

I've never said you are or were, Randa thought, more impressed by the hostility than the denial. Was it only Claude's philandering Bill had been hired to check on?

In too great a hurry to lift her drink from under the potted palm, Julia, draping the towel over her shoulder, walked to the path that led off the deck toward the house. For a moment she hesitated, stared at the ground, turned as though to say something, changed her mind and walked away.

"Nice talking to you," Randa said to the retreating woman, half laughing.

She walked over stepping stones to her car, convinced that Julia's discovery of Vicki Bryant's involvement gave significance to things she had known but hadn't wanted to think about. Now she had no choice.

And it was all related to four years ago in Hawaii.

An hour later, as Randa walked into her kitchen, she noticed the red light blinking on her answering machine. Maybe it was Lee.

It was Buckles.

"Our absent leader hasn't authorized anyone to consult with you," the voice said, "and has had no contact with a swift-running beast. Nobody from that herd has contacted me. You done right."

She didn't know why he left messages like that. Any idiot interested in what was going on could figure out what he was saying.

The message didn't please her. Horse had known she would not deal directly with him unless authorized, so he had lied

95

about having cleared things with Chubleigh. It was arrogance. It was patronizing. Because he was a federal officer and she was only a sheriff's deputy, he didn't think the formalities were required. Well, to hell with him.

She made herself a small salad with lots of black olives, which she loved. She sprinkled parmesan cheese over everything; then, after sitting on her lanai watching two laughing girls going downriver in a long canoe, she went inside and phoned Bill White, telling herself she was not asking a private detective for assistance, which was forbidden by protocol, but was interviewing a witness who obviously knew more about what was going on than he intended to tell her. For the moment she was less interested in what he knew than in his ability to lead her to Vicki Bryant who might have gone back to wherever she had come from. If she knew she was being followed, she could be anywhere. All Bill seemed to know was that she had checked out of the Beach Motel the day Woody Barstow was shot. It didn't mean she had left the area.

Randa waited through a thirty-second promo Bill had put on his machine. When he didn't pick up, she left a message.

He called shortly after eleven while she was stretched out on her sofa watching the local news and wondering why Lee hadn't called. The signal was scratchy. He was on his portable.

"I'm down a little road just past the parking lot of the Beach Motel. Vicki Bryant's in a room with the guy you've been looking for. Lee Fronzi's in there with them. His wagon, I can see it from where I'm standing. They've been in there more than a half hour."

Then Lee wasn't in Georgia and may never have gone there. Oh, my God!

Because every cop and deputy on the beach knew she was hunting for Abu Mosul, it was not surprising that Bill knew about him. And not surprising that he had chased him down.

What Bill expected to gain she could only guess. Maybe he just wanted to discredit Lee. Maybe he was finding out things for Julia. Whatever his reason, he had succeeded in convincing her that Lee was in trouble. She dreaded finding Lee with Vicki Bryant. She dreaded having to question him. But at least now he couldn't pretend he wasn't involved.

She wondered: had Claude Lazard been in regular contact with Vicki Bryant since the murder of Woody Barstow? Did Lee actually go to Georgia to be with his brother?

"Stay there," she said. "I'm on my way."

She changed shoes, put on working slacks and a short-sleeved shirt, strapped on her pistol and headed out.

The street was near a bird sanctuary at the far end of the island. A street lamp shed a pool of light on seagrape trees at a gravel turnaround a couple of hundred feet inside the road. Her headlights picked up the railing of a foot bridge that angled into the sanctuary. A car was tucked into the woods near the bridge. Its interior lights were on. The driver's-side door was open.

Through trees a hundred yards down a worn path she could see two lighted windows in the Beach Motel and reflections on the window of what looked like a pickup truck. Nothing was moving.

She sat at the wheel and watched the lighted car near the footbridge. She lifted her flashlight off the passenger seat. She considered calling for backup but didn't want deputies roaring in with blazing rooflights.

She fitted the flashlight under her arm and quietly closed her door and locked it, crunching gravel as she walked in front of her car to a strip of grass that led down the edge of the roadway.

With dry seagrape leaves brushing her face, she peered into the back seat of the car, then the front seat. She was offended by the stale odor of cigarette smoke. The glove compartment was open.

She went to the driver's side, climbed in and found an envelope in the glove compartment addressed to Bill White. There was a round, yellowish stain on the envelope. She raised it to her nose and smelled gun oil.

She got out and closed the door. Again she considered calling for backup. But what would she tell them, I'm nervous? If nothing was wrong here, especially because she was a woman, she'd never hear the end of it.

She had gone no more than twenty feet down the long path when she heard a gunshot coming from somewhere near the motel, not loud, like they're portrayed on TV, more a snapping, puncturing sound. But it was clearly from a handgun.

CHAPTER ELEVEN

She dropped to a crouch. Her foot slipped and she fell into a nest of saw palmetto fronds, feeling the pain of a sharp edge slicing her forearm. She waited more than a minute, her hand in sticky blood gripping her arm. She ran cautiously down the path to the motel parking lot.

A door opened and an elderly man in a T-shirt came out. She yelled, "Get back inside!" and ran past him to the second lighted unit, slamming her palm on the door. "Open up!"

She pushed her badge at a man's face in an opened crack in the blinds. "Open up!" The door opened and she shouldered the man aside and scanned the room and rushed past him to the bathroom. No one there, no one behind the shower curtain. She opened a slider and went outside to a lighted patio and pool. No one out there. Beyond the pool and a deck and a hedge there was a second parking lot past the end of the building—two cars under a street light, neither of them Lee's car. She went back inside.

"What's going on?" the man said, noticing the blood on her forearm.

He didn't look Middle Eastern, but he was bald and about the right age.

"Are you Abu Mosul?"

"Who?"

"Are you Abu Mosul?"

"No. What's going on?"

"You here alone?" The room looked unused, not the site of a recent meeting.

"What's going on?"

She went outside and ran to the far end of the lot and scanned the units. No windows lighted up. There was only one car and a red pickup truck, both in front of lighted units. She swept her flash over the underbrush. She pushed past pine boughs and shined her light around. Heard something. She looked toward the sound, her pistol tight in her hand, her body drenched in sweat.

She saw the white shirt, then the blood stain, then the face of Bill White. He was on his back, his head slanted off a cypress trunk. She stepped into shallow water, crouching over him. The right side of his shirt was soaked with blood. She felt for a pulse. One of his legs started twitching. His eyes popped open, bewildered, not seeing anything. She moved the light off his face, saw the butt of his automatic still in a shoulder holster.

"It's okay, Bill," she said, suddenly light-headed, frightened for him, the leg quivering as she pressed her hand into it. "Oh, my God, you poor . . . I gotta go for help."

She backed out of the underbrush and ran all the way up the path to her car and called in, grabbed a wad of tissues from a box in back and pressed it into the cut on her arm. When she got back to Bill, he was unconscious. His leg had stopped twitching. She could barely get a pulse.

She was kneeling over him in soggy moss, slapping at mosquitoes when the crime-scene unit arrived. She saw Fog Rudenski get out of the truck, then the forensic tech—big, broad-shouldered Al Martinez. Surprised he was on duty.

The ambulance came roaring in behind them.

"In here!" she yelled, waving her light, cringing from the beam of the paramedic's big torch as he ran toward her, flashes of light like bats flying through the trees.

A deputy's cruiser skidded into the lot, the rider leaping out before the wheels stopped. She kept him out of the trees and showed him where to hang yellow tape, then led Fog down the row of darkened windows to a girl standing at the opened doorway of the office.

"What's going on?"

"Abu Mosul," Randa said. "Where's his room?" noticing a woman in a robe and pajamas peeking out the doorway of a back room, her hair wrapped in a kerchief, a woman in her fifties.

"I'm the owner here," the woman said, staring at Fog's badge as she moved toward the desk in flopping sandals.

The girl was working the computer. "No Abu Mosul."

"Vicki Bryant?" Randa asked. "I know she was registered here."

"Vicki Bryant, Vicki Bryant," the owner said, touching the girl's arm, urging her aside, bony fingers tapping the keyboard. "Yes, I remember. Paid cash. Checked out last Thursday."

"This Abu Mosul," Randa said, "is a small man, bald, probably has an accent."

The girl looked hesitantly at the owner. "The man in 107?"

"What's he done?" the owner said. "I don't let trash in here."

Making sure that 107 was the seventh unit down from the office, Randa sent Fog down the pool side. She went out front and called a deputy over from the ambulance. "In case this gets nasty." If Mosul was in there, he had to be deaf, dead, unconscious, or cowering in fear, maybe with a gun, else his window would be lighted.

She hit the wooden door with her knuckles, waited, hit it again. The window lighted up.

"Police!" she said. "Open up."

The door was cracked open. A face under a balding skull peered out.

"There's been some trouble out here," Randa said, standing aside so that he could see the ambulance and the police cars. "We're questioning—"

"I didn't see anything!"

"Would you remove the chain, please."

"I don't know what happened. I can't tell you anything."

A high, whiney voice with an accent, plainly Arabic.

"We are listing all occupants of this wing of the motel. If you have a driver's license . . ."

"I'm registered in the office," he said.

The office had him registered as Douglas Trent. "I need to verify your name."

The man looked nervously at the deputy, more scared of him than of Randa. "Just a minute." He closed the door.

Because bullets could fly through the panels, she stood next to the deputy out of harm's way. "If he comes back with ID and isn't threatening, you walk away. He may be more than a witness, and I don't want a lawyer saying he was intimidated. If I go inside, I'll leave the door open. You wait by the ambulance."

The paramedics, she noticed, were coming out of the underbrush lugging a stretcher. A medic told her he doubted that Bill would make it to the hospital. "His lungs are filling up with blood."

She went back to the room where the man was showing the deputy his driver's license. He removed a green card from his wallet. The name Abu Mosul was on both documents.

"So who is Douglas Trent?" she asked.

With an indifferent shrug: "I'm a businessman. I didn't want my name. . . . It's not against the law."

"It could be," she said, scanning the room.

The two beds had been sat on. There were plastic coffee cups on the nightstand between the headboards, one of them imprinted with lipstick. The room smelled of cigarettes and wine.

Abu looked relieved when the deputy walked away.

"Your guests," Randa said, pointing at the cups. "No. Leave the door open."

He came away from the door. "Guests?" looking puzzled for a moment, then smiling. "Oh . . . yes, there was someone here."

"Did the woman have a name?"

"I suppose so. I didn't ask. One doesn't ask their names."

She gave that a tight lip and walked past him, looking at the beds, at the cups, at an ashtray with four butts in it, all stained with lipstick.

Fog had come to the slider. She let him in and told him to go out to the ambulance. "Stay with Bill as long as you can. He may know who shot him. I'll join you at the hospital."

She sat on the nearest bed and pointed the little man to a chair. "You understand," she said, "that you're free to ask me to leave. Right now I have only a few questions, but I'll want to see you at the sheriff's headquarters in the morning."

"Why? I didn't see anything. I have no idea what happened out there."

"It's not about 'out there'," she said.

"The woman? Is it the woman? I didn't know her. Why would I know such a person?" laughing as though to share the absurdity.

"This isn't a game, Mr. Mosul. We both know the woman is Vicki Bryant. We both know you've been in contact with her for some time, not just this evening."

He seemed to grow older as he stared at her, then at something beyond her, then at his hands folded in his lap. He raised an ankle to his knee and picked at his sock. He finally looked up. "May I ask what this is about?"

"Right now it's about Woodrow Barstow. You were seen with

him less than a mile from here in a bar called The Brig."

"Seen with him? No. I knew Mr. Barstow. I saw on television what happened to him, but no, I couldn't have been seen with him. I haven't—"

"You were seen at a table with him just before he was shot. We have witnesses."

"They're wrong! I've never been in that bar, and I haven't seen Mr. Barstow in more than a year. I had no idea he was in Florida."

He spoke so matter-of-factly, with nothing of the earlier attempts at deception, she would have believed him if she hadn't known better. Could he be telling the truth?

She decided, for now, to let it go. She didn't have time for more questions, and this wasn't the place for it. She wanted to get to the hospital.

"Don't try to get cute with this, Mr. Mosul," she said, getting up, handing him a card from her folder. "I want the truth when I talk to you tomorrow."

"I'm telling the truth! I've never been in that bar or saloon, whatever it's called. I haven't talked with Woodrow Barstow in more than a year. And not here, not in Florida."

"Which one of the cars out there is yours?" she asked, weary of the denials.

"The blue one. It's rented."

"Tomorrow morning at the sheriff's headquarters," she said, walking away.

"Your witnesses are wrong! I wasn't there!"

The voice haunted her as she crossed the parking lot to where Bea Kim was standing at the yellow tape.

"What the hell was Bill White doing here?" Bea said.

"Checking on the guy in one-oh-seven," she said, turning, pointing at Abu in the open doorway. "Go over and take a good look at him. He's Abu Mosul, the little baldheaded guy your

104

waitress saw."

Bea walked to the doorway, talked with Abu a few seconds and came back. "Could be the one," she said, "although the guy the waitress described was wearing a baseball cap. She never said bald."

"Never said bald?"

"No. Maybe he was bald, but she didn't say so."

"Where did I get that notion?"

"Beats me. I didn't hear a call for this. You got here first?"

"I heard the shot," Randa said. "I didn't see the shooter. He or she could have run down there," pointing toward the sanctuary and the canal, "or gone past the office to a waiting car. I saw taillights, nothing I could identify."

Eventually Randa would explain Bill's role in this but not until she knew more about the car that could have been Lee's. Maybe Bill just wanted it to have been. He didn't say he had seen Lee in it or in the motel room.

And you didn't say a word about Lee to Abu.

If, when Bill called, he had been standing where he was shot, where was the car he said he was looking at? The car that sped off came from the other side of the office. Was Bill over there when he called? Why had he gone to that side if he was here to watch Abu Mosul's room? Was the car that sped off Lee's?

"You sure that waitress didn't say the man with Barstow was bald?"

"Very sure."

Glancing at Abu, Randa said, "I just can't picture this guy in a baseball cap."

Bea shrugged. "What happened to your arm?"

"Underbrush in there. Saw palmetto."

"Another thing," Bea said. "That second waitress? She said the guy was wearing a dark jacket. How many guys wear jackets in Florida this time of year, especially in a rat hole like the Brig?

105

You could get in there wearing nothing but a jockstrap."

"Don't try it," Randa said.

As she drove to the city she again asked herself why she hadn't mentioned Lee to Abu. Had Lee actually been there?

Aw, Lee, what the hell are you doing?

CHAPTER TWELVE

Randa had to wait at the emergency entrance for a man to transfer out of a wheelchair into the back seat of a silver limo before she could pull into the broad space under the portico.

Fog was at the glass doors waiting for her—hands at his sides, head tilted, sadness in dark eyes watching her get out of her car, talking across her roof.

"He didn't make it."

She was saddened but not surprised. She gave the announcement a silent moment as she walked into the lighted vestibule, her soaked slacks chafing her legs, mud caked on her knees.

"Died in the ambulance," Fog said. "Coughed up some blood. Never said anything. You gonna look at him?" said with a lot of fatherly kindness in his expression.

"No." Viewing the body would only deepen the wound and do nothing for Bill.

"He got family here?"

"Just his ex-wife," Randa said. "I'll call her."

She felt no affection for the woman who had reviled her when she and Bill were seeing each other, but even a worst enemy doesn't deserve to get bad personal news from a public source like television.

"Thought we might need these," Fog said, handing Randa a ring of keys. "I gave the car keys to a guy's bringing the car in."

"Watch mine," she said, looking back to make sure the doors were closed and the lights were off. It wasn't a sheriff's car, and

Chubleigh wouldn't pay to replace a battery.

She went to a phone at the end of the lobby and made the call, talked a few minutes, then rejoined Fog at the door.

Fog asked, "How'd she take it?"

"She thanked me for telling her."

"I guess she'd spent years afraid of a call like that."

"I suppose so. You had any sleep?"

"You need something?"

"I want you at Bill's office first thing in the morning. It's in the Edison Building, that strip of storefront offices next to the bank on Palm Court. I'll get there as soon as I can. I'm too tired to do it now."

While she was strapping herself into her car, Fog tapped on her window and came around to the driver's side.

"I'll need those keys."

"No," she said, picking at wet cloth on her knees. She couldn't wait to get home and get her soiled clothes off. "You wait outside and don't let anyone in."

"Like Tyonek Horse? I picked up something about him. Had a few beers with an FBI friend. Want to hear it?"

"If it doesn't take too long."

"He said they're not as hot on this as Horse is. And the navy isn't either. He said they're just keeping Horse busy until he retires. A kind of courtesy, I guess. He lives alone. The job's his whole life. The new SAC doesn't seem to like him."

"Shouldn't he be on disability? I've wondered about that."

"I think they went over the special agent's head on that one, somebody up in D.C., a friend, I guess, some big shot in the Hoover building got this assignment for him."

"I don't have time right now, but Olivia Mannheim didn't hurry down here from D.C. to keep us out of a case nobody cares about. Maybe your friend doesn't have the whole picture. Maybe he was trying to mislead you."

"I didn't get that impression, but . . ." He shrugged. "I suppose."

"Let's talk about it in the morning. Get some sleep. Bea can handle the crime-scene chores. I guess she couldn't find Kappy."

"Probably home in bed with Irene. It's where I'd be, a nice-looking woman like that," big teeth shining in a grin.

Something to sleep with seemed to be his first thoughts about women, not that he was inconsiderate or abusive, just horny. He enjoyed appearing to be a sexual adventurer, but she was sure he didn't cheat on his girlfriend, Rita Salazar, whom he had been living with for nearly three years, an oncology nurse.

One time on a ride to Clewiston he explained why he hadn't married Rita.

"It's because of Dolly Madison."

That astonished her. She didn't think he'd ever heard of Dolly Madison. "The president's wife?"

That stumped him. "The president? What's he got to do with it?"

She laughed. "Never mind."

"Caught Dolly's father poaching is how I met her. We lived together some eight years. I loved her but never married her, and when she died I thought it would insult her memory if I married someone else."

"You tell Rita that?"

He laughed. "Hell no. Think I'm crazy?"

When she pulled into her riverside parking lot, she found Lee's convertible in his favorite spot near the lemon tree. And she found Lee asleep on the living room sofa in the blue pajamas she had given him for Christmas, lying flat out, her afghan across his legs.

She stood in the hall outside the doorway of her bathroom with a hand on the light switch and watched him for nearly a minute—the man with whom she was sharing her bed and her life. She wanted to lie next to him and wake him with a kiss. But she couldn't because she was tired. At least that's what she told herself.

She went into the bathroom and closed the door, stripped off her clothes, and patted her legs with a soft towel. She stroked a salve over the chafed skin, put antibiotic ointment on her forearm, taped gauze over it, and went into her bedroom without looking at Lee.

She had been in bed no more than two minutes when she heard the knob turn and a sticky sound as the door came open. She shut her eyes in the darkness and felt the mattress sag and felt Lee's breath on her face, his lips on her cheek. When his arm slid under her, she turned away.

"Is it safe to say you're too tired?"

She said nothing, drew her legs away from his prodding knees. She would have given anything to turn and flatten her belly against him. But she couldn't. She prayed he would leave her alone.

"Guess we're both too tired," he said, turning away, a hint of bitterness in his tone. He knew she was awake.

And she stayed awake for what seemed hours, alternating between feeling sorry for herself and arguing that she had no hard evidence he had done anything wrong.

In the morning she was in slacks and jacket at her kitchen counter filling her portable coffee cup when he came to the doorway barefoot, yawning, scratching his belly.

"What happened to your arm?"

"Sliced it on a saw palmetto. Nothing important."

"I thought this was your day off."

"I have to go in." She looked for deceit on his face but could see none. The last thing she wanted was an argument, but she had to test him. "Things okay in Georgia?"

"Same old . . . you know. Couldn't wait to get back."

That he had come back to Vicki Bryant and not to her floated briefly through her mind, but she dismissed it. Not the issue.

She turned to the sink when he came over and slid his hands under her arms and embraced her.

"You were out late," he whispered into her ear, "and obviously very tired."

"Bill White got shot last night."

He pulled back. If he was faking surprise, he was very good at it. His reaction seemed genuine.

"Bill White? The one you—"

"The private detective Julia hired," she said, searching his eyes, finding no evasion in them.

"Really? But he's a cop."

"He retired last year. He was a private detective."

"How'd it happen?"

"Someone shot him outside the Beach Motel," she said. "He was checking on Vicki Bryant."

He lost control of his expression and, as if to hide from her, turned his back and filled a paper cup with water, held the cup to his mouth, and stared out the curtained window.

Tears filmed her eyes as she watched him. "We've got a lot to talk about," she said. "But I don't have time now. You haven't been honest with me, Lee."

Until this moment she had had only Bill's word that Lee was in the motel room with Abu Mosul and Vicki Bryant and that he had been with Vicki and Claude Lazard at a restaurant. Now it was confirmed.

Still gazing out the window, he said, "I haven't lied to you."

"I don't want to talk about it now. There are people waiting for me. I don't know when I'll be free, but I'd appreciate your finding time—"

"I haven't lied to you, Randa. I can explain."

She gave that a stolid look and walked past him into her bedroom. Her hands trembled as she gathered up her things. She tried to calm herself by communing with her image in the mirror, but the face in the mirror wouldn't help.

He was still at the sink when she walked to the outer hallway, not looking at him.

"Let me explain," he said. "Okay, I've been hiding things. But I—"

"Not now."

"But I—"

"Not now."

For the first time since they had started living together she left her apartment in his presence without looking at him or kissing him goodbye. She got into her wagon and didn't look back until she was moving toward the gate.

He wasn't in the doorway. He had stayed inside. Tears formed in her eyes.

She drove across town to headquarters telling herself it was a waste of time to fret over something she knew so little about. There was no reason to think him guilty of any wrongdoing. And if he had been with Vicki Bryant, whoever the hell that was, she would have smelled it on him: the shower wasn't used last night; the towels were exactly as she had left them.

She stared glumly through her windshield, both hands gripping the wheel, her face a mask of stone.

She hadn't entered Lee's name in any of her reports. She hadn't mentioned him to Fog or to Buckles. She had tried to hide him. And now when she was asked why Bill White had called her to the motel, she could not leave Lee out of it. He was in that motel room, and it could have been his convertible that had sped out of the parking lot. She wouldn't allow herself to think it could have been he who had fired the shot.

It will come out, Randa, whether you say it or not; and if you leave his name out, you're guilty of a crime.

Never before in her career had she even thought of covering up for anyone. It shamed her now that she had considered it.

Love! Who the hell said it makes you happy?

She went straight to her cubicle in the squad room. She had mail but couldn't read it, messages on her machine she couldn't listen to. She just sat there opening envelopes, staring at words on paper.

Her phone rang. It was Buckles.

"Tyonek Horse is in with Derek. I'm sure they'll want to talk to you. So come talk to me."

She went straight to the women's room and sat in the narrow booth studying scratches in the white paint on the door. She gave herself about a minute at the mirror while she washed her hands. She took several deep breaths and walked up the corridor and slowly, reluctantly, opened the door to the major's office.

The formal austerity of the room, the undecorated walls, the ugly furniture, even the smile on the man at the desk did nothing to cheer her.

"You get a shot for that?" he said, pointing at the bandage on her arm.

"It's nothing," she said, dropping into one of the cushioned chairs. "A saw palmetto."

"Don't fool with it," he said. "It could get infected."

"What's the FBI want?"

"Information about Bill White, I imagine. Is there a connection between Tyonek and Abu?"

"You're better positioned to know that than I am. All I know is Bill tailed Vicki Bryant to Mosul's room and called me." She took a deep breath, paused, stared at the edge of the carpet,

113

finally raised her eyes. "Bill knew I was looking for Mosul and looking for Vicki Bryant." She was tempted even then to say nothing about Lee, but she couldn't betray herself. "He also knew that Lee Fronzi was in that motel room. I think that's his main reason for having called me."

"Fronzi? What the hell . . . ?"

"I don't know what he was doing there. I haven't had a chance to talk to him. It's the second time he was seen with Vicki Bryant." And that came out loaded with guilt.

Her gaze faltered. She looked down at her hands, waiting for the ax to fall. He knew she should have mentioned Lee's involvement in her reports, but all he said was, "That puts you in a bind, doesn't it," probably remembering last year when Chubleigh had raised hell because she had brought Lee on a manhunt.

"Nothing I can't handle."

Chubleigh would immediately have upbraided her, but Buckles wasn't Chubleigh. He had been a cop for more than eighteen years. He knew the effect it would have on her and Lee's reputations if she were officially reprimanded.

"How involved is he?"

"I don't know. I'm going to have it out with him this evening."

He gave that a lot of thought. She hated the way she felt, hated the vulnerability, hated avoiding the major's eyes.

The buzzer sounded. He got up and came around the desk, took her arm, and walked her toward the door.

"Don't mention Lee to Derek," he said. "We'll talk in the morning."

114

CHAPTER THIRTEEN

The artificial hand, like two curled steel fingers, rested on Tyonek's knee. His real hand, the left one, rested on his other knee. He was in the chair Olivia Mannheim had sat in, his ankles crossed and tucked under the seat like a schoolgirl's—not the way men usually sat.

Randa took the chair across from him. Buckles sat next to her, leaning forward, elbows on his thighs, chin on the heels of his hands, fingers stroking his eyes. It's how he usually sat when preparing for boredom.

"We've all met," Chubleigh said, folded hands bouncing on his desk, looking at each of the faces, eager to get started. "So let's get right into what we're here for."

Apparently he knew about the incident at her apartment. Buckles told him? Tyonek?

"Cooperation," Tyonek said, directing himself to Randa with a smile, urging something of the kind from her. The smile reflected neither warmth nor humor, only teeth too big for his face.

She gave him a nod.

"I figure you got the impression the other day I had some kind of approval from the sheriff," he said.

"That's what you told me."

"Oh, no. I only meant I was sure the sheriff wouldn't mind if we talked. Just trying to save time. You must have misread me." Again the patronizing smile.

I didn't misread you, she thought, and I'm not misreading you now. And you've just called me a liar, watching triumph sneaking into his eyes. He apparently believed he had outwitted her. She doubted he could outwit a clam.

She noticed dark creases outside his eyes. He squinted a lot, maybe needed glasses. She couldn't remember whether Chi Chi Rodriguez wore glasses. Maybe not. There was less masculinity in his face than in Chi Chi's, but they did look alike, remembering following Chi Chi around a Seacrest golf course, laughing when he played to the crowd.

"Agent Tyonek Horse here would like to know whether you think the shooting last night had anything to do with the Barstow case," Chubleigh said. "Any reason to believe it does?" looking at Tyonek.

"Not hard to figure," Tyonek said, leaning forward, feet thrusting from beneath the chair. "I know you and Bill White were deputies together. I thought maybe he was there on your behalf, maybe working for you."

He knew it would diminish her in Chubleigh's eyes if she were thought to enlist help from a private investigator. Why was he trying to cut her down?

Buckles put a hand on Randa's arm and said to Tyonek, "You have no call to say that."

"I wasn't criticizing her. I just couldn't figure out why she got there so fast."

"You were at the crime scene?" Randa asked.

"Just monitoring police calls, talking to people. I understand Bill White called you."

"I don't know where you heard that. But yes, he did."

"Just doing you a favor? Like I said before, Sheriff, I'm not here to tell you how to run your department, but in a sensitive matter like this, I would think—"

"It's what *I* think that matters in this office," Chubleigh said, offended by the criticism. "And what I think is you couldn't get a warrant to search White's office so you came here thinking my standards aren't as high as some federal magistrate's. And you probably don't see that as an insult. If you had probable cause, you'd be at White's office right now."

"I didn't get a warrant because I don't want to go that route," Tyonek said. "The same reason I haven't got the injunction Olivia Mannheim threatened you with. I don't operate that way. I cooperate. I don't want to fight you. I want to combine our investigations," playing boy scout sitting there with the sun shining on him through the high window.

Chubleigh ignored him and looked at Randa. "You got White's keys? They weren't on him or in his car. And Rudenski doesn't have them."

So Tyonek went to Bill's office and Fog turned him away. That's why he's here. She glanced at Buckles. He nodded. He apparently knew about it.

"What is it in White's office you're looking for?" Chubleigh asked.

Tyonek sat back, giving both Randa and the sheriff a long, searching look. "If I had a free hand in this, I'd tell you everything you want to know. But you know how the Bureau operates. You know I can't disclose—"

"What I know, Mr. Horse, is that you've got to persuade me you have a legitimate cause to poke into my homicide investigation. Maybe you got away with confiscating evidence in Hampton, but we're a different breed of cat over here."

"I wasn't part of that," Tyonek said.

Why, Randa wondered, was there a crew of FBI agents going through the Hampton apartment, whereas here there's only one? Why hasn't the FBI special agent in charge contacted the sheriff? Maybe Fog's informant is right. Maybe Barstow's death isn't important to anyone but Horse. But why, if that's true, was

Mannheim sent here?

"We're trying to help you, Sheriff," Tyonek said. "We want to cooperate. Why would we want to hurt your reputation by getting a restraining order?"

"Cooperation works two ways," the sheriff said, looking at Buckles, then at Randa, knowing they knew why he was being hard on Tyonek.

Last summer Randa's assistant, Skip Morrow, was killed in northwest Georgia while investigating a building that, unknown to anyone in the sheriff's department, was a storage facility for illegally imported drugs. It was also unknown to them that the building was the focal point of an FBI sting.

It was actually Randa who had sent Morrow to check out the building. But, ironically as it turned out, the sheriff, believing he could make points with the governor, took credit for sending Morrow up there, and accordingly caught the blame when it was revealed that Skip had blundered into the FBI operation.

Instead of the commendations he had expected to gain, all hell came down on Chubleigh's head. Words like "incompetent" and "stupid" flew at him from as high up as the United States Attorney General's office. Even the governor, whose curiosity had prompted the search in the first place and for whose approval the sheriff had become involved, publicly denied any knowledge of the matter when it became known that the man who owned the building was a major contributor to the governor's war chest.

It didn't surprise Randa that Chubleigh was hostile to the FBI, and it didn't surprise her that the FBI was undisturbed by his hostility. If they had told the governor what was going on in that building, the whole disaster could have been avoided, and Skip Morrow would be alive. So much for cooperation.

"I just don't understand your attitude," Tyonek said. "You know this is a matter of national security."

"We're all under the same flag," Chubleigh growled.

"But I—"

"You throw your high standards in my face and expect me to jump. You don't give a flea's tit about my standards. You seem to think I don't have any."

"I'm trying to cooperate!"

"Then stay away from White's office or come up with probable cause for getting in."

Having said that, he got up and turned his back and went to the window, hands in his pockets, waiting for them to leave. He wasn't the most brilliant man Randa had ever worked for, and certainly not the most courteous, but he was clearly the most stubborn.

The move to the window baffled Tyonek. He looked wonderingly at Randa. She just smiled and got up. "Meeting's over," and headed for the door.

"But you haven't answered my question!"

Randa waited.

"Do you think White's death is connected to the Barstow case?" Tyonek asked.

"Why would you ask that?"

"Obviously I'd like to know. It wouldn't hurt you to . . ."

"You wouldn't have gone there, Mr. Horse, if you didn't think so. You knew Abu Mosul was in that motel. Why don't you try being honest with us? All this interagency rivalry—"

"What makes you think that?"

As he stared at her, he seemed poised as though undecided whether to attack her or to run. Something very strange about this guy. He's an investigator with the massive authority of the federal government behind him. Why doesn't he use it? Saying he's in Cherokee City just to kill time doesn't explain anything. The Bureau is too famously short-handed to waste an agent.

"You told Captain Frye you 'spotted' Abu here in Cherokee

City," she said. "Apparently you wanted to get Woodrow Barstow over here. Why did you go through Frye? Why not contact Barstow on your own?"

" 'Go through'? I didn't 'go through' anyone. I happened to mention it to the captain, who's a friend of Barstow's, also a friend of mine, and he passed it along. I didn't have any reason to get Barstow over here."

There was a lot of hostility in this man, maybe caused by the nature of his assignment, maybe by something else. She watched him head for the door, noticing that he tucked his prosthesis into his jacket pocket before he went outside. That gleaming steel probably got uncomfortably hot in this Florida sun.

To Buckles she said, "When I called in the shooting of Bill White, I didn't mention any names. I said a man has been shot and I need an ambulance. It wasn't my call that brought Horse to the crime scene. I didn't see him there, you know. He must have come after I left. So how did he know I got there 'fast,' as he said?"

"I don't know. But you gave an address," Buckles said. "He probably knew it's where Mosul was staying. And don't be so hard on the guy. He's getting no cooperation from us and apparently no respect from the Bureau."

"Why would a nighttime shooting outside a motel interest the FBI? I'm convinced this guy wanted Barstow in Cherokee City and used Abu Mosul as bait. What's the connection?"

"I think he's just trying to find some meaning in what he's doing here," Buckles said. "If the FBI thought there was something going on here, they'd've sent more than a one-armed short-timer."

"The NCIS believed he would take over the investigation of Barstow's homicide. She came here especially to identify Barstow's remains and to convince the sheriff that he should turn things over to the FBI. Mannheim wasn't indifferent to our interest in the case; she definitely wanted us out of it. And with all of that, this FBI man has either been made impotent by his superiors or he's incompetent. Or—the alternative I'm beginning to like—they're all waiting for something to happen. And maybe he doesn't know it."

"Here?"

"There have been two homicides, Major. Both of them connected to a man who was working for Saddam Hussein, and all we get is one FBI agent asking whether we see any connection between the murders. He didn't want to know whether there was a connection; he wanted to know whether we thought there was. He's not monitoring a crime scene. He's monitoring us." With that she picked up her bag. "Something fishy's going on."

"Maybe Derek senses the same thing is why he's being so stubborn about this."

Randa laughed. "Yes, that's so uncharacteristic of him."

She was halfway to the door when Buckles said, "Oh, be sure to pull everything out of Bill's office. Horse might still try for a warrant. And be careful how you handle Fronzi. Derek has a long memory," he said, referring to the manhunt Chubleigh had become incensed over. Because Lee had been in her car on that venture, Chubleigh was accused by the press of giving special favors to a rich businessman. Publicity like that doesn't win elections.

As she went into the squadroom, she noticed Abu Mosul on the waiting bench. He got up, but she waved him back down.

"Be with you in a minute," she said. Did Horse see him? Not if he didn't come into the squadroom.

She was reading the screen of her computer when Bea Kim leaned across her shoulder and whispered, "It wasn't him the waitress saw. She was here when Mosul walked in. She said it wasn't him."

"Where is she now?"

"I sent her home."

"She's sure?"

"Seemed to be. And she agreed the guy was wearing a baseball cap."

"Why does she remember him?"

"I don't know, but she was firm. 'Definitely not him,' is what she said."

Randa worked at her desk for twenty minutes before she got up and led Abu Mosul into the conference room. She pointed to a chair under the bulletin board. She closed the door and sat across from him. The room smelled faintly of sweat—a closed room, no windows, no ceiling fan.

"I understand you're in this country on some kind of special status."

Mosul nodded. He appeared subdued and nervous. Conviction of even a misdemeanor could threaten his immigrant status, she imagined.

"It's pretty unusual these days for a man who was part of Saddam Hussein's regime to be allowed to roam freely in this country."

"I've been cleared—'vetted,' I think they say. And I wasn't that high up, never sat around the long table." And he snickered sheepishly.

"So what's your status now?"

"With them? Nothing. Now I'm a consultant for the CIA. In another year I hope to become a citizen." He was apparently working hard at being an American. After only four years in this country he had lost a lot of his accent. When she pointed this out, he said, "Foreign accents are valuable only if you're a pretty girl or you're rich. An Arabic accent these days could get me lynched."

"You lied about hosting a meeting in your room, Mr. Mosul.

Let's clear that up. You lied about knowing Vicki Bryant. Who is she?"

He seemed to shrink a little. "Misdirection is not a lie," he said. "I was misdirecting you. She's a friend of a man I'm trying to do business with. I have no personal—"

"Who is this friend?"

"Claude Lazard. He's in the arms business, like me. It's why I'm in this country. The CIA . . . I'm a consultant on Middle East defense systems; that is, I have been these past three and a half years. Lately I've been trying to get back into private trade. That's why I'm here," sitting like a meek schoolboy, hands resting on his knees, fingers tapping. The fingernails looked manicured.

"And the man who was with Vicki Bryant?"

"He's a friend of Lazard's."

"Why was he there?"

"He came with her. Her boyfriend, maybe. I don't know," dismissing Lee as though he hadn't spent weeks with him on a submarine.

"Why was she there?"

"She's a very nervous woman. Doesn't know anyone. She thought . . . I guess she and Lazard have been lovers and broke up because his wife found out about her."

"Why come to you?"

"I don't know. I guess Claude told her about me. Maybe he said we were good friends."

"How did Vicki know where to find you?"

"She saw me at the motel. About a week ago. She had a room there."

"And she just popped in with this man?"

"I was astonished. I had no idea she knew me."

"At last night's meeting, they were in your room how long?" thinking about the four stained butts in the ashtray.

"Maybe an hour," Abu said. "They left maybe twenty minutes before all that commotion outside."

"Before you heard the shot?"

"I didn't hear a shot. I didn't know anybody had been shot until you told me."

"Why did you lie about the woman?"

"What am I supposed to do? Why get her involved? She had nothing to do with what happened out there."

"How do you know that?"

"They were gone. I heard the car drive off."

"You heard the car drive off, but you didn't hear the gunshot that was right outside your door?"

The question seemed to unnerve him. "What can I say? I didn't hear it."

"So why did you lie to protect that woman you call a stranger?"

"If it came out I said she was in my room, it would hurt me with the people I'm trying to do business with. I didn't want my name linked to her."

"Why not if you thought she was an old friend of Claude's?"

"That's what I thought before she came to my room. By the time she left, I knew different. She's apparently quite promiscuous. I assume not very stable."

"And she asked you to help her get back together with Lazard right in front of this man you say might be a boyfriend?"

"Who knows how people live these days?"

"Do you know where I can find her?"

"No. She said she moved out of the motel a week ago. She didn't say where she went."

"You've been here how long?"

"Two weeks tomorrow."

"How soon after you got here did you talk to the FBI?"

The question startled him. He apparently hadn't been

prepared for it and probably didn't realize the local police knew about it. And of course she had been told only that the FBI had "spotted" him in Cherokee City.

"I went to them so they wouldn't question why I was here. It's complicated. International trade in armaments is tightly regulated, especially now, as you can imagine. I'm not a citizen and I'm from the Middle East. I don't want trouble. I wanted it understood that I am here for very legitimate reasons."

"Why would they think you weren't?"

He sighed, looked past her at the wall. "There is a man here. You must know about him."

"Give me his name."

"Raphael Cardozo."

"You're here to deal with Cardozo?"

"His daughter, Claude Lazard's wife. She runs the business now. But he's there, and I know from my CIA connections he's being watched. I know how it might appear if I'm seen with him. I can't afford . . ." He raised his arms in a gesture of helplessness. "I walk on eggshells. September eleventh has put a curse on my business."

"Who is Cardozo being watched by?"

"I presume the FBI, maybe others."

"You said yesterday you hadn't met with Woodrow Barstow."

"Yes. I knew he was here only when I learned about his death. I wasn't in that bar. I swear."

"But you knew him."

"In Washington. I had many talks with him. I first met him in Hawaii four years ago. I presume you know that."

"And you first met Vicki Bryant there?"

"No. She was there? I never saw her there. I only just met her here, last night."

"You met Claude Lazard in Hawaii? And the man who came with Vicki Bryant?"

"I knew them . . . yes, in Hawaii."

"Tell me about Hawaii," she said, sitting back, wondering how, with a straight face, he could say he had no idea who Lee was and then admit he had met Lee in Hawaii. Was he lying about not knowing Vicki Bryant in Hawaii?

Most of what he told her she already knew. He had been delivered to the Israelis by the Jordanians and had been held in a Tel Aviv jail for more than a year.

"It wasn't my activities they cared about," he said. "They knew me. People I had made arms deals with. They knew I was honest. They knew I had been helped out of Iraq by the Jordanians. They didn't care about that. It's what they thought I knew about Nassar Massud. I once worked with him, that's all. I didn't know anything . . ."

"Who is Nassar Massud?"

"Some kind of spy or something. He's . . . he was killed in an airplane crash in Mexico. They thought I knew things about that. I didn't. I don't. I'm an arms trader. Entirely legitimate. Non-political."

"Why did the CIA want you?"

"The same reason. Find out what I knew. It was nothing. I knew nothing about Massud. Never heard of him."

"But they held you?"

"They gave me a job as a consultant on Middle East defense systems. It's my area of expertise. I was in the Iraqi ministry. I assume you know that."

"You're a Baathist?"

"No. It's a myth that everyone who worked for Saddam agreed with him or even liked him. I loathed him."

"And now you're free?"

"Now I'm trying to re-establish myself. Selling arms is a very lucrative business."

Randa wanted to deepen her understanding of Lee's role in

all of this, but she decided to wait. She had heard enough for now. More questions might spook him.

"I'm assuming you're not planning to leave Cherokee City," she said, getting up, watching him push back his chair.

"Not until I finish my business here. When I'm ready to leave, I'll call your office. I don't want any trouble. I want to co-operate. What I'm doing here is completely aboveboard. I want you to know that."

Clearly, Randa thought, it's what you want me to believe.

"We'll talk again," she said.

CHAPTER FOURTEEN

It was nearly ten that evening when Randa walked down to the bench on the river and sat with legs tucked under the seat, arms folded under her breasts, breathing deeply of warm river odors while watching the shiny back of a manatee that had just risen to the surface, a big seacow out there drifting with the current, maybe like her, wondering what the hell it was all about. There was no one across the river in the illuminated tennis court that cast pools of light on the moving water.

Lee had left a message on her machine while she was in the shower: "Have to check on something in Quantrill. May take a while. Please don't go to bed before I get there. We have to talk."

Yes, we have to talk.

Usually around this time of evening they would be on her living-room sofa, the television tuned to something they weren't watching, voices they weren't listening to, bodies feverishly entangled.

Before coming down here she had gone over papers she and Fog had picked up at Bill White's office: two booklets of field notes and a five-page report that may or may not have been sent to Julia. Appended to the report were negative results of website efforts to find Vicki Bryant.

There were only mild surprises in the documents, nothing about Abu Mosul. Lee was mentioned only as having been at the restaurant with Claude Lazard when Vicki Bryant was there, nothing to suggest he had been previously acquainted with Vicki or was in any way involved with her. Either Bill had lied about Lee's involvement or had not wanted anything remotely libelous to appear in his report. That Woodrow Barstow had followed Vicki to the restaurant was not mentioned.

She and Fog searched every inch of Bill's office but found nothing to link him to the Barstow investigation.

The only local mystery the report cleared up was that Vicki had checked into a Royal Inn in Seacrest after she had left the Beach Motel, and again she hadn't listed an automobile tag number or a street address in Denver, and the police there had never heard of her.

What interested Randa most was that Bill had kept everything out of his report that might have shown a connection between Vicki and Barstow. She remembered Julia's surprise when she learned that Vicki had been followed by him. And she remembered watching the surprise fading into apprehension as they talked about it. If Julia was guilty of no wrongdoing, why was she scared? For her father? For Lazard? For Lee? Was the Barstow part of Bill's investigation kept out of the report because Julia had not wanted her concern about Barstow to appear in writing?

Randa was in her living room watching the eleven o'clock news when she saw a streak of light from the parking lot slide across her television screen. She went to the window. Lee's convertible was out there at the lemon tree, headlights shrinking to tiny dots, then blinking out. In the vestibule outside her kitchen she fingered the window curtain aside and, with a small feeling of dread, watched Lee approach her door.

She stepped back, searching his eyes when he came in. He gave her a brief worried look but made no attempt at a greeting.

"There was an accident on forty-one," he said, going into the kitchen.

"Anyone hurt?"

"Couldn't see. I was way back in the line. Didn't see an ambulance, just a couple of patrol cars."

He spent a long time at the sink, his back turned as he washed his hands and dried them on a paper towel.

She asked, "Have you eaten?"

"I had something up there."

"Coffee? I could make coffee."

"No thanks."

He tossed the crumpled towel at the wastebasket and missed, went over and picked it up and dropped it from shoulder level, arm extended like a golfer dropping a replacement ball into soft grass.

He finally turned and looked at her. "I don't know what you're accusing me of, but I haven't tried to deceive you."

She hadn't expected him to blurt out a confession. He was a wealthy, successful man who would not easily admit to a weakness, especially to someone whose esteem was important to him. She had no factual knowledge that he had done anything wrong. She prayed he hadn't. But she had to act as though he might have, else she would learn nothing. Right now she could not act like his lover. She had to address whatever explanations he might come up with like a cop. She had been trained to know that a successful questioning depends on leverage. If you don't have it, you act as though you do.

At this moment she realized more keenly than ever before how deeply being a cop defined her. She was surprised, maybe dismayed, by how easily she could set aside her affection for this man. She wasn't sure she liked what she was learning about herself, but it was there. She led him into the living room where she sat across from him on the sofa, watching him drop into a chair Charlie Hawkins had given her, one of those overstuffed things she could still see Charlie pushing into the room. "Is this a great chair or what?" he had said, grinning, plopping down, elevating the footrest with a big lever on the side. She hated it but would never part with it.

"I don't know what the hell you're up in arms about," Lee said. "I didn't have a chance to call you when I got in. Zoe said Vicki Bryant was looking for me. She needed a ride."

"Vicki Bryant. Is that her real name?"

"Why? You think it isn't?"

"Sounds made up. You knew her in Hawaii?"

"Don't play games with me, Randa. You wouldn't ask unless you knew," leaning forward, elbows on his knees, getting into it. "You think I'm screwing around with her? She's a bony, homely nobody. What the hell would I want with her?"

He didn't ordinarily put people down like that. She didn't believe he thought she was jealous. She believed he was trying to misdirect the inquiry. It didn't matter. She knew where she was going.

"The man who was murdered on the beach was following her," she said. "He was a retired investigator for the NCIS."

"Stalking her? That's an irony."

"Why?"

"That's what she's doing."

It wasn't, but she let it go for the moment. "She's the subject of a federal investigation. And you've been seen with her, and that puts you in the middle of this."

"How? So I knew her. So what?"

"You knew her in Hawaii. Tell me about that."

"How's it put me in the middle of anything?"

"Tell me what happened in Hawaii."

"Nothing. She came out there to see Claude. He kissed her off. Now she's here trying to connect with him. Okay, I met her out there, but it has nothing to do with why she's here. And I didn't 'know' her. I'm trying to persuade her to leave. I'm trying to protect Julia. Vicki doesn't mean a damn thing to me."

"You went with her to a room at the Beach Motel occupied by the man you brought to Hawaii in your submarine. You know the man. It wasn't just an innocent encounter."

"That's what this is about? You think I'm some kind of a suspect?"

"I didn't say that."

"Then what the hell are you saying?"

"I'm trying to find out what's going on."

"You're saying you don't trust me. That's obvious."

"You knew her in Hawaii."

"She came there to see Claude. They knew each other when he was at the Pentagon. They lived together. He said he kissed her off when we went back to sea. Now she's stalking him."

"Lee, she's not stalking him. He's been paying her motel bills. He's been chauffeuring her around. He wants her here."

Lee got up and went to the window, stood with his hands in his pockets, both hands bulging like fists.

She gave him a little time. She was having trouble accounting for the anger. It wasn't like him to lose this much composure. It should be obvious to him that she had to ask these questions.

"Two people have been murdered," she said, "and you're in the middle of it. I want to help you. We both know there's more to this than Julia's love life."

After a while he went back to the chair and sat with knees spread, hands dangling in front of him, a wounded, almost defeated look in his eyes. It was strange to see him acting like a misunderstood boy.

"I probably don't know any more than you do," he said. "I'm trying to find out. That's why I went with Vicki to Mosul's room. I suppose I should have told you."

"You know something was stolen. You were questioned about it by the NCIS agent, and maybe the FBI."

"They questioned everybody, not just me. They were after me because I had brought Julia out there."

"Before or after the voyage?"

"After. When we got in."

"How was she involved?"

"She wasn't. I found out the navy was going to dump some surplus small arms. I thought she'd be interested. She came out to see what was available. It just happened at the wrong time for her. She had nothing to do with any missing components."

"Fill me in on that."

"This going into some kind of record? I'm not supposed to talk about it. I'm not even supposed to know about it."

"You were there."

"I was the supply officer. I had nothing to do with ordnance. It was Claude. He handled all of that."

"Why wasn't Abu Mosul flown to the United States? Why a submarine?"

"It was an exchange. We gave them something; they gave us Mosul."

"Why aren't you supposed to talk about it? What's the secret?"

Lee frowned, lightly tapped his fingers together and stared at the floor. "What we gave them were upgraded components of a weapons system we did not want anyone to know about, especially the Arabs. That's why we took him aboard off the coast of Africa."

"And something of what you delivered had been stolen?"

"Exchanged, apparently. We didn't know there was a problem until we got back to Pearl."

"Explain that."

"The stuff we delivered was sealed under government inspection at a factory in Virginia—high-tech aiming devices. It was under seal when they brought it aboard the boat and never touched until their people came aboard and took it. But they claimed that what they had been promised wasn't in the crates. They said we substituted something inferior. I don't know anything more than Claude tried to explain. But the bottom line is if something was missing, it happened at the factory or after the Israelis got it."

"And this had nothing to do with Julia?"

"No."

"Or Vicki Bryant?"

"We didn't even know we were shipping out when she was there. How could she—"

"What was on the manifest?"

"I don't know how that was handled. That would be for customs officials. I suppose the Israelis must have wanted to see some kind of a list. All I know is Claude signed the stuff aboard and check-listed the crates when they were off-loaded. And they were sealed. He couldn't have taken anything out of them."

"And these acts of innocence caused you and Claude to leave the navy?"

"I left the navy because my brother asked me to."

She let that go. She wasn't getting the truth. She was getting a story he had worked out for himself over the past four years. If what he had said were the truth, naval investigators would have lost interest in him years ago. And maybe they weren't interested in him. But if that were true, why wasn't he being more open?

"Did Barstow contact you here, when he came here?"

"No. Those guys aren't interested in me."

"What guys?"

"I don't know. Whoever you're talking about."

"I've mentioned only Barstow."

"Then it's only him. There were others . . . out at Pearl, a whole swarm of them."

"The FBI?"

"No," he said, but mention of the FBI didn't surprise or upset him. Had he ever been contacted by Tyonek Horse?

She let it go. "Is the navy still looking for those parts?"

"I don't know, but they're no longer state-of-the-art."

"You keep up with that?"

"Just through Claude."

"Then you knew what was in the crates."

"I suppose he did. I didn't."

"If the crates were sealed and remained sealed until the Israelis picked them up, why did he have to know what was in them?"

"His responsibility as ordnance officer. No captain would permit anything aboard his boat he wasn't sure was safe."

Randa decided to get into something else. "Why did Vicki choose you instead of Claude when she needed a ride to Abu's room?"

"I don't know. Maybe she couldn't find him. She didn't want me in the room. I had to actually force my way in."

"So what was the real reason she was there?"

"I don't know. All they talked about was Claude."

"But you knew that wasn't the real reason."

"I don't know what I knew."

You know you're not telling me the truth, she wanted to say, but decided not to. She got up. "I'm going to make some coffee and heat up a cranberry scone," she said. "Want to join me?"

"No. I'm okay."

"It's decaf."

"No thanks."

When she came back into the living room with a loaded tray, he was stretched out on the chair, head back, face turned to the ceiling, eyes closed.

"Sure you don't want anything?"

"No, I'm fine," not looking at her, not moving his head, fingers tapping the fat chair arms. With his face averted, he said, "It's going to be the same thing, isn't it."

"Same thing as what?"

"The sheriff. You and me together. He's going to want it stopped."

A year ago the sheriff forbade her to see Lee because she had brought him with her on a manhunt. She was tempted to ask whether he wanted to stay away from her, but she said, "It's been mentioned."

"I can imagine how it looks, things point at me. But I'm really just trying to protect Julia."

"But not from a philandering husband," she said. "Lee, if Vicki Bryant didn't want you to meet with Abu Mosul, she wouldn't have called you. She would have called a cab."

"Yeah," he said resignedly, sitting up, his face in his hands. After a while he looked up at her, tired of the evasions. "I've explained everything that needs to be explained. If you can't accept it, I'm sorry."

"Two men have been murdered, Lee. You're going to have to tell me what you know."

"I had nothing to do with any murders."

"Lee, you were with a man the federal authorities have been watching for four years, a man you spent several weeks with on a submarine. You weren't in his room just to innocently accompany a woman you say you hardly know. Tell me what's going on? I'm trying to help you! If this case is taken away from me—and it very well might be—there won't be a damned thing I can do for you. If you're innocent and Julia is innocent, what are you hiding?"

He didn't answer. He got up and went to the window, stood there a long time staring into the parking lot.

When he turned, he avoided looking at her. "I'm sorry I'm making it tough on you. If you weren't a cop . . ."

"Lee, what's going on?"

"I can't tell you anything more than I have."

"Why don't you trust me?"

"I suppose I could ask the same question, couldn't I." He turned away. "I'm going to get my things." He went into the bathroom and came out carrying the leather kit he had kept toilet articles in. He didn't look at her.

She said, "If this investigation is taken out of my hands, you'll be at the mercy of people who don't give a damn about you."

"Maybe I already am," he said, walking into the entryway.

She watched him open the door. Completely baffled and hurt, she watched the door close behind him. She heard his car start up. She went to the window and watched taillights flare at the gate, headlights illuminating the distant road. She had learned nothing of what she had most wanted to know except that something out there was more important to him than confiding in her. He didn't trust her.

After a half hour of trying to come to grips with it, she phoned Gloria.

"You busy?"

"What's up?"

"Nothing," Randa said. "Can I come over?"

"Of course. What's wrong?"

"Everything's wrong."

Gloria laughed. "Come on over. We'll talk."

"I just want to come over. I don't want to talk."

"Then come over and we won't talk."

"It's after midnight."

"Come on over."

CHAPTER FIFTEEN

When Randa pulled into her reserved parking slot behind the headquarters building, Fog Rudenski, waiting for her, stuck a leg out of his Taurus and came across the hot asphalt with his hand at his mouth gripping the white handle of a lollipop. The relentless sun was still eastward, burning down on them.

"Hit some pay dirt," he said, sliding the candy to his cheek, holding her door open while she gathered papers and a handbag off the passenger seat. "Abu's got a friend, a guy in his fifties, doesn't look American—little mustache and goatee, the clothes, the shoes, how he handles himself. They talked nose to nose over lunch in that same Royal Inn Vicki Bryant was staying at. And there was another guy, maybe a bodyguard or something, had to be six-five. I brought Al Martinez a bottle the big guy tossed into a saw palmetto—prints on it for the file."

He tapped her arm as they stepped onto the walk at the building entrance. "A sec," and went over and tossed the lollipop into a trashcan, came back and trailed her into the cooled air of the building.

Randa said, "You get a name?"

"Couldn't. Afraid to spook him."

"Is Vicki still there?"

"Didn't think it would be wise to ask."

"Okay," she said. "Look, I have to . . ." She pointed down the hall at Major Buckley's office.

"They spent an hour at Clay's Marina in South Cherokee

City," Fog said. "Stood outside Abu's car, just talking and pointing."

"At what?"

"Boats, I guess. Nothing else out there, a couple of mangrove islands. I was watching from the street. They seemed to be checking the place out. Can't imagine why it took an hour. Anyway, Abu left them at the Royal Inn. I couldn't get a name or anything. Abu knows me, so I had to wait for him to clear out. By then they were gone. The desk woman had no idea who I was asking about."

"She didn't remember the big guy?"

"They probably weren't guests there."

"Any word on Vicki Bryant?"

"Unless she took a boat out of here, she's still in the area. Nothing at the airport or car rentals. Could have taken a bus, I suppose."

"Write up what you've got and leave it on my desk," Randa said. "I don't know how long I'll be with Buckles. Who's watching Abu?"

"Bea. He's in his room. She's watching the car."

Almost as an afterthought Randa said, "If you get prints off that glass, make sure that Interpol gets a look at them."

"Interpol?"

"If that friend of Abu's is an Arab . . . yeah. Interpol."

"Why not let the FBI do it?"

"You do it," Randa said, realizing she had made a switch in her thinking.

She went down the hall and tapped on the major's door, opened it and went inside to a faint odor of sardines—the major's morning snack. He looked up from what he was working on and pointed her at a chair, leaned back and yawned into his hand, creating a friendly air the way he looked at her but not with sexual interest: he'd never shown any interest in her that way, maybe because she'd never shown any interest in him.

She settled into one of the cushioned chairs he said he had picked up at a yard sale but actually received as a gift from a politician whose son he had rescued from a D&D. It was a comfortable-enough chair, but, like everything else in the room, too old-fashioned.

"I had a long talk with Lee," she said.

"He's staying with you?"

"No."

"Derek asked about that."

She grudgingly accepted the intrusion. "All I'm sure of is he knows more than he's willing to talk about. He says he's protecting Cardozo's daughter Julia, but I don't know about that. I'll put it in my report."

"Protecting her from what?"

"The guy she's been living with. Maybe something else."

She was finding it easier to be objective about Lee, but it hurt. Buckles seemed to understand. He didn't pressure her.

"Have you figured out," he asked, "why Barstow isn't mentioned in Bill's notes?"

"I think Julia wanted the information, but didn't want it in the report. She knows something's going on and feels threatened, maybe for herself, maybe for her father. Something's in the works. She clammed up the minute I connected Barstow with Vicki Bryant. That scared her."

"Think there was a separate report?"

"We looked but didn't find one. It's possible she didn't want Barstow mentioned in Bill's report because she intended to stick it in Lazard's face before she dumped him. Maybe she doesn't want Lazard to know she's worried about the Barstow connection."

"Is it possible that Bill didn't want Julia to know he was

checking on Barstow, that he was doing that part of it on his own?"

"All I'm really sure of is that Julia was interested in a whole lot more than Claude's philandering. Conceivably, Bill was holding that back for more money. But if we want to swing this in a different direction, it's plausible that Bill was shot because he was poking his nose into a friable area."

He smiled. "You like that word."

She returned the smile.

"Where's Fronzi in this?" he asked.

"I don't know. I got hints he's trying to find out what's going on so he can intercede for Julia. I just don't know." And she hoped Buckles wouldn't press for more. She hoped to learn everything about Lee's involvement before things had gone too far. It occurred to her that she might be doing for Lee what Lee was doing for Julia. Maybe there was a stronger loyalty to family in Lee than she had been led to believe. He seemed to be risking a lot for her.

Buckles leaned forward with elbows on his desk. "I think you're right about things coming together here. Why else would Tyonek assume that Barstow would run over here just because Abu Mosul was here? And why else would the FBI be hanging back? There's been no injunction, and they're not actively hunting for Barstow's killer. They're like owls in a tree watching mice coming into a clearing. Just waiting. And it's related to what the FBI was looking for at Barstow's daughter's apartment, don't you agree?"

It's what I said to you the other day, Randa reminded herself. She said, "You think somebody's trying to unload what was allegedly stolen from the Israelis? Maybe through Cardozo?"

"I had a long talk with sources in Seacrest," Buckles said. He opened a drawer, took out a sheet of paper and leaned it across his desk to her. "Maybe this Duke Butterworth can tell us what went on in Hawaii. Maybe we should start from that point, get into what seems to be at the root of this."

"You sending me to Hawaii?" She was joking. She didn't expect to be sent anywhere.

"Savannah," he said.

And that surprised and pleased her. She preferred Hawaii but either place would be a lift. She could use a few nights away from her apartment.

"As you can see there," Buckles said, waving a finger at the paper, "he was a drinking buddy. Retired now. Runs a pump company, marine pumps. Got a place on the river. Ever been to Savannah?"

"Once." With Charlie Hawkins, part of a tour through what he called "the nostalgic South"—east to Savannah, west to New Orleans in time for Mardi Gras where his wallet got lifted.

"Check with Mary. I want you up there by nightfall. He expects you at his shop sometime in the morning, says he's leaving on a fishing trip, be gone for a week."

While he talked about his source in D.C.—apparently an old friend—she thought about what she was going to wear, something a man wouldn't do, she supposed, remembering Charlie's monotonously gray suits and gray socks, black shoes and red ties, nothing more colorful except things she had given him he never wore.

"I guess you know it was Horse they assigned to check on Barstow and that girlfriend, Paris something. I understand he pleaded for the assignment, didn't want to be 'cashiered,' as he called it, thought he was going out in disgrace because of his arm. He wanted to redeem himself."

"What'd they suspect Barstow of?"

"I couldn't find out. But I guess it's connected to that girlfriend—name's Courtland, Paris Courtland. Derek's eager to break this case. Maybe he'll spring for a trip up there. There has to be a file on Courtland. They won't release it to us, but maybe you can coax them out of a peek."

"Use my feminine wiles?" she said, laughing.

"Something like that."

She told him about the stranger Fog had seen with Abu at Clay's Marina in South Cherokee City. "Don't know what they were doing there, but I don't think Abu sells boats."

"And the FBI is just sitting back?"

"Makes you wonder, doesn't it?"

He smiled. "See you in a couple of days."

She got flight information from Mary and went down the hall to the squadroom where Fog was working on his report. He told her the lab had been unable to lift any usable prints off the wine glass. She told him about Georgia and maybe going from there to D.C.

"I'll call you," she said.

"Where you going now? There's someone you might want to talk to. Kappy's got him in the chat room."

"Who?"

"Calls himself Porter Johnston. He tried to sell a watch to one of Kappy's sources, a Seiko, the name Kirby etched on the back plate."

She spent a half hour with the man, a thirty-two-year-old junkie well known to the police, a beach prowler. He admitted to having taken the watch off the wrist of a corpse he had found on the sand. He said he had heard a shot and had seen a "shadowy figure" run past the lighted windows of a nearby cottage. Kappy said the beach patrol had not reported any lighted windows on that part of the beach.

She took Fog aside. "Hold him for first hearing. He's lying."

"As a suspect?"

"I doubt he's capable of murder, not the way this went down. That beach was pitch dark. How could he see a watch out there?

So did he steal it before or after Barstow got on the sand? Did he stumble over the body in the dark? Or did he see the man fall? Don't worry about the 'shadowy figure.' That's nonsense. See if you can find something stronger than theft or possession of stolen property."

Since the police knew the man to be homeless, she didn't anticipate any trouble holding him.

Within an hour she was at home wrapped in a towel at the opened mirrored doors of her closet gazing with dismay at things on hangers she had once loved and now hated. She had nothing to wear and no money to buy anything. She moved things on hangers down the pole, finally choosing four outfits, including a blue linen suit still in a cleaner's bag. It didn't matter what she wore, she told herself. Who would be looking at her? She caught an image of her saddened face in the mirror and started laughing.

She fell asleep on the plane and was groggy in the taxi and on the elevator in the hotel trying to figure out what the bellman was saying about a light on the wall that flashed whenever a ship came up the river.

In her room, looking down at a long, lighted street peopled by what from even eight stories up she could tell were tourists from the way they strolled hand in hand pausing at windows. She talked to herself about a crawling nervousness she always experienced when alone in a strange city. It made her think of her mother's insecurity when they had first come to Rhode Island—nights of crying that had terrified Randa, who would have been alone in this strange country if her mother, like her uncle, were to die.

Although she felt thoroughly American, she wasn't sure she had entirely shed that fear. She wondered whether it had any connection to her desire to be married and have children. When you live alone in a rented apartment you don't feel that you belong to much of anything. And that led to thoughts about Lee.

She fell asleep propped up on pillows watching the remnants of an old Clint Eastwood movie.

CHAPTER SIXTEEN

In the darkness of the small cove, as Claude idled the engine of *Julia's Folly* and bumped the heavy timbers of the slip at Clay's Marina, Claude felt the boat tilt. Someone had come aboard. He turned nervously from the helm just as a man appeared at the top of the ladder. He couldn't make out who it was, only a dark silhouette.

"She wants her boat back."

It was Lee Fronzi.

"What the hell?"

"She wants the boat back," Lee said, coming onto the bridge. He reached past Claude for the key.

But Claude had the key in his hand. He shoved it into his pocket. "What're you doing? Come on!"

"Give me the key!"

Claude pushed Lee aside and went down the ladder to the cockpit. He wrapped the stern line around a cleat on the slip, and went forward and secured the bow line.

"In the cabin," he said, glancing at boats to the left and to the right. He couldn't see anyone, no lights on other boats. It was three in the morning. He doubted anyone was around. Coming into the marina he had searched the road and the parking lot and seen no vehicles except his own over near the chandlery. But there were plenty of places out there to hide a car. Fakhri, the big Arab bodyguard, was always snooping around. Twice Hammid Ramzi had asked who Lee was. He

146

snapped on the light in the small galley that partially illuminated the edges of the bunks and the table and chairs at the forward bulkhead.

"She told you to stop using her boat," Lee said.

"Keep your voice down."

"Get your own fucking boat!" Lee yelled.

"You're tired, man. You need some sleep." He moved past Lee and closed the sliding door. "I'm not hurting anything. I'll get the boat back to her."

"Rent one!"

Claude took a deep breath, held it, and let it out noisily. "*This* boat," he said. "I need *this* boat."

"Why?"

"The Coast Guard is used to seeing me in it. You don't want them butting in any more than I do. Julia'll get her boat back."

"Look," Lee said. "I don't give a shit about that. I don't care what you're doing. I just don't want Julia involved. Now, give me the key."

"I'm not hurting anything, Lee. There's nothing criminal going on here."

"Bullshit. Raphael doesn't believe it. Julia doesn't believe it. They haven't called the cops because they don't want any trouble. But you're up to your neck in something stupid. Give me the key."

Just as Lee got up, the sliding door opened and a large man came into the cabin. Claude pushed Lee off. As Lee stumbled, the giant called Fakhri gripped Lee's collar, pulled him backward with his left hand and drove a knife into Lee's back. Claude heard a quick intake of breath, then watched Lee collapse to the deck. In stunned horror he watched Fakhri lean down and slide the blade through Lee's throat, making sure he was dead. Blood pooled out across the deck.

"Jesus! Oh, my God! You fucking crazy idiot! What did you do?"

Fakhri turned to the sink in the galley and rinsed off the knife. Without a word he went outside and Claude felt the boat sag when Fakhri vaulted the rail.

In frantic bewilderment, Claude whirled around in little circles, too frightened to think. *This is crazy! Oh, my God!* staring at the body on the deck. *Oh, my God!*

He knew he couldn't take the boat into the gulf and dump the body overboard. He wouldn't know how to sink it. The Coast Guard was out there. He'd get caught.

He stared at the bloody cut on Lee's neck. This was insane! He wanted to run. He had to do something. He couldn't leave the cove with Lee's body in the cabin.

With trembling hands, he knelt over the body and put his hands under Lee's armpits. He dragged him onto the aft deck, looked around, couldn't see anyone. He pulled the body onto the slip, tried lifting it, then held Lee's collar and dragged him into the parking lot. He ran back to the boat and untied the lines. He knew a place down the coast where he could boon-dock in mangroves while he cleared the cabin of blood.

I don't know what to do! Maybe I should bring the body down there. No. They'd see me! I have to get away.

That crazy, fucking idiot!

CHAPTER SEVENTEEN

Randa was enjoying a cheese omelet and toast and coffee at a window table overlooking the Savannah River. She had slept late and phoned the pump shop to be sure the man was here. He sounded cheerful and young. He offered to pick her up, but she said she'd take a cab. In a car with a stranger, she preferred the back seat.

Duke Butterworth's shop was a converted filling station on a narrow road a few miles up river from Randa's hotel. There were weeds in broken pavement, a dented pickup truck in front of closed garage doors, rusted oil drums alongside a broken fence. The words "All Pumped Up" were lettered on the large window of the office. Above them in block letters was the name Duke's Pumps. Except for the sound of hammering inside the garage, she might have thought the place abandoned. It wasn't the kind of place she'd expect a retired naval officer to own, but who knows?

As she opened the office door she ducked from a black and yellow spider rocking at the center of a web high inside the doorway. The office smelled of crankcase oil.

"It don't bite," came from a girl in shorts and halter sitting on a large wooden desk, knees spread, hands gripping the edge of the desk outside her knees—a pretty girl, maybe nineteen with blonde hair wrapped around her head. "He's in there," jerking her head toward the doorway to the garage.

Duke Butterworth was in a grease pit under a white boat

149

suspended above him on a carrier trailer.

"With you in a sec," he said, shooting a quick courtesy glance at her, grinning. He hadn't shaved in maybe a week and there was a streak of green paint on his bald scalp. He had a small face and small regular features. Although some women would find him cute, he didn't come close to what Randa looked for in a man. If she hadn't known his background, she would have concluded that his entire substance was right there in the grin.

When he climbed out of the pit and came toward her wiping his hands on a paper towel, she noticed a gold ring in his left earlobe. He had to be at least forty-five.

"Duke Butterworth," he said, gesturing her toward a chair where the girl, moving off the desk, almost knocked the handset of a telephone off its cradle. She went to the window and lifted a can of Squirt out of ice in an old-fashioned drink dispenser.

"We going or not?" the girl said, ignoring Randa, impatient and petulant. "This isn't my idea of fun, you know, hanging here. I could've gone to Beaufort with Angie. Should've."

"So go," Duke said, glancing apologetically at Randa.

"Like how?" the girl said, spilling Squirt on her chest, slapping at it.

"Look, I got something to do right now. You want to wait, wait. You don't, don't."

"Fuck you," the girl said. She set the opened can on the lid of the dispenser, splashing her drink all over the lid. She stormed out of the office.

"I oughtta know better, right?" Duke said. "Act my age, as they say," and he laughed, apparently looking for approval, maybe admiration.

He pointed at a chair that was angled off the corner of the desk while he sat across from her, his head under an ancient, faded Marilyn Monroe calendar. As she lowered herself onto a crushed mat on the chair seat, she noticed a tattoo on his left arm of a naked girl under a palm tree fingering the word Aloha shaped by tresses of long yellow hair.

"They said a sheriff's deputy, a sergeant. A detective, right?"

"Randa Sorel." She got her folder from her bag, opened it, showed him her photo ID and badge.

"How's Lee these days? Kind of lost touch," he said.

"He's fine."

"Rich, isn't he? We never knew that out there. He just seemed like one of us, pitching liberties, chasing broads, getting drunk. Hell of a guy. When I found out his old man was loaded, I almost flipped. He in some kind of trouble?"

"We're just following up on that inquiry the navy made in Hawaii."

"Ah, that," he said, sinking into his chair, lips pressed into a sour acceptance. "That one-armed guy came here six months ago asking about that. I'd've thought it was all on the record. Been over it a dozen times. Lee knows as much as I do. You must've questioned him."

"Can you tell me what was stolen?"

"I never thought anything was. It's like I told that one-armed guy. What's his name?"

"You probably mean Tyonek Horse."

"Yeah, that's it. How could I forget a name like that? He some kind of an Indian?"

"A Native American."

"Yeah, that's what I thought. You couldn't get close to him, you know? Like he was over there and I was over here. You know what I mean? Not friendly. Afraid he might scalp me," and he laughed, showing very even white teeth. She wondered whether the teeth were real. Nothing else about him seemed to be—a man hiding within what he thought was an impressive exterior.

"When did you talk with him?"

"A couple of months ago. He asked the same questions they did in Pearl."

"What questions?"

"You know, about whether anyone aboard the boat tampered with the crates. They wanted my records of people checking out tools. That's most of what they asked me—the NCIS guy and the Indian."

"Were the crates tampered with?"

"No. Couldn't've happened. We didn't have the kind of sealing materials the navy used in Virginia. We couldn't've opened them without . . . you know, it showing."

"The NCIS guy. Was his name Barstow?"

"Could be. I'm not really big on names. I remember faces. Your face," and that came with a smile. "I'll remember your face." When she ignored that, he added without a trace of umbrage, "I thought the Israelis made it up, you know, hoping to get a second one."

"A second what?"

"Damned if I know. Ask Lee."

"You think he knew?"

"Never questioned it, like I told the Indian."

"Wasn't he a supply officer?"

"Yeah, but he knew a lot about high-tech ordnance. The skipper used to go to Lee a lot. He never liked Claudio—what we called him. A chick in a bar always called him that." He got up and went to the dispenser for a drink. "Get you something?"

"No thanks."

He came back to the desk tilting a wet can to his mouth.

"You knew Lee pretty well, didn't—" She was startled by a buzzing in her handbag. Her portable. She put it to her ear but heard only a growling maze of static.

"Bad location for those things," Duke said. "The tower's too far away or something. Everybody's bitching about it. Me, I use one of these," putting his hand on his desk phone.

She thought it was Mary but the voice was eaten up by static.

"I'm getting poor reception," she yelled into the phone. "I can't make out what you're saying. I'll call you as soon as I can."

Another voice came on, maybe Buckles. She again yelled that she'd call back. She listened a few seconds, then shut it off and put the phone into her bag.

"I guess there's not enough traffic to make them put up another tower. I don't know what's going on," Duke said.

"Out at Pearl did you know a woman named Vicki Bryant?"

Randa was worried about the call, wondering what it was about. Was it urgent or just telling her about her flight to D.C.? Because she didn't want to talk business in front of this man, she decided to wait. She'd call from the hotel.

"The one-armed guy, the Indian, he asked about her. There was a woman from stateside out there like what he described. I never caught her name. Kind of lanky, flat-chested, not very good-looking. I saw her a couple of times with Lazard, if that's the same one."

"Before or after you took that cruise?"

"I didn't see her when we got back. She might've been there, but I thought she just came on vacation. That was a couple of weeks before we went out. I think they knew each other up north somewhere."

"Was Claude happy to see her?"

"Yeah. He was all over her. And it was funny because he could've got better than her at a kennel. She was a real bow-wow. Horse-faced, you know what I mean?"

"Did Lee know her?"

"Could've, I guess."

"Before you went on that cruise, when that woman was there, how much advance notice did you get?"

"Usually they gave us plenty of time, but for that one, maybe because we were to meet the Israelis, not much."

"And Lee wouldn't have had any advance notice?"

"Maybe. Supply officer. Maybe he'd get the word early."

Something else Lee had lied about. To get away from it, she asked, "Did Lee have a regular girl out there?"

"Not for a long time, just pickups. But when we got back from that cruise there was this one came to see him from the mainland, from Florida, I think. We always kidded him he never went with the same one twice. Then this one came along—not bad-looking, kind of skinny. But they got close, and he tried to make us think she was his sister-in-law."

Like a stone dropped on her heart. "Remember her name?"

"I met her only once. They kept to themselves."

It was a struggle getting the next question out. "But they were lovers?"

"I never got inside their motel room, but for two weeks, he wasn't in the BOQ. That was down the coast at Andrew Hull Foote sub base.

"Once, I remember, he was with her in a restaurant, waiting, standing there with his hand on her ass, and she was leaning up mugging him. I remember there was an admiral and his wife watching and not liking what they saw." The memory made him laugh.

"Can you describe her?"

"About thirty, not bad-looking, but not what I like. I like them like you." He laughed. "You know, everything in good proportions."

She gave that a weary and hopefully discouraging response.

"She was blonde," he went on, "maybe fake, had a Southern accent. Oh, and she had something to do with small arms, talked about it, surplus rifles or something, I remember. She was like a business woman."

And he had his hand on her ass! She wanted to scream that it wasn't true, that it wasn't Julia Hodges. But she just sat there in silence despising the grin on the man's face.

"She someone important?" he asked.

"Important to him, apparently." She took a deep breath and moved around in the chair. "Does the name Paris Courtland mean anything to you?"

"Never heard of him."

"It's a woman."

"Never heard the name."

With pain crawling through her belly, she talked another half hour about Barstow's inquiries but learned nothing of value.

"Did Lee discuss with you why he decided to quit the navy? Was it over this?"

"Once you're on their shit list . . . him and Lazard both felt they were dead in the water. You must have heard about the fist fight."

"No."

"In the officer's club at Foote. Lee and his girlfriend . . . I don't know whether they broke up or what. But old Claudio moved in. What I heard, Lee caught them belly to belly and chased Lazard half across the base into the parking lot, knocked him down, was all over him, yelling he could kill him. They had to get the shore patrol."

"Fighting over her?"

"He wouldn't talk about it, but I never saw him with her again. In fact, I guess I never saw her again. Maybe she cut out. He stayed drunk for a week. They told him his career was dead."

Randa cut the session short. She accepted his offer for a ride and only half listened to his chatter as they drove in the battered pickup to her hotel. Upstairs in her room she stood at the window watching people waiting to board an excursion boat docked alongside a sitting area that separated the street from the river, people who seemed not to have a care in the world, men and women standing together, holding hands, some with children, people who loved each other, people who belonged together, people who had real lives.

It wasn't until she had showered and lain down for a while that she made the call to Cherokee City.

"Sorry you had to hear it on the phone," Buckles said. "It happened last night at that marina in South Cherokee City."

"What happened?"

A pause. "You didn't get my message?"

"What message?"

"Aw, Jesus, Randa. I thought my call . . ."

"I couldn't make anything out. What happened?"

"It's Lee Fronzi." A pause that seemed eternal, then Buckles said, "He was killed. I'm sorry, Randa."

Everything inside her froze. The meaning of the words wouldn't break into her mind.

"It happened late last night," Buckles said. "He wasn't found until this morning. We've got the whole crew over there."

She only vaguely heard him explain what the medical examiner had told him. An artery in his neck. A knife wound in the back.

"You okay?"

"I'm coming home," she said.

"His brother and his brother's wife . . . I think they're at his townhouse."

She packed, paid her bill, and took a cab to the airport. She couldn't get a flight directly to Cherokee City and had to wait three hours for a flight to Marchland, sitting alone in a waiting room.

In Marchland she called a friend at Florida Highway Patrol and within an hour was in a patrol car speeding south on

Interstate 75. She was shivering in the passenger seat, her hand over her eyes. She couldn't stop crying.

CHAPTER EIGHTEEN

"I can't let something slip past us up there," Sparzo said. "This is a third killing and different from the other two. What do Chubleigh's people say about it?"

They were in Sparzo's office. A female agent, Moira Pelletier, was sitting next to Tyonek, a black woman with a southern accent, shiny black hair pulled back into a bun, dark eyes intently watching Sparzo, occasionally glancing at Tyonek. He had seen her in the office but didn't know her. He had no idea why she was here. Sparzo had given no explanation.

"I have an appointment with the sheriff tomorrow morning," Tyonek said, nervously nipping cloth on his knee with the steel fingers. *Why is she here?*

"He was stabbed in the back and his throat cut. That's not a run-of-the-mill homicide," Sparzo said. "That sounds like terrorism. Something's going on up there I want to know about?"

"All I know is there was bad blood between him and Claude Lazard. Out in Pearl—"

Sparzo waved that off. "That has nothing to do with this. Lazard has been living with Cardozo's daughter for what is it, three years?"

"My friend says they broke up," Moira said, glancing at Tyonek. "I don't know them personally, but I've heard of them."

"Who's your friend?" Tyonek asked, giving her an uneasy up and down.

"A girl works at the country club Mrs. Hodges plays golf at.

She's manager of the little restaurant they got out there. She heard this Claude guy moved out a few days ago."

"You get up there much?"

"I was raised there. I heard you were watching them is all. I mentioned it to him," tilting her head at Sparzo.

"Anything about the victim, Lee Fronzi?"

"I don't know any of those people. I just saw it in the newspaper and remembered my friend telling me about Cardozo's daughter. It said the victim was related to them by marriage."

"Is something going on with him you know about?" Tyonek asked.

"Like what?"

"Anything at all."

"You think there is?" Moira said.

"That's why I'm there . . . to find out."

Sparzo said, "Unless we go in there full force—and I don't have resources for that—I don't see any reason to assign another agent. D.C. gave you the ticket for this, but Moira could go up there and hold your ladder if you need help."

Not very successfully hiding his irritation, Tyonek said, "And she's here because you wanted her to meet me?"

"She's a top-notch agent and she knows a lot of people in that community."

Tyonek let it go. Best to treat this lightly. He tapped Moira's knee with the claw and grinned. "The minute I sense a problem, I'll send for you."

In the corridor outside the office, he asked Moira to go light on her inquiries. "I don't want to spook anyone up there in case something is perking."

"You think something might be? All those killings don't tell me much. People getting shot or stabbed up there all the time, especially in the section I come from. Couldn't pay me to go back and live there. You know, I tried Puerto Rico. It's worse

159

over there."

Tyonek smiled. "Does *he* think something's going on around Cherokee City?"

"All I know about what he thinks is he wanted me to witness warning you so he can blame it on you in case something is." She smiled, gave his arm a friendly tap, and walked away.

He stood there admiring the swaying of her hips as she glided down the corridor. He tucked the image into his memory bank.

Wrapping himself in the seat belt out in the parking lot, Tyonek wondered whether this Moira Pelletier could become a threat. Was she brought into that meeting to let him know he no longer had a free hand in Cherokee City? Or was she there, as she said, to provide proof that Sparzo was doing his job?

Tyonek yelled inside his head: Damn that son-of-a-bitch whoever it was! They're here! They've come down from Marchland, and I didn't see it! Lee Fronzi did. Why else was he at that marina? He was checking on them? This could spoil everything!

With anger churning in his gut, he drove across town, clearing his mind of the meeting with Sparzo by telling himself Randa Sorel couldn't have seen him shoot that detective. She had to have taken a good half hour from the time White called to the moment she came into the gravel road where Bill had parked his car. And no more than ten minutes, if that, had passed before he pulled the trigger. She couldn't have seen anything but the body slumped against the Cypress tree. When he escaped through the patch of swamp to the edge of the canal and down the muddy path to where he'd parked his car, he told himself they'd find a .38 slug in White's heart with nothing on a database to identify it.

That damn fool had intended to use me to justify breaking into Mosul's room!

He remembered the silly look of surprise on Bill White's face

160

when he stared at the .38 police special, his mouth open in surprise when he took the hit. He remembered watching Bill sag against the Cypress tree with pulsing blood spreading over his white shirt.

Now as he approached the seagrape trees in the parking lot outside Abu's room, he searched the swampy patch of trees where he had shot the man, pleased that the newspaper writer had said there was no evidence linking the death of White to the earlier shooting on the beach.

Is it possible White had lived long enough to tell someone who had shot him? Wasn't that the kind of information the police would withhold from the media? He'd know the next time he went into Chubleigh's office. Their faces would show him.

Abu opened the door a crack and peered out, wide-eyed.

"Let me in," Tyonek said. "I don't want to be seen out here."

"Of course, of course." Abu hurriedly closed the door. He removed the chain and stepped back as Tyonek burst inside, shoving the claw straight into Abu's belly. "I want answers. Who's here and where are they?"

"Nobody! What are you talking about?"

"Don't fuck with me. I can bring you down. I can put you in irons. You can yell your fucking head off I'm in this with you but nobody'll believe a little whining Arab. Now, where are they?"

He had crowded Abu to the far wall and was jabbing him with the claw, yelling into his face. He gripped Abu's chin with the claw and twisted it cruelly, staring into Abu's wildly gawking eyes.

"That marina. Why'd you tell them about it?"

"They knew he was using the boat."

"You told them?"

"I didn't think! Please! For God's sake!" grasping the claw. "You're hurting me!"

Tyonek let go in disgust, stepping back as Abu slid down the wall and sat, knees drawn up, whimpering.

"You didn't have to do that," he said, rubbing his chin. "You have no reason—"

"Who did it?"

"Let me up."

"Get up. I'm not stopping you."

Choosing a chair six feet from Tyonek, who was sitting on the bed, Abu, still rubbing his chin, said, "They sent somebody down from Marchland—those people I told you about. I don't know his name. Claude was making a trial run. Fronzi was waiting for him. He went aboard. There was a big argument and this idiot from Marchland stabbed him."

"On the boat? The body was in the parking lot."

"Claude dragged it out there."

"Why? Why not dump it in the gulf?"

"He said—look, all I know is what Claude told me. He thinks the man stabbed Lee and cut his throat to show Claude—they're ruthless, these people are ruthless." He nursed his chin, eyeing Tyonek as though for pity.

"Why not take it out in the gulf?"

"I don't know. Claude was afraid to."

"So now what's he gonna do? He can't use that marina now."

"Maybe he's renting another boat. He'll let me know."

"I still don't understand why he needs a boat."

"Just to distract them. She wants them to think she's where the crates are. She doesn't trust them, and obviously for good reason. Now he's afraid that idiot will follow him if he uses a car. If she even sees that guy, she'll run away from this. She won't tell us where the stuff is."

"Killing Fronzi was stupid," Tyonek said.

"They're stupid."

"Who told them about him? Was it you?"

"Of course not. Why would I?"

"When you hand them the stuff, why will they let you get away? You know who they are. They know you've worked with the CIA. They get what they came for. Why not kill you on the spot?"

"I won't hand them the stuff. I don't know where it is. When the money's in the bank, Claude'll call the woman. She'll tell us."

"Where do you think it is?"

"Port Mangrove. In a locker up there, an hour from where she'll be, and I don't even know where that is."

"And they'll have to drive up there to get it? Why not take you along, make sure it's where you say it is."

"They wouldn't have to. Where am I going? They'd hunt me down. They're very resourceful. And if some of the Marchland people are there, they wouldn't want me to see them."

"Where's the woman? The diamonds will be in the bank in Seacrest," Abu said. "She's got to be somewhere around there. I suppose she wants them to think she's in Mangrove Harbor."

"How long's the box rented for?"

"A year," Abu said. "They don't rent it for less time than that, and you have to have ID and an account."

"And only the guy who rents it can open it?"

"Claude. He's the only one."

"And in the morning when the bank opens, you pick the rocks up and go with Claude to the woman's place and get your half. Then you come down to that little restaurant on 41 where I get mine."

"It's foolproof."

"Don't kid yourself," Tyonek said. "Nothing's foolproof. And if something does go wrong, you're in prison, remember that."

"You don't have to keep saying it."

CHAPTER NINETEEN

Although Buckles's office door was ajar, Randa walked past it to the women's lav and, in the small booth, held her face in her hands and tried to slow down the beating of her heart. She washed her hands and assured the eyes in the mirror that she was okay—she could talk about Lee's death.

She avoided glancing at Buckles's doorway as she went down the corridor to the squadroom. Two men at desks at the far end paid no attention to her as she went to her cubicle, put her handbag into the bottom drawer of her desk, and sat there looking at the manila folder propped against the monitor of her computer.

As expected, it was Lee's file. She read every word on the facing sheet (the responding officer's offense report), which described in detail his initial observations at the crime scene—the condition of the victim's body, scuff marks in the gravel leading from the slips, a variety of measurements. She read the casualty report and several supplementary reports, one from Bea Kim, who had gone to the scene and had accepted responsibility for the investigation on Randa's behalf.

She read again the description of the wounds: a penetration into the victim's back that corresponded to a blood-soaked cut in the fabric of the gray jacket and a white shirt; a long incision in the left side of the victim's neck apparently made while the victim was alive. But no blood in the gravel.

The body had been discovered by a cleaning woman on her

way to work at approximately six-fifteen in the morning. There was no night watchman on duty at the marina. No witnesses to the murder had been found.

Bea Kim had located the manager of the store. He claimed to know nothing of what had happened and did not know why the victim had been in the parking lot. He was acquainted with the victim's name but did not know him personally and had never done business with him. The owner and manager of the marina, George Stetson of 314 Myster Place, Boliva, had not been located.

Buckles looked up when Randa came into his office.

"You okay?" he asked, watching her settle into a chair, holding her bag in her lap, maybe aware that she usually set the bag on the floor but right now needed something to hold on to. "I'm sorry I had to break it to you like that," he said.

"It's okay. I'm fine."

He seemed to doubt that. "We could hear you pretty clearly," he told her. "Mary and I both assumed you got the message okay. I'm sorry that—"

She waved him off. She didn't want to talk about the phone call. She didn't want to be here, but it was her job.

"Two things," she said, forcing herself to mention at least this much. "It doesn't look like he was killed where the body was found—no blood on the gravel. The drag marks come from the direction of the slips, but no big spill of blood on any of them."

"It happened on a boat?"

"And that marina is where Fog saw Abu and another man."

"And that tells us Claude was linked to Abu and these strangers on some very dangerous business."

"And the FBI isn't rushing in. What's that tell us?" Randa took a deep breath. Buckles allowed her a few moments.

She tightened her lips, changed the subject. "You said his

brother is here?"

"He's—I guess he's still there—at Lee's place in Seacrest. The wife and the wife's sister. You plan to . . . ?"

"I don't know." She had thought about meeting with Dominic and Rita, but the more she thought about it the less she wanted to. She was afraid she wouldn't be welcome. She wasn't part of the family. Joining them at a time of mourning might be awkward. She had no role in Lee's life the family would respect. She was just the girlfriend.

She could almost hear Gloria scolding her for putting herself down like that. *For God's sake, Randa, have more respect for yourself! You're important to him!*

"I'd like to go home for a while," she said. "I can catch up with Bea in the morning."

"No problem," Buckles said.

It isn't the same as when Charlie died. She had had, at least briefly, the sympathy of Charlie's mother, who had come to Florida from Philadelphia to attend the funeral. For a while they had exchanged letters, but last year Randa's Christmas greeting had not been reciprocated.

"I'll be in in the morning," she said.

At her apartment on the river, she puttered around her kitchen warming up a casserole she had made a few nights ago. She sat alone at her small table and slowly swallowed her food. Descriptions of the crime scene lingered in her mind as she ate. After clearing the table and putting dirty dishes into the washer, she went into her bedroom and undressed. She noticed her white walking shoes and Lee's next to each other at the slider of her closet. She started to cry and curled up on the bed and cried herself to sleep.

She woke up around midnight thinking about the circumstances of Lee's death, then angrily shoved those thoughts aside, reminding herself she had only the responding officer's cursory description of what he had seen. The ME's report would be more detailed.

If it happened on a boat, why was Lee on the boat, late at night? My God, what were you mixed up in?

She went into the kitchen and noticed the light blinking on her answering machine. There were two calls, both from Gloria who had just heard the news of Lee's death on her car radio. Although Gloria might still be up, Randa didn't return the calls. She ate half a bran muffin and watched the remnants of a talk show on television, then a full-length movie. She took two aspirins around three in the morning and went back to bed.

Around noon the following day, Randa was with Bea in the parking lot of the marina in South Cherokee City. A seagull fluttered down to the stump of a piling no more than ten feet from Randa and began pecking at something buried in breast feathers. There was a soft wind coming in off the cove, strong sunlight glinting on the water. The air was heavy with odors of decomposing fish.

"From what Archie said," Bea was saying, her hand toying with the temple of her sunglasses, "it was a long blade, sharp as a razor. Couldn't tell where the assailant was standing. Dr. Fouts said he died instantly."

Randa glanced beyond the gull at a man in scuba gear falling backward off the stern of a white Sea Craft, a girl in a yellow two-piece bathing suit leaning over the rail watching him.

The wind coming in off the mangrove islands tossed strands of hair across Randa's eyes. She pushed them aside.

"I think I've been in Florida too long," Bea said. "I'm beginning to enjoy the smell of the gulf."

Randa gave that a smile. "Fog learn anything in Seacrest?"

"He thinks he knows who Buckles talked to in D.C."

"Anything on Vicki?"

"Not that I know of."

"Did the brother give any hint about why Lee might have been here?"

"He just stood outside the ribbon," Bea said, "and stared at where the body had been found. He never said a word."

"And there were no women with him?"

"Not that I saw. I wouldn't have known he was Lee's brother except Fog told me."

"Did the brother ask for me?"

"Maybe he asked Fog."

There was nothing more she could learn from the crime scene. The techs would doubtless pick up things. "See if you can find the other boat owners," Randa said. "There's got to be a witness around here somewhere. People aren't supposed to stay in these boats at night, but sometimes they do—a good place for getting out-of-the-house sex. If you detect the slightest vulnerability, push hard."

"You going down there now?" Bea asked.

"I suppose I should," Randa said, smiling at the questioning look that came into Bea's eyes. Bea knew nothing of Randa's relationship with the Cardozo family.

"You're a mystery," Bea said.

Randa nodded sadly and walked to her car. Years ago a guy in college had made a similar comment in the back seat of a convertible in a parking lot on Doake Street.

Heading south, Randa tried to remember what Lee had said about Julia's youthful marriage. It had resulted, apparently, from a pregnancy in her junior year at a Georgia prep school. Because Julia was seventeen and the man, an assistant track coach at a neighboring school, was twenty-four, Julia had the option, as Lee put it, of charging him with statutory rape.

Instead she married him. She miscarried two months after

the wedding and petitioned for a divorce a week after that. Why she kept the name Hodges, Lee had no idea.

It seemed odd now that Randa hadn't asked what Julia's maiden name had been. And odd, perhaps, that Lee had not told her. Maybe it had nothing to do with her father's criminal connections: maybe she wanted to swap her ethnic name for one more acceptable to the yahoos.

Lee's townhouse was fifteen feet from a wire fence that bordered the tenth fairway of the Leaping Dolphin Country Club. It was a two-story, two-bedroom affair. Each bedroom had its own bath, its own walk-in closet. An enclosed pool and a sundeck overlooked a garden. Beyond the garden was one of the several "lakes" that decorated the grounds and gave excess water a place to go in a downpour.

Dominic was in a lounge chair near the pool. He was in swimming trunks and white sandals. He took a cigar from his mouth when he spotted Randa coming across the lawn.

"Randa," he said, swinging fat legs around, gripping the edges of the lounge chair, pushing himself to his feet—a big man, easily six-four, easily two hundred and fifty pounds, very hairy. Unlike Lee, who favored his mother, Dominic got his build and his looks from their father, a Sicilian carpenter who had wandered up the coast of Italy and married the daughter of a Genovan shipbuilder before migrating to the States. According to Lee, his mother was part Swiss.

Randa's hand felt small in Dominic's thick fingers and rough palm. "It's been a while," she said.

He smelled heavily of cigars.

"Hell of a thing, ain't it?" Dominic said, waving Randa toward a padded deck chair. "Get you something? Booze? Iced tea? Plenty of everything in there."

"Nothing right now," Randa said. "Is Rita here?"

"They're down the beach. They took the golf cart or I'd—"

"That's okay," Randa said. It was Dominic she wanted to talk to.

"So, when'd you hear? They said you were in Savannah."

"Yesterday around noon," Randa said, pleased that he had asked for her.

As she watched him fit a cigar to his lips, take it out, inspect the ash, knock ash onto the patio tiles, she marveled at how different he was from Lee—more the construction worker than executive. She watched him pick a throwaway lighter off a table and spend thirty seconds burning the end if his cigar with a small flame.

"Yeah," he said, "hell of a thing. The guy spends sixteen years in the navy, not a scratch, comes home and gets it in a parking lot. It don't make sense. They say some god regulates things down here. But if it's true, he must be stupid you see all the crap that goes on."

He reached both hands behind him and gripped the chair arms. Grunting loudly, he lowered himself and raised hairy legs to the leg rest. It took him a few seconds to catch his breath.

Wondering about the health of his arteries, Randa asked, "When you saw Lee the other day . . ."

"What other day?"

"Sunday."

"No. I didn't see him maybe in two weeks," Dominic said.

That hurt. That lie was bigger than the others. Lee not only hadn't gone to Georgia but had spent a night here . . . with Vicki Bryant? My God, how could I have been so blind?

Something of her pain probably showed on her face.

Dominic said, "You okay?"

She nodded, embarrassed.

"I called him," Dominic said, "what was it Saturday or something, and he said he couldn't come up. He was working

171

on something."

"Related to business?"

That brought a knowing smile. "Let's cut to the . . . what's it mean 'cut to the chase'? People say that. What's it mean?"

"I think it comes from an impatient movie director. Those old cowboy movies."

"Like get to the interesting stuff. I always wondered," he said, dragging smoke into his mouth, plumes of smoke pouring out his nostrils. "It's this other shit you want to know about, right? Claude Lazard and that dancer?"

"Dancer?"

"Dancer, prancer," waving his arms. "What the hell, the broad from D.C."

"Vicki Bryant? You know her?"

"All I know she was in Hawaii with Lazard. He dumped her out there."

"And took up with Julia?"

"Didn't know you knew that. But that was later."

"When they came back from the voyage to Africa. I guess it upset Lee a lot. Wasn't there a fight?"

He leaned across the small table and tapped ash off his cigar. "I'm surprised he told you."

"He didn't."

"Aah . . ." He sat back and studied her face, then gazed past her at something in the distance.

"That business in Hawaii," Randa said. "What was he actually accused of?"

"I never could figure it out. Lee said it was bullshit the navy played the flop on the Israelis. Never happened, he said."

"The flop?"

"Substituting something cheaper. He said it was a cover. The navy was watching every move they sealed those crates. Couldn't've happened. They watched every inch of how it was done—manufacturing, packaging, the whole thing."

"Something happened. The FBI is down here. Navy investigators. They wouldn't be here if something wasn't going on."

"And Lee's blood pressure wouldn't have been in the trees. Zoe called me. That's why I wanted him to come to Georgia, play some golf, get away. He said he couldn't leave."

"He told me he was trying to protect Julia. Protect her from what?"

"I don't know. She finally kicked Lazard out of her house. Maybe it's to do with him, something, you know."

"It involves your father-in-law. I'm pretty sure of that."

"Maybe. One thing I can tell you: Raphael Cardozo booted Lazard off Julia's boat and told him never get on it again. I don't know what that was about. Lazard was trying to hog it, I guess, taking it out at night. Maybe meeting broads. Who knows?"

Randa remembered the scene at Cardozo's estate.

"He resented Lazard, didn't he?"

"He protects his daughters. Asks Rita all the time if I'm treating her right," laughing.

"He's involved in something, Dominic. The FBI is watching him. The navy had been keeping a man on him. What can you tell me about this guy Abu Mosul?"

He looked puzzled.

"An arms expert," Randa said.

"Never heard of him."

They turned their heads toward the screened lanai. The two women had just come onto the patio.

CHAPTER TWENTY

Julia gave Randa a weak smile as she dropped into a chair at a table several feet from where Dominic was sitting. She apparently wanted to be by herself. Without looking at anyone, she got a cigarette from a pack on the table, put it to her lips, and teased it with a small flame from the throwaway lighter, sucking smoke into her face. She looked disheartened.

Rita, Dominic's wife, seemed less distraught. She was a self-assured older sister, a take-charge kind of woman, dark-haired, fortyish, energetic. She seemed a bit hefty for the crop T-shirt and red shorts she was wearing, but she looked comfortable. The sandals looked funny on her short legs. One thing, and maybe the most significant thing: everything on her was expensive: gold bracelets, big rings, capped teeth that glowed like little treasures inside painted lips.

"Hoped you would come, Randa," she said, extending a jeweled hand. "Can you believe it? Can you believe such a thing could happen?"

"It's hard," Randa said.

"How do you accept something like that?" she asked, as though truly looking for answers.

Randa could give her none and hoped there wouldn't be a lot of talk about Lee's death.

"Rita, get me a beer, will you?" Dominic said.

"I look like your servant?"

"No, she's better looking. Come on, you're up."

Julia pushed her chair back.

"You going inside?" Dominic asked. "Get me a beer, will you?"

Without a word, without looking at anyone, Julia walked to the screen door and went into the lanai. They watched her open the slider and disappear into the main room.

"What's she pissed off about?" Dominic said.

"Leave her alone." Rita had something else she wanted to talk about. "So, did you tell her?" she asked Dominic.

"Come on," frowning. "What for? It was nothing."

"It wasn't nothing. What's the matter with you?"

"Tell me what?" Randa said.

"A guy tried to break in here last night," Rita said. "He was jimmying a downstairs window."

"You saw him?"

"Just a blur. He ran off when I snapped the lights on."

Dominic said, "He heard Lee died and thought nobody'd be home is all it was."

"You should have reported it," Rita said.

"What for?" Dominic said. "What they gonna do? He didn't take nothing."

"What time of night?" Randa asked.

"Maybe two o'clock, two-thirty," Rita said. "It woke me up. I'm a light sleeper. Julia, too. She was right behind me. A guy running off is all either of us saw."

"Isn't there someone on the gate at night?"

"He said no strangers came in after twelve. I asked him."

"Don't mean anything," Dominic said. "Anyone can jump the fence the other side of the lake there. But look, nothing happened. I went through this before. The cops come over, they look around, they talk among themselves, they tell you they'll keep an eye out. Was anything stolen is all they care about. It's statistics. They want to know how many times it happened for statistics, that's all. The more crimes, the bigger their budget. They ain't gonna do anything."

Randa said, "Want to show me the window?"

Rita cocked her head at Dominic who swung his legs around, rubbed his eyes with the heels of his hands, and got slowly to his feet.

"I'll show you," he said. "But it's nothing. Marks on the sill like he wedged a crowbar under the window, maybe a tire iron, something like that."

In the house, Julia looked up from pillows at the end of a long sofa. She was watching television, legs drawn up. It was the sofa Randa and Lee had twice made love on.

"Showing her the window," Dominic said to Julia.

"But not upstairs. I don't want her upstairs," Julia said, speaking as though Randa wasn't standing right there.

"She just wants to see the window."

"I also have to look through things in his office," Randa said. The office was upstairs.

"No! It's private!" Julia got to her feet, almost but not quite blocking Randa's way.

"I'm not here as a friend, Julia. I'm a police officer. Lee was the victim of a homicide."

"His things are private!"

"Not anymore."

After a moment Julia's gaze faltered. "Don't you need a warrant?"

"Who do I serve it on? Lee's not here and ownership right now is in limbo." She doubted the family had any more right to be here than she had. "I'm investigating a murder, Julia."

A fierce defiance momentarily entered Julia's expression, but it melted when Rita touched her arm.

"She wants to find out who killed him just like we do," Rita said.

Although Julia seemed to doubt that, she did step aside, letting Randa get past her.

The calming effect Rita had on her sister was interesting. Would she act this way if she were involved in whatever Julia was worried about? She seemed innocent enough, but you never know.

"I'll look at the window when I come down," Randa said, fearful that Julia might dash upstairs and remove something.

As Randa walked past her, she noticed Rita's restraining hand on Julia's arm.

Randa spent an hour in the small office, originally a bedroom. She found nothing in the file cabinet except outdated business records. A picture of Lee's submarine hung on the wall and a framed newspaper clipping of Lee's son in his baseball uniform. On the desk next to a table lamp she saw a small framed snapshot of a man, possibly Lee's father. Randa had been in this room only once before. The other few times she had come upstairs, she had gone directly into the bedroom. She found nothing new in there.

So what's up here Julia didn't want me to see?

She shrugged and went downstairs.

"You learn anything up there?" Dominic asked when Randa appeared on the stairs.

"Not a thing," she said, giving Julia a questioning look. "Which window is it?"

While she and Dominic and Rita were inspecting the window, Julia joined them. She told Randa that Lee had often said he did not want a funeral ceremony and wanted his body cremated.

"When'd he say that?" Dominic said.

"A long time ago. His ashes will be scattered at sea."

And I will not be invited to that family outing, Randa told herself, ashamed that Julia's attitude had made her feel like dirt.

177

It wasn't until she was well away from the country club that she pulled off the road and gave herself up to a prolonged session of sobbing. Julia had made her feel like a nobody, and that had hurt more than anyone could know.

An hour later when she walked into Buckles's office, she was greeted with: "We got you on a flight to Reagan National. It takes off at 4:15."

"How long's he give me up there?"

"Whatever it takes, I guess—within reason. He's pissed off. Tyonek got snotty with him this morning. Derek threw him out of his office."

"Tyonek want anything special?"

"The same thing—access to our files, a free hand, no interference."

"Did he ask about Lee's death?"

"He mentioned it but apparently doesn't think it's connected to anything he's interested in. At least that's what he wanted me to think."

"They've gotta have something going," Randa said, "and we're in their way."

"That's what it looks like."

"And Tyonek Horse is their lookout."

"That's how I read it."

"And this newspaper reporter in D.C., Doug Flaherty, how well did he know Barstow?"

"He worked on a story about him is all I know. Only he changed jobs. Edits a newspaper in northern Virginia.

"How about your friend, the FBI guy. Do I talk with him?"

"Not without I clear it."

Randa laughed. " 'Without'?"

"Get out of here," he said and waved her off.

Chapter Twenty-One

Next morning, after an uneventful flight and nine hours of sleep in a motel, Randa drove a rented SUV to a small city twenty miles southwest of the capital where she found Doug Flaherty smoking a cigarette at a sidewalk table outside a small café—a lean man in his fifties sporting a golf shirt and shorts and sandals. The instant he saw her, he crushed out his cigarette, got up and, with a big smile, held out his hand.

"Would you rather go inside?" he asked.

"This is fine." The seat, uncushioned, was made of interlaced steel straps, not very comfortable, but tolerable. It was a nice day and he probably wanted to stay outside to smoke.

After chatting about D.C. and Dupont Circle and embassies down Massachusetts Avenue, they got around to Woody Barstow.

" 'An occasional recrudescence' is what he called it," Flaherty said, laughing. He had a small mouth and little bands of metal holding his teeth together.

"The drinking or the women?"

"I was thinking about the women. He had to have them. A wife wasn't enough, apparently."

"Paris Courtland was . . . ?"

"I'm not sure what she was. He claimed she gave him technical assistance, but she didn't know half what he knew about naval ordnance or anything else, from what people told me. That was the argument that got him fired . . . well, not fired. 'Coerced into retirement' is more accurate."

"How long did she work for him?"

"She took up with him during the investigation of the Israeli dispute. He hired her a couple of years later—about three years."

"She helped his search for the missing components?"

"No, that was a misunderstanding. There were never any missing components."

"Really? I thought Barstow was brought in just for that. That's what I've been told."

"I think they needed him to explain the discrepancy between what the Israelis had expected to get and what they actually got. I don't know how the word got out that something was missing, but people picked up on it and thought it's why Woody stayed on. But it was something else."

"Like what?"

"I don't know. They wouldn't let me read his reports. My source there said there were big gaps, maybe classified information, I don't know. But I never got an explanation as to why he hadn't been reassigned after they turned the investigation over to the FBI. Whatever he was doing, it had to be of interest to them, but I couldn't find out what it was. My editor lost interest and put me on something else."

"What was the FBI's interest?"

"I couldn't find out, but I think it had something to do with a scientist who worked at Peenzo Industries in Virginia. People out there said they spent a lot of time asking questions about it. Maybe suspected terrorism stuff. There was a lot of xenophobia, as you know, back in those days. A lot of what people call racial profiling. Maybe he was a victim of that. I think he was Taiwanese."

"What happened to him?"

"He died."

"Natural causes?"

"Far as I know."

She spent a moment watching two young men spreading a blanket out near a fountain, one of them kneeling, toying with the other one's face, exactly like boy and girl stuff.

"Does it make sense to you that the accusations against Barstow were right, that he found what he was looking for and just didn't report it? The FBI ransacked his daughter's apartment. They had to be looking for something."

"He wouldn't steal anything. I know he was accused of that; but, believe me, if he had found whatever they were looking for, he would have brought it in and slammed it down on the director's desk. He was a very proud guy. He was a weird duck, but he wasn't dishonest."

"Except with Paris Courtland?"

"No, I don't think that was dishonest. I think he kept her on his payroll to watch her. She had a pretty good job at Peenzo. What the connection was between that and the Israeli thing I couldn't find out. She was witness to every stage of the planning and production and packaging of whatever they shipped out. Because his investigation came on the heels of that probe, I suspect there was a connection. I just don't know what it was. But he wanted Paris Courtland with him. As you probably know, she wasn't here very long before the FBI got on his tail. They said they were looking for infidelity and boondoggling, but I think it was more than that. But boondoggling was the reason he was asked to resign."

"What do you mean 'she wasn't here very long'?"

"She had left Peenzo Industries and he tracked her down somewhere out west and brought her back."

"Where out west?"

"I don't know. Colorado, I think."

"Denver?"

He shrugged. "Could be."

"Describe her."

181

"Tall, skinny, flat-chested, curly brown hair, spaces between her front teeth, big wet lips. What else? Didn't smile much. Leaned in squinting when she listened to you. Wore dark-rimmed glasses sometimes, sometimes went without them, maybe used contacts. A mannish air about her."

"A lesbian?"

"Who knows?"

"I may know her," Randa said.

"She's in Florida?"

"I don't know where she is, but I think I've been looking for her."

Flaherty had no idea what that meant. She was tempted to enlighten him but, mindful that he worked for a newspaper, decided not to.

"Something I don't understand," she said, changing the subject, "is why they'd use a submarine to carry ordnance or whatever it was halfway around the world. Why a submarine? Those things are slow. Why not fly it over there?"

"Secrecy, I suppose. But delivering ordnance was not the mission. It just happened that the *Tarrantine* was due to go out."

"Is that a special kind of submarine?"

"It's an SSBN converted, used mostly for information gathering."

"Nuclear?"

"That's what the N stands for. 'SSBN' means 'submersible ship ballistic missiles nuclear.' "

"I thought they were called 'boats'?"

"Not officially. The navy calls them ships. 'Boats' is what submariners call them. Probably started back in the nineteenth century when they were small. Calling them boats makes you appear 'salty,' " wiggling his fingers outside his ears.

"There must have been some substance to the claim that

Israel was short-changed."

"Yes. The Israelis were miffed that what they got wasn't state-of-the-art. But our more advanced stuff hadn't yet been fully tested. Whether that was the reason they didn't send them, who knows?"

"How did the FBI get in on it?"

"I don't know. But it was their investigation that caused the dismissal of Paris Courtland."

"Was that Tyonek Horse?"

He seemed surprised. "You know him? He's in Florida?"

"We think things are coming together in Florida."

"What things?"

"We don't know."

Flaherty gave that a long, questioning stare. "And that's why Woody went down there?" A nagging old question seemed to have been answered. "I never understood why he would go to live with his daughter when he could have moved into a swanky life with a fabulously rich widow right here in Spring Valley. I don't know what the attraction was, but she came to the office looking for him all full of disappointment when she found out where he had gone."

"A mistress?"

"People thought he was going to marry her after his wife died."

"And now you think he went to Florida to pursue his case?"

"Proving the navy wrong was about the only thing I can think of that would have made him give up Marlene West. He spent a lot of nights at her . . . I guess you'd say 'her estate.' "

"Sounds like you spent a lot of time on this," Randa said.

"More than my editor liked, but poking into government secrets is as good as this job gets."

Two young men sauntered past their table holding hands. For several minutes she had been watching a middle-aged man ogling a boy standing under the marquee eating an apple.

"This a gay hangout?"

"Looks like it, doesn't it," laughing.

"What can you tell me about Tyonek Horse?" she said after a moment.

"Not much. They said he was a kind of loner."

"How did he lose his forearm?"

"I have no idea. I didn't see much of him."

"Does the name Abu Mosul mean anything to you?"

He almost jumped out of his seat. "Is he in Florida?"

"That surprises you?"

"Yes, it does. I thought Woody Barstow lost interest in him way back. I've never met him. I just know him as a so-called expert on Middle East defense systems. But considering the current paranoia—a lot of it justified, no doubt—I guess it's not surprising that they have him on a leash. He's in Florida?"

"I believe Barstow followed him to Florida." She might have mentioned that Tyonek Horse alerted Barstow to Abu's presence in Cherokee City, but she was here to gather information not to provide it.

"Hah!" Suddenly sitting up straight. "This is getting good," he said, leaning forward as though afraid some words might slip out of Randa's mouth unnoticed.

"Does the name Vicki Bryant mean anything to you?"

He shook his head. "Who's she?"

"I'm not sure. But Barstow was interested in her."

He pointed at a pack of cigarettes on the table. "Do you indulge?"

She shook her head and watched him feed a cigarette to his lips, lean into a small flame, sit back and haul smoke into his lungs, unabashedly giving himself a nicotine fix.

"This woman Marlene West," Randa said. "Is she still around?"

"I don't know." He pushed his chair back. "Let's find out."

He excused himself and walked past the boy under the marquee and went inside the building. A motorcycle roared past with a girl on the tandem seat hugging the driver. Randa turned her face away from the exhaust fumes. When Flaherty came out of the café holding a slip of paper, the boy with the apple crossed the street and joined the man who had been watching him. They strolled off together toward the fountain.

"I imagine she still lives there," he said, handing Randa the paper on which he had written the address and phone number of Marlene West. "It's one of those big houses behind an iron fence and a few acres of lawn. Not hard to find. Just give this to a cab driver."

Randa sat forward on the rear seat when the cab turned into the driveway of Marlene West's estate. Massive iron gates opened as though in response to an electronic signal. She could see the house. It stood on a rise among trees dominating an acre of lawn—a broad building two stories high, sandstone walls and white-framed windows and a tall, steep slate roof.

When the cab pulled into the circular drive, a woman came out the front doorway under an arched portico. She greeted Randa with a handshake and a warm smile. Her fingers were cold.

"I guess you had no trouble finding us," she said. She was in her late thirties, tall with a lean face neatly framed by straight black hair cut at the jaw line. She introduced herself as Joletta Cambrini and said she was Mrs. West's secretary. It was she who had taken Randa's phone call.

They went into the house and walked through a large galleried rotunda past chairs and plush-cushioned divans Randa couldn't imagine anyone sitting on. There were paintings on every wall, landscapes, many of them English hunting scenes.

185

Marlene West was waiting in a room by a window overlooking a garden. As she extended her hand and smiled, she apologized for not getting up, said she was having trouble with back spasms. "Old age creeping in," she said with a thin smile. Randa suspected she was no more than in her early fifties.

She was not at all what Randa had expected. She was overweight, had fatty eyelids, and steel gray hair slightly curly that hung to her shoulders. There was something of the earth mother about her, an abundance of bosom, thick arms and strong-looking hands, not the style of woman one usually thinks of as a mistress. She didn't look like a rich woman. She looked like a farmer's wife posing as a rich woman.

"Sit here," she said, indicating a small cushioned chair at the other side of a tea table. "Can I get you something?"

"No, I'm fine," Randa said. To avoid Mrs. West's penetrating gaze that made her uncomfortable, she looked around the room at polished French-looking furniture, bronze sculptures on a mantle above a stone fireplace, framed landscapes on richly papered walls. She wondered why people of wealth surrounded themselves with expensive things. Just because they could? Did they need constant reminding that they were rich? But how would I know? I've never had a dime to spend on much more than rent and transportation.

"You said you wanted to talk about Woody Barstow," Mrs. West said.

"He was a close friend?"

"Bosom buddies." she laughed. Her whole body laughed.

"And you know how he died."

"His daughter, Kirby, called. She thought I would want to know. It was thoughtful of her, don't you think? You've met her?"

"Yes," Randa said, "she told me about the invasion of her home . . . the FBI. I guess they were looking for something."

"Did they find it?"

"Apparently not what they were looking for, although they carted away a lot of paper."

"Did they mention a valise?" Marlene asked.

"A valise? Not that . . ."

"And you're here looking for it, whatever it is."

"Why a valise?"

"Because that's what that little weasel one-armed FBI man wanted. I'm sure you know about him."

"Tyonek Horse?"

"That sounds like the name. He flashed something at me, some kind of ID thing. He said he was from the FBI, a disgusting little person," waving her hands as though to scatter off fragments of his memory. "Is he really an FBI man? I didn't think they hired foreigners."

"He's a Native American."

"An Indian? Really?" She made a grunting sound of baffled acceptance. "Yes, I remember the boots. It makes sense."

"He called on you?"

"He pushed his way past Joletta, almost knocking her down," glancing solicitously at her secretary who was sitting across the room smiling. "An arrogant little monster."

"What did he want?"

"A valise! He accused me of hiding it. He said Woody brought it to my house and that it belonged to the government."

"And there was no valise?"

"Not that I ever saw. And I've searched the house, even the attic. There's no valise in this house."

"Did he say what was in it?"

"He just said he wanted it. When I threatened to call the police, he got angry. I think it scared him. Why would he be afraid of the police, unless he wasn't what he said he was?"

"Maybe it wasn't fear. What did he say?"

"He made some meaningless excuse about keeping the police out of it. When I talked to Woody—and I'm not sure Woody knew him, although he had told me he was being investigated. But he said the same thing. 'Don't call the police! It'll just make things more complicated.' So I didn't. It's all so confusing. Government workers! They're all liars. I hope you're not like that."

"Just federal workers," Randa said, laughing.

As though on cue, maybe getting a signal from the kitchen, Joletta left the room and came back with cookies, cups, and a tea service on a tray. She set the tray on the table, poured tea after getting nods from Mrs. West, and went back to her chair across the room, perching there like a little bird, feet together, hands folded in her lap.

"Did you ask Woody about the valise?"

"He didn't say anything about it, but he wanted a description of the man. From his reaction I gathered he had seen him or someone acting suspiciously, maybe following him around."

Randa gave that a moment. "Did you know Paris Courtland?"

"No. He told me about her, and I gathered he had brought her back from Denver to keep tabs on her. I don't know what she was supposed to have done, but it had to be something. All I could get from Woody was he didn't like her and didn't trust her. So why keep her on unless she knew something that was valuable to him?"

"Did he retire because they made him fire Paris Courtland?"

"No, because they had no respect for him."

Randa sipped her tea and watched a bird sitting on the sill outside the window. The bird flew off.

"Did Woody ever mention a scientist named Henry Wang who worked at Peenzo Industries?"

"Briefly," Mrs. West said. "He didn't say much about him

except that Paris had worked with him and had been in charge of disposing of his things when he died."

"Things at Peenzo?"

"And at his home in Lee City." She reached for a cookie. "She left Peenzo shortly after Dr. Wang died, and I think it's connected to why Woody fetched her from Denver."

"That was about a year ago?"

"More or less. And that's when things started to go downhill for him. I became aware of Woody's problem when Tyonek Horse came here looking for a valise."

"The accusations against him and Paris Courtland had already started?"

"And the heavy drinking," Mrs. West said.

And then he went to Florida, Randa said to herself, satisfied that she now at least had a handle on the sequence of Woody Barstow's activities since Hawaii.

She finished her tea and after declining an offered cookie, she thanked Mrs. West, followed Joletta to the portico and walked down a path to her rented car.

At her hotel that evening, after working on a report that would justify prolonging her stay in the D.C. area, which she prayed the sheriff would allow, she sat on the edge of her bed watching Mary McDonnell moving around in a wheelchair on the TV screen. She was watching the movie but fixing in her mind the sequence of Woody's activities. He had been assigned to duty here in D.C. when he came back from Hawaii. He worked on something for about three years possibly connected to the Israeli incident. When Dr. Wang died, Paris Courtland resigned from her job at Peenzo Industries and went to Colorado. Woody brought her back to D.C. and gave her a job, presumably to keep an eye on her. At about that time, the FBI assigned Tyonek Horse to investigate Woody's behavior. Shortly after that, Paris was taken off Woody's payroll and he was forced to resign. He moved to Florida to live with Kirby and, when Ty-onek tipped him off that Abu Mosul was in Cherokee City, he came to Cherokee City where he was murdered.

So the big question here is: What was going on between Ty-onek and Woody? If Tyonek had been interested only in Woody's supposed abuse of his budget, what reason could he have had for relaying to Woody through Captain Frye that Abu Mosul was in Cherokee City? Were they working together?

Thinking about all of this, she went into the bathroom and showered, put on linen slacks and a matching taupe shell and sandals, and took the elevator down to the restaurant. After a relaxing meal of chardonnay and marinated salmon, she went back to her room and left a message on Doug Flaherty's cell phone asking him to call her in the morning.

"I want to visit Henry Wang's shop in Lee City," she told him.

She watched television for an hour, then darkened the room and went to sleep. She was awakened around eight-thirty in the morning by a phone call from Flaherty.

"Give me a half hour," she said.

Chapter Twenty-Two

It was only a short drive through the hills of northern Virginia, to the small town of Lee City where a woman named Jocelyn Kite had rented a room and a basement shop to Henry Wang.

"Went to a bluegrass concert over here at Sandburg last week. Authentic American," Doug said, steering his old car with his right hand, his left dangling out the window holding a cigarette. Although she was not comfortable inhaling the stale odors in the car, she was enjoying the green hills they were riding through. At her end of Florida, everything was flat.

"I'm not really into that," Randa said.

"Do you like jazz?"

"Only when it has a melody."

As the car turned a corner and moved slowly up a winding road Randa was reminded of rural areas west of Providence in Rhode Island. Her mother had enjoyed riding through those wooded hills, they reminded her, she said, of England.

"This it?"

"It's her name on the mailbox," Doug said, crushing his cigarette in the ashtray as he steered up a narrow gravel drive.

A large barking dog loped across a patchy lawn followed by a black woman in a blue old-fashioned house dress. She was barefoot.

"Oh, don't mind him," she said, swatting the dog's rump, sending it back to the house. "He just showing off." She searched both their faces as they got out of the car, maybe

191

deciding whether to trust them. "Ain't much here," she said, leading them toward the back of the house. "That woman carted most everything off. Nothing left but benches. She took the tools and boxes and other stuff she could lift. Don't know what you expect to find, but you free to look."

"His room?" Randa asked as they walked around back of the house and approached a small attached shed that sheltered a stairway leading down to the cellar.

"Someone else in it now. Can't let you in there," the woman said.

She unlocked the door and pushed it open, slid her hand along the wall and snapped on a bank of fluorescent overhead lights that fiercely brightened the room. The air carried a faintly metallic smell.

"He had the lights put in," the woman explained. "Hurt my eyes if I worked here. And that bench," pointing across the room, "like those lights weren't enough, had little lights hanging over it where he worked. That woman took them. She took everything except I had to sweep it out."

The stone walls of the room were painted white. The cement floor was white. The glass in a casement window over the bench had been painted white.

"He did all that, first thing he got here. Didn't like people prying," the woman said, noticing Randa looking at the window.

"Have any idea what he was working on?" Randa asked.

"None of my business," the woman said. "He kept this room locked. Long as they pay the rent and don't break things, I don't care what they do."

"What did you find in here after he died?" Doug asked.

"I didn't know he dead until that woman came here. She said it happened at work, then she hauled everything out except that bench. I never made out what any of it was. She said it was government secrets. And so did that man I told you on the phone. He didn't like everything was gone and asked questions about the woman more than about Dr. Wang."

"What kind of questions?" Randa asked.

"Was she alone. Did she say where she was taking the boxes. Stuff like that. He said he was FBI, but I didn't believe they'd hire a man who had only one hand. What would they want someone like that for?"

If Tyonek Horse had been interested only in Woody Barstow's relationship with Paris Courtland, why had he come here?

When they were outside, standing near Doug's sedan, Mrs. Kite said, "Right out there," pointing at a large field, "that's where I seen him for hours staring into the sky. Don't know what he was looking at, but he stood there, elbows out, hands in his back pockets looking up. I couldn't see anything up there. Wasn't no bird he was looking at. Don't know what it was."

"And you didn't ask him?"

"None of my business."

Later, in the car, heading back to the city, Doug said, "Maybe he was just out there taking a leak."

"Or maybe he just wanted the sun on his face. One of those slow-motion Beijing happiness things. What was his specialty?"

"They wouldn't tell me. All they said was 'naval ordnance.' Most of what they do is classified."

"Why did he work at home?"

"I think it was on his own time. I couldn't find out."

"But Paris Courtland knew."

Doug nodded. "And probably Woody Barstow did. And Tyonek Horse."

Doug looked genuinely disappointed when she turned down his offer to take her to dinner. He was a nice-enough man, and he had done her a big favor driving her to Lee City, but she preferred, at least that evening, to be alone. Thoughts about Lee had been creeping through her fatigue. She was feeling sorry for herself, no kind of company for a man she had only a professional interest in.

After dinner in the hotel restaurant, she bought a paperback novel and upstairs, lying in bed, got to page thirty-seven before she fell asleep. In the morning after showering and putting on jeans and a blue shirt, she phoned Buckles and filled him in on what she had learned.

"What did Bea find out at the marina?"

"She said there was a man asleep in one of the boats but he didn't hear anything. Did you find out anything about Vicki Bryant up there?"

"Maybe a lot," Randa said. "I think you'd better check again with the police in Denver. This time do the search for Paris Courtland."

It took Buckles a few seconds, but he finally said, "Aah . . . you think so?"

"It's the same description, and it makes sense. It'll all be in my report. Any chance I can stay up here? I'd like to talk with that friend of yours in the Hoover Building."

"You'd better come home," he said. "Someone here wants to see you."

"Who?"

"An FBI woman. Says she knows you."

"Got a name?"

"Probably," and he laughed and hung up, annoying her. Just to annoy her is probably why he held back the name. She shook her head. Men. They're all ten years old.

She had time to visit the World War II memorial before she took a cab to Reagan. When she got home around ten that evening, she found a brown two-door parked near the lemon tree. A woman got out. She didn't recognize her until she got up close. It was Moira Pelletier.

"A long time," Randa said.

Moira held out both arms. "I'm so sorry about Lee. It's so sad."

Her embrace and the mention of Lee's name brought tears to Randa's eyes.

"Come in, come in," she said, her hand on Moira's back, urging this old friend of Gloria's toward her apartment door. "This time of night, it's got to be something urgent."

"Not glad to see me?"

Randa smiled. "Always glad to see you. Just tired. Airplane rides . . ."

"I take pills when I go up. Sleep most of the way."

"Are they habit forming?"

"Paying for them ain't," Moira said. She was a university graduate, but for some reason she enjoyed occasionally slipping into street patois. Gloria said it was to protect herself against guilt, something about having betrayed the community by joining the cops. But who knows?

They small-talked while Randa dropped luggage onto her bed and made coffee in the kitchen, fighting off a mild resentment of this intrusion. She really wanted to be alone, wanted to shower, wanted to climb into bed.

When the coffee was made and poured, they went into the living room. Moira sat in Charley's chair, Randa on the sofa opposite.

"There's nothing official about this," Moira said. "It's just you might hear about me snooping around . . ."

"How would I hear that?"

"The Indian. You met him. He wants this place to himself."

"Tyonek? You're going to work here separate from him?"

"Oh, he knows I'll be here. The SAC told him so he wouldn't be surprised."

"Or alarmed," Randa said.

Moira's eyes narrowed. "Why'd you say that?"

"It would be a big help, Moira, if you guys would tell us what's going on. All this turf foolishness is a pain in the ass. I don't want to get into it right now. I'm too tired. But it's possible that Bill White and Lee Fronzi might still be alive—"

"Hold on," Moira said, raising both hands. "What are you talking about?"

"What's Tyonek doing here? He isn't investigating a murder. He says he is. The navy said it's why he's here. But he doesn't seem to give a shit about a homicide investigation. Why is he here?"

"They told me . . . I been in Miami. All I know is they said he's just riding out his short time, waiting for his pension."

Maybe. And maybe Moira didn't know what was going on.

"Okay, but now you're here. Why? And don't bullshit me, please."

"They said he was supposed to investigate a murder? That NCIS man?"

"Woodrow Barstow," Randa said. "A woman came here from D.C. and said the FBI was taking over the investigation. Tyonek pretended to have just been assigned. But we know he's been chasing Barstow for at least a year. We know it has something to do with a Dr. Wang who worked for a naval ordnance manufacturer in Virginia. We know that a woman named Paris Courtland is down here calling herself Vicki Bryant and that she's mixed up in something you people are interested in."

Moira sat back with her mouth open, both hands in the air. "I swear to God, Randa, I don't know a thing about any of that. I'm not supposed to say, but they sent me here to find out what you people are doing. All's I know is that the Indian isn't telling them anything they want to know. I supposed they thought he was sleeping on the job."

"It's a two-way street, Moira. And you can tell your SAC

what I said. We don't want any more people killed. Maybe Tyonek is here as a lookout. Maybe he's here for other reasons. But it could save lives if you'd let us in on it."

"I don't know anything about what you're saying," Moira said, sitting there frowning, annoyed. "You know, I think that bastard thought we were just going to sit here you and me and make hen talk—two women, right? And I'm supposed to run back down there and tell him what we gossiped about. That man is prehistoric."

Randa got out of the chair, took a deep breath. "I'm sorry I can't be more hospitable, Moira. But I'm exhausted. If you want to talk tomorrow, give me a ring." She went to the desk in her bedroom, came back with a card. She handed it to Moira and walked her to the door.

"I'll call you," Moira said. "And I'll try to find out what's going on. I hate being used like this."

CHAPTER TWENTY-THREE

Randa reached for her cell phone, missed, and knocked it to the floor. While leaning across the mattress, she glanced at her bedside clock and saw four lighted hyphens on the dark face. She apparently had slept through a storm.

"Ten-fifteen," Buckles said. "You're not up?"

"I'm talking to you. What's going on?"

"There are two guys here looking for you. Chubleigh wants you to come in."

"What two guys?"

"FBI."

Randa closed her eyes and sank back on the rumpled sheets. "Me and my big mouth. Am I in trouble?"

"Not with Chubleigh. Did you talk to that woman last night?"

"I unloaded a lot of frustration on her. She must have reported it," noticing a black dot in the corner of the ceiling, probably a spider.

"Well, Chubleigh's not unhappy. He thinks you broke through the wall."

"They waiting there for me?"

"On the nervous chairs outside his office."

While Randa showered and dressed and downed a few ounces of orange juice, she tried to remember what she had said to Moira last evening. She was sure she had said too much, but if it didn't rile Derek Chubleigh, what the hell.

★ ★ ★ ★ ★

They were waiting for her in the chairs in front of Chubleigh's desk, two men in gray suits with white button-down shirts, red ties, black socks, and black polished shoes. They turned their heads in unison when Randa came in. She nodded at Chubleigh and sat to the left of his desk, angled out so that she could easily watch both men and the sheriff.

"So let's get right to it," Chubleigh said, not bothering to introduce her. He was leaning forward with elbows on the desktop, hands together, evidently anticipating some fun.

"These two gentlemen are from the FBI. They think you're sticking your face into their affairs and want me to take you off the case."

"And why is that?" Randa said, calmly regarding the men. She was acting. Whenever she was brought into this office and directed by Chubleigh to say things, she felt like a puppet being manipulated by a moron. She went along because it was her job.

The one nearest her, a smallish man nearly bald with heavy-lidded eyes, was apparently the spokesman.

"As we told the sheriff," he said, "we're taking over your investigation. You are to stop whatever you've been doing. You're interfering with something you know nothing about, something extremely sensitive."

Randa could find nothing in Chubleigh's expression endorsing what had just been said.

"Just doing my job," she told the man.

"Now it's *our* job," he said, dismissing her as you might an unruly child.

"Oh, well now," Chubleigh said, "let's not get carried away here. You haven't persuaded me to decide anything. I call the shots in this office."

With impatient annoyance, not the best attitude to confront

Chubleigh with, the man said, "You know we can stop you. All I have to do is place a call to a federal judge."

Chubleigh bristled. "So do it instead of sitting there threatening me. But I don't think you will. You've had plenty of chances."

"I'm trying to persuade you, Sheriff. I don't want to resort to—"

"Bullshit. You're afraid it'll get on the news. What are you hiding? We talking some kind of corruption here?"

"There wouldn't be any publicity, Sheriff. A federal judge would make a call to your office and tell you to stop. No one but you and him would know about it."

"Those reporters out there aren't stupid. You take me off the case and leave Tyonek Horse up here sitting on his ass, nobody doing anything to solve three murders? They'll do their own investigating. There's already a reporter from up in Virginia on his way down here."

This was news to Randa. And maybe it wasn't true.

"I've ordered Sergeant Sorel here to vigorously investigate these homicides, which is my responsibility. You can consult with her. We want to cooperate. But goddamnit I'm not taking her off these three homicides unless you give me a good reason." He turned to Randa. "Do you think Tyonek Horse is trying to solve these murders?"

Randa shook her head.

"And you think he's waiting here for something to happen?"

"It looks that way," she said, inside the puppet laughing.

Chubleigh turned back to the two men. "You want my co-operation, why don't you dish out a little of your own. We're all citizens of the same country. We all pledge allegiance to the same flag."

Both men sat there mute as marble. Finally, the bald one tapped his partner on the knee. Both men got up. With defiant exasperation, the bald one said, "We tried." He nodded at

Randa, glanced sadly at the sheriff, and led his partner out of the office.

When the door was closed, Chubleigh turned to Randa. "Now, what in hell is it you said to that woman?"

"I was tired," Randa said. "I'm not sure I remember, but I guess I told her we couldn't protect our people unless she or someone told us what's going on. I mentioned Paris Courtland down here calling herself Vicki Bryant. I said we think something's about to happen."

"Good. Now I want you to write it up. And put in everything you can remember. But don't talk to that woman again."

"You don't have to worry about that."

Although Randa knew that Moira, coming here at night pretending to be on a friendly visit, had just been doing her job, she nevertheless felt betrayed. She was one of them, an FBI agent. They don't trust us, or they think we're incompetent. And that angered her. The anger degenerated into fatigue as she sat for several hours at her computer trying to remember everything that had happened during the last two days.

Late that night, she was awakened from a bad dream by footsteps in the kitchen. Irrationally her first thought was that Lee had come in. She reached for her bedside lamp, tapped the button but the light didn't come on. The clock face was blank—no numbers, no little hyphens. She was swinging her legs to the floor when something huge charged into the bedroom and slammed a wet, chemical-soaked cloth into her face. A firm hand gripped the back of her head. She tried to yell. She struck out with both fists. She tried to twist her face aside. She couldn't breathe. The odors in the cloth smothered her. She lost strength and became nauseous and sagged onto the bed, thinking rape. She tried to drive a knee into the bulk that hovered over her and heard a man's voice saying something from a mile away. She felt herself sobbing as she faded into unconsciousness.

CHAPTER TWENTY-FOUR

She stared up through dreamy eyes at fluorescent tubes imbedded in a tiled ceiling. She tried to sit up, but agonizing pain in her skull stopped her.

She moaned against the pain and dazedly wondered where she was. She was fully dressed but in clothes she hadn't worn since going to Maine last winter—hiking boots and a denim shirt and jeans! She was still wearing her pajamas! Her mind swirled in a delirium of panic. My God, what's happening? She frantically scanned the room, rolled onto her side, lowered her legs and slowly sat up, the room swaying as she winced from the pain that gripped her head. Gradually she steadied herself.

She was in a small room with bone-colored walls and a door ten feet from the bed and narrow casement windows high up the wall. There was no furniture in the room except the bed. The air held the imitation pine odor of cleaning fluid.

She pressed fingers into her temples, slowly rolling her head, rotating her shoulders. She got up. Stood for a moment fighting vertigo. She took a deep breath, went over and tried the door. It was locked. She rapped on it. A sudden irrational spurt of anger made her pound on it with her fist.

"Open this door!" she yelled. There was no response. "Open this fucking door!"

Her heartbeat accelerated as she waited, leaning her hand on the door, looking down. She went back to the bed and stared up at the windows. She pushed the bed to the wall, stood on the mattress, and craned her neck to look out. She saw trees, hardwood trees. They didn't look like Florida trees. She couldn't see the ground. She tried to break the glass. It was thick. She couldn't budge it. She got down and sat on the other side of the bed and lowered her face to her hands. Her heart was beating rapidly and she started feeling sorry for herself. She was in pain. She was scared. For a moment she was lost in despair. She raised an edge of a sheet and wiped tears from her face, turned her head and stared helplessly at the door.

I don't know where I am! This is crazy!

She had no recollection of an abduction, but obviously she had been abducted. She gently probed herself and was sure she had not been raped.

"Who the hell is out there!" she yelled, her adrenaline rising.

She strode to the door and pounded on it. "Let me out of here!"

The doorknob moved. She stepped back. The door opened toward her. Two women in brown shirts and denim slacks were facing her in a large room—both young and slim, the one nearest her a redhead. There were windows behind them, a small field and trees beyond the windows, a door to the right on the outside wall some fifteen feet away. She could smell brewed coffee.

"No one's here to hurt you," the redhead said. "Go back and lie down."

She was about Randa's size, maybe five-nine. The second woman, standing to the left, a few feet behind her, was holding a stun gun Randa recognized as one she had tested for Buckles at a police gun show.

"If you need something—"

Randa stepped into the redhead, both hands slamming her shoulders. She tried to put the woman in front of her as a shield, but the second woman moved quickly to the side and fired a barbed, electrically charged projectile directly at her. It was like being walloped by a truck. Her knees buckled. Both women caught her before she collapsed. The projectile had fallen away, but she was still shaking from the impact as the women dragged her into the small room and laid her on the bed.

"That was very foolish, Randa. We don't want to hurt you."

The second woman, gathering up the long wire and the projectile, said, "If you want something, knock on the door. But don't try that again. Stay in this room."

"Who are you?" Randa said, frightened and humiliated, pressing her hand against her rapidly beating heart.

"If you want anything, knock on the door," the woman said. She left the room. The other woman followed her outside and closed the door. She heard the lock snap into place.

Lying half on the bed, both feet on the floor, craning her neck to watch the closed door, at the edge of throwing up, Randa remembered a dog trembling on the ground after being hit by exactly the same barbed projectile. I am that dog, she thought, tears flooding her eyes. She raised the hem of her shirt and the pajama top and found red marks just under her rib cage. She held her hand at her heart, remembering what the demonstrator had said about induced fibrillation. Her heartbeat was fast but strong. The rhythm seemed regular.

She pulled herself onto the bed and lay there more humiliated than hurt, taking deep breaths, trying to compose herself. She got up and stood for a moment assuring herself that she could walk, could run if she had to. Gradually her fear changed to anger. A memory of her apartment moved into her mind as though from a dream—a dark form looming over her, an evil smell clamped to her face. She again gently explored herself for pain. She was sure she had not been raped. But it was a man who had assaulted her. Was it a man who had dressed her? She sat down and closed her eyes. It didn't matter. She had to get out of this. She had to find a way.

The shorty pajamas bunching up under her slacks made her uncomfortable. The base of her tongue tasted foul.

What did she remember about the stun gun? It was the latest version, supposed to be less powerful than the original model. Civilians could buy it. Police in many states were equipped with it. It could hurl a barbed projectile on a wire some twenty feet, delivering an electrical current that could penetrate two inches of clothing. The impact could cause permanent damage. It could kill.

I need a shield, she told herself, looking around. Tensing her neck against the pain, she slid to her knees and looked under the bed into strong odors of cleaning fluid. Nothing there, not even dust. She looked at the metal screening on the air ducts. They wouldn't help. If her food came in on a tray. . . . That would be the time to strike—slap the tray into the first woman's face, push her into the one with the gun, then run to the door.

It wouldn't work. I would never reach the door.

This isn't some dirty little cult, she told herself, remembering the ordeal of Patty Hearst. This place is neat. These women are trained. Their uniforms may be plain, but they're uniforms. There are no insignias on their shirts. These people come from a well-disciplined organization.

She had recently read about a neo-Nazi group of skinheads called the *Bruders Schweigen,* a kind of international Ku Klux Klan. But people like that—what would they want with me? Like McVeigh, they hate the government, but why me? I'm not important.

Am I in Idaho? Are these people terrorists? They know my name! Did they kill Lee? "We don't want to hurt you," the woman had said.

Then why bring me here?

Oh, goddammit, this isn't important! I have to get out! But how?

She wanted a mirror. She wanted to see her face. She fretted over that for a few seconds. She ran her fingers over her cheeks, tapped her hair.

Okay, I'm a mess. So what?

The door opened. She sat upright. The woman with red hair came inside carrying a tray, a thin plastic tray that wouldn't shield anything. The one with the Taser waited in the doorway. She was shorter, darker.

"Where are we?" Randa asked.

The redhead set the tray on the bed. "Hope you like chicken salad." There was a folded paper napkin under two white-bread triangular sandwiches on a paper plate. Steam was curling off the dark surface of coffee in a paper cup.

It's a weapon!

"Is this chicken kosher?" Randa asked.

The woman shrugged. "I have no idea. Are you Jewish? I'm sorry, but it's all we got. It tastes good."

So they're not German skinheads, she thought and started laughing. Why would they be? It's just something I read. They're not threatening or swaggering or posturing. They don't act like terrorists. This seems like just a job to them.

"Who are you?"

"That's not important," the woman said. "Look, we don't want to hurt you. Just don't try anything stupid. We're a hundred miles in the woods. No roads out there. We'd just have to go looking for you. And those woods are filthy with mosquitoes."

"What do you want with me?"

"Nothing. Just relax."

The moment the women were gone, Randa cleared her throat and spat into the napkin. She dropped the crumpled paper to the floor. Most inelegant, she thought—what her mother would say.

The man at the testing had said it was possible to intercept the projectile but you'd have to be damned skilled or damned lucky. And this was from a farmer out west somewhere who had tested the gun on pigs, never used it on a human.

When she finished the sandwich, she went over and rapped on the door. She heard a key enter the lock.

"You have milk or something? The coffee?"

"Sorry," the woman said, rising on tiptoe to look past Randa at the bed. "I can make you another sandwich."

"No thanks." Randa went back to the bed. She sipped at the coffee. Unsoftened by milk there was a bitterness to it, but it was coffee and it helped cleanse her throat.

I'll probably have only one chance to break out of here. If I fail, they'll put restraints on me. It'll have to be at night. They'll likely take turns sleeping. There'll be only one to deal with.

She lay back, considering for a moment whether the pillow beneath her head would stop the current. Probably not.

It'll be dark.

She stared through the casement windows at the sky. There were no clouds. Maybe there'll be a moon.

She went to the door and knocked and waited, holding the crumpled napkin in her hand.

"What do you want?" through the door.

"I need the bathroom," which was true, and she wanted another look at the room.

Five minutes passed before the redhead opened the door. The shorter woman was leaning on the sink holding the Taser.

"The door on the left," the redhead said, pointing.

There were two doors on that inner wall, both closed. She caught the time on a clock over a counter near a hand pump at the sink. It was five-fifteen. On her way back to the bedroom, she noticed wheel tracks in the clearing, automobile tracks.

She doubted they were a hundred miles in the woods. Even so, where would I go if I got out there? Even with a moon, I'd get lost.

Back in the room with the door closed and locked, she noticed that the tray and the paper cup were gone. She remembered in an old Tarzan movie this guy saying that animals rest when they know that fighting is useless. They're smarter than we are, she thought, lying down, closing her eyes. The headache was less severe. She wanted a pill to reduce the pain but was afraid of what they might give her. Her stomach had settled. She told herself she would be all right. After a while she fell asleep. When she woke up, the ceiling lights were on, but it was dark outside the windows. She wanted to know whether both women were up. She went to the door, realizing that her headache was gone.

"You got something to read? I'm going nuts in here."

There was no response.

"Hey, come on!" she yelled.

"Go back to bed. It's late." It was not the redhead's voice.

"How late? What time is it?"

"It's almost morning. Go back to sleep."

"I've gotta go!"

She waited several minutes before the key entered the lock. She watched the knob turn. She yanked the door open and lunged at the gun. The woman, startled, tried to pull back but Randa ripped the gun from her hand. It flew across the floor. The woman ran after it. Randa got to the outside door. It was locked. She turned, feeling foolish, expecting the projectile to fly at her. But the woman couldn't make the gun work. She slapped it against her leg. It went off. The projectile ricocheted off the floor and banged into the wall. Randa grabbed the wires and pulled the gun from the woman's hand. The woman scuttled like a crab to the sink. She pulled open a drawer. Randa piled into her, reached across her just as the woman grabbed a gun, a real gun, a semi-automatic. Randa hit the woman's hand, snatched the gun from her and backed off.

"Open the door!" she said, waving the gun at the wall.

"This is wrong. Don't do it. You've got the wrong idea," she said, frightened, staring fearfully at the gun.

"Unlock the door. I'm a police officer and you're in big god-damn trouble."

"You don't understand," the woman said.

"Unlock that door!"

Because there might be another gun in the drawer, Randa waved the woman aside. There was no second gun, but there were keys, house keys and one plastic-handled car key.

"Get on the floor," Randa said.

Dropping nervously to the floor, the woman said, "This is wrong, Randa. Don't do this. It isn't what you think. They just want you out of the way."

"Who does?"

"Nobody wants to hurt you."

The door next to the bathroom came slightly open. Randa grabbed the keys and fired a round into the wall. The door closed.

"Don't come out here!"

"For chrissakes, Randa, don't do this!" the woman screamed from the floor.

The second key she tried unlocked the outside door. She raised a switch on the wall and lights flooded the clearing outside. She got out of the building and was tempted to run straight into the woods but how far would she get? There was only a sliver of moon. She had seen wheel tracks that went around the front of the building. She ran through thick grass to the back and found a pickup truck snuggled against the cement-block foundation. She raced to it, got the key into the ignition and started the engine.

The redhead, holding a gun, came in front of her as she switched on the headlights. Randa moved the truck forward, cramped the wheel to avoid the woman, putting her on the passenger side against the building. As she drove across the clearing, she saw the woman in her rearview mirror standing against the building, the gun hanging at her side.

She didn't shoot at me!

She bounced the truck over deep ruts down a narrow dirt road. In less than twenty minutes she was on a paved road where signs directed her to a highway leading south into Georgia. Because she had no money and no ID, she stayed on the highway until she found a settlement large enough to have a police department. She knew she was in northeast Georgia where there had been recent reports of police abuse, not a place to be caught driving a truck with no license, no ID, and no money.

The name of this city, Cardwall, hadn't come up in any reports she had seen. What she did see now was not encouraging—broken sidewalks, tilting telephone poles, collapsed beer cans in the gutter, a drunk in a doorway eyeing her. The police station was in a two-story brick building next to a pool parlor. She had to step over a hound asleep in the doorway. A girl at a desk behind a railing looked up from something she was reading.

"Yes?" the girl said.

"Is the chief in?" Randa said. "I'm a Florida deputy sheriff. I need some assistance."

The girl gave her a questioning onceover. She pressed a button on an intercom console. An annoyed male in a rasping voice answered her.

"What you want, Hazel?"

"There's a woman here says she's a deputy sheriff from Florida."

"What's she want?"

"Wants to talk to you."

A tall black man emerged from a doorway. His head was shaved. His blue shirt was open at the throat with a badge sagging off a pocket.

"You're the chief?"

"Billy Johnson," the man said, regarding her skeptically. "You got ID?"

"No. I was being held by some people north of here. I took their truck."

"What you mean 'being held'?"

"I was abducted. I know it sounds insane, but I really am a detective sergeant in Cherokee City County, Florida. Could you possibly put me in touch with the state police here, a Lieutenant Stanley Krupinsky. Do you know him?"

"This is Cardwall police," Billy said.

"If I could use your phone. Please, I'm not lying. They dressed me . . ."

He opened a gate in the barrier, walked past her to the door and looked out. "That your truck across the street?"

"I drove it here, yes."

"Wait here." She watched him cross the street and look inside the truck's cab. He came back holding a small plastic envelope. He closed the door and pointed at a chair. "Sit down over there. You got keys to that truck?"

She was holding the key.

"Let me have it," he said, looking at her closed hand.

"All I want is to talk to the state police. If you would let me use the phone."

"You got the key there?"

She opened her hand. He took the key.

"You got ID, a license to drive that truck, anything?"

"I told you I was abducted. If I had stolen the truck I certainly wouldn't have come to a police station. Please, let me use your phone. I can clear all of this up."

He went behind the barrier and took something from the envelope, put it on the desk in front of the girl.

"Call this in."

"If you'll let me make a call," Randa said, starting to get up.

"Stay right there," Billy said.

She reluctantly sat back down. At another time she might easily have accepted this man's caution, but right now she was in no mood for it.

"Look, I just want to make a phone call."

He ignored her. At least five minutes went by before the girl lowered the phone. "It ain't listed stolen," she said.

She took the envelope from his hand and went through some papers.

"It belongs to the state of North Carolina," she said, "Department of Surplus Properties."

Billy looked at Randa. "You drove here from North Carolina?"

"I'm not sure. It was north of here, in the woods, in the mountains. Look, I can clear all of this up with a phone call."

Billy wasn't eager to help her, but he seemed not to know what else to do. Finally he asked, "Who is it you want to call?"

After an interminable half hour, Billy held the phone out to her. She got up.

"Stan? Is it you? Boy, am I glad to hear your voice."

"Probably Nantahala National Forest," Stan said—a big man sitting across from her in a booth at The Corner Dynette just outside Atlanta. He was tapping his forefinger on the rim of his coffee mug, a thoughtful expression on his long, homely face. "The National Guard built an airstrip with a house sounds like

213

the one you described. It's mainly for firefighters and game wardens, but other fed and state agents use it."

When he asked why she thought it was the FBI who had kidnapped her, she briefed him on the situation in Cherokee City. He had read about the unusual spate of homicides in that small city but hadn't realized that the stabbing death in the marina parking lot was of the man Randa had introduced him to last year at Redmond Hospital in Rome. Lee had brought her there in a helicopter to see her deputy who had been shot in the hills near Cartersville.

"Sorry to learn about your friend," he said, reaching across the table, tapping her hand.

"Thanks."

"A random killing?"

"I don't know, Stan," she said in a tone meant to discourage talk about Lee.

Stan gave her a long look and changed the subject. "Tyonek Horse. You don't trust him?"

"I don't think he's in Cherokee City killing time waiting for a pension. They don't have enough manpower to waste it like that."

"He's up to something?"

"We think something's about to happen. I think it's why they wanted me out of their way. We just don't know what."

"Then what's this Tyonek doing?"

"The sheriff thinks he's a lookout. It's what I used to think."

"And now?"

She shrugged. "I don't know. Something fishy's going on."

With Stan's help, she got a seat on a flight to Cherokee City late that afternoon and was greeted at the airport by Buckles who wanted to take her to a downtown restaurant for dinner.

"Not dressed like this," she said, laughing. They settled for cheeseburgers and shakes at a Lingo's.

"The chief blew his stack," Buckles said.

"He knows it was the FBI?"

"The minute he heard what had happened, he called the SAC, and he was really pissed."

"Because of what they did to me?"

"Because of the insult to him. But he did want to know whether you had been injured."

"That was nice of him."

"They actually Tasered you?"

"Like a dog," she said and explained as best she could what it had felt like.

Outside in Buckles's car, he said, "Bea Kim came up with something. That witness in the next boat got liar's remorse. He told her he heard some men arguing that night around two-thirty or so. Didn't know what they said but it was loud, said he didn't go on deck to look. But he said he'd seen *Julia's Folly* using the slip next to him. Bea learned that the slip was leased for two weeks by a guy called himself Joseph Smith."

"When does the lease expire?"

"Day after tomorrow. But if you're thinking of checking out Cardozo's daughter's boat, I don't think we've got enough for a warrant."

"I don't think we need one," Randa said. "Can you send a crew out there?"

"Want to make sure first?"

"Cardozo will beg me to examine that boat if Lazard was using it."

She couldn't believe that Claude had murdered Lee. He wasn't capable of anything like that, and he wouldn't have used a knife. He wouldn't have cut Lee's throat.

But somebody did. Some inhuman bastard was desperate to put Lee out of the way.

Thinking of Lee brought an avalanche of tears. All the way to her apartment she sat next to Buckles with her hand over her eyes sobbing.

"You okay?"

"I didn't listen," she said. "I didn't believe him. I didn't give him a chance."

The anguish of self-incrimination came like a sword into her heart. She couldn't stop crying.

"Aw, Lee. I'm so sorry."

CHAPTER TWENTY-FIVE

Randa was perched on the stern rail of *Julia's Folly* enjoying the gentle rocking of the boat, looking at pink clouds stretched across the evening sky and tips of waves reflecting pink all the way to the horizon. A soft breeze was coming in off the gulf. A beautiful Florida evening.

"Down in the cracks maybe they'll find it," Raphael Cardozo said. He was in the fighting chair, his hairy arms folded across his chest, his legs crossed at the ankles, the breeze toying with hairs on his scalp. There was fatigue in his eyes she hadn't noticed before. He had readily agreed to allow her crew to inspect the boat—partly, she believed, because he wanted to nail Claude Lazard, partly because he was tired of what he called "this turmoil." "It's supposed to be the fucking golden years," he said.

"If there's blood in there, they'll find it," Randa said.

Occasionally a voice leaked from the cabin where Al Martinez and his forensic crew had been working for nearly an hour.

"I never thought he had it in him," Raphael said.

"I don't think Claude did it—not the way it was done."

"But he had this boat."

"That's why we're here," Randa said. "But go back to what you were saying. Claude explained what it was?"

"No. What he said was you could get where the enemy was without going there. Trying to be cute. Julia asked if it was navy stuff. She said she'd need papers, receipts or something. That's when he shut up."

"But he wanted you to help him?"

"He never said it. But you knew it's what he wanted—our contacts, you know?"

"And that was several months ago? Before or after that woman came down?"

"I don't know when she got here."

But it was before Abu came to Cherokee City, she told herself. Aloud she said, "When did he start using this?" meaning the boat.

"Nights, you mean? A couple days before you were out here. Before Julia went to Europe this last time."

"Before Woodrow Barstow was killed."

"You getting anywhere with that?"

"We're learning."

"Your sheriff think I had something to do with it?"

"I don't know," Randa said. "But *I* don't."

Big Al Martinez came out of the cabin waving an evidence bag.

Raphael got out of the chair. "Find Lee's blood?"

"We won't know for maybe a week," Randa said.

"On TV they do it the same day."

Randa smiled. It took two trips on the tender to get them all ashore, giving Randa a chance for a private conversation with Al.

"Did that note I left you help?"

"What note was that?" Randa asked.

"We got a report back from Marchland. The markings on that slug they pulled out of Barstow match those on a bullet they found two years ago in the right femur of a woman in Virginia."

Randa's mind immediately raced to images of Paris Courtland, Claude Lazard, Woodrow Barstow . . . and Tyonek Horse—the only four she could think of who linked the D.C./ Virginia area with Cherokee City.

"That's important," she told Al. "Thanks."

She walked with Raphael to the parking space near the pool and waited until the crime-scene van was gone before she asked, "I want your honest opinion, Mr. Cardozo. Was Lee part of anything criminal?"

"Not that I know of."

"He said he was staying close to Claude to protect Julia."

"Then that's what he was doing. He was always good to her."

"Yes, I know," Randa said, watching a funny look come into his face, probably in response to how she had said it. She thanked him and drove back to the mainland.

Later from her kitchen, after changing into jeans and one of Charley's old shirts, she put in a call to Major Buckley and told him what Big Al had told her.

"That FBI friend of yours in Virginia—can you put him on it?"

"I'll try," Buckles said.

She was making a turkey and Swiss sandwich when someone knocked on her door. She hurried into her bedroom, got her semi-automatic, made certain it was loaded and carried it to her front hallway, holding it at her side.

"Who is it?"

"Moira Pelletier."

"Just a minute." She walked the gun back to her bedroom, came into the hallway and opened the door, greeting Moira with a face of stone. "Those goons with you?" not looking into the yard, looking directly at Moira, an unexpected bitterness in her voice.

"I never knew they'd do that," Moira said, making no move

to come inside, her dark eyes loaded with regret. "All I did was tell them what you told me, Randa. I never meant you any harm."

Although Chubleigh had expressly forbidden her to talk with Moira, she decided it would be foolish to deny herself what could be an invaluable source of information. If Moira was afflicted with remorse, as she seemed to be, she might open up a little.

Let's see what happens. "Come in." She stepped back.

After Moira glided past her—she walked like her joints were greased—Randa scanned the parking area. Nothing unusual out there. She closed the door and made sure it was locked. In the kitchen she pointed Moira to a chair at the table by the window.

"You hungry?"

"I just ate," Moira said, "but you go ahead."

"Coffee?"

"If you're making some."

In a deadening silence, Randa filled the tank of the coffee maker, put grounds into the cone, snapped on the switch. She wrapped her half-made sandwich in foil and tucked it into her refrigerator to eat later. Anger was still in her voice when she said, "Black or with milk? I don't have any cream."

"Black is fine," Moira said. "If I had known what they were going to do . . ."

Randa waved that off. "Weren't they getting regular reports from Tyonek?"

"Yeah, but something happened. The Coast Guard told us something he never reported, and they said Tyonek had never contacted them. That's when they put me on him."

"So are you going to tell me what the Coast Guard told you?"

"Aw, don't be sore at me. I've never kept anything from you." She waited for Randa to accept that, then said, "The boat where it happened? They'd been watching it for several days, watched it making night runs up the coast to a dock on Mangrove River. They saw it the night Lee was killed. Only that time it came out of South Cherokee City and went down the coast and got lost in some islands. Tyonek never said a word about that boat. So now we question everything he reports. That's why I was sent here."

"To watch him?"

"To find out what's going on. Either he's covering something up or he's just not doing his job. I'm not sure of this, but I suspect they think he's holding stuff back so that he can make a big bust all by himself."

"And you want my opinion?"

"If you've got one."

"Then square with me," Randa said. "Because if you don't, you might as well go home. I'm going to find out who killed Lee Fronzi whether the FBI likes it or not. You want something from me. . . ."

"I'll tell you what I know. I know that dock on the Mangrove River is rented until tomorrow night. And I got a bunch of shit on Abu Mosul you might be interested in. He's also been lying to us."

The "also" wasn't lost on Randa.

"What about him?" she asked.

"We know he's been in touch with some people in Marchland we been watching—one of those so-called charity things that could be a money laundry. One of them called Hammid Ramzi was in a restaurant with a man sounds like Abu Mosul—a little bald man who talks Arabic. If it was him and he's connected to those people, it could be a violation of his permit."

"We saw Abu with someone at Clay's Marina," Randa said.

"When was that?"

Randa told her what Fog had reported.

"What I need is connections with Raphael Cardozo," Moira

said. "Abu told us he was trying to work something out with him. He admitted working through Claude Lazard. You know, the SAC got a little worked up over that bulletin you put out on him."

"Why?"

"He thinks Claude is a point man for Cardozo. He wants him free."

"You know what that means to me? It means you're not the only agent working on this."

"I'm the only one I know about," Moira said. "Except for the Indian."

They were distracted for a moment by a flock of Ibis settling into a nearby field, beautiful birds with long curved beaks pecking at the grass.

Randa said, "Raphael Cardozo isn't involved in any of this. Neither is Julia. I think she suspected Claude was using her for something shady and kicked him out. And it wasn't because he was fooling around with a woman. It was because he was bringing suspicion on her father."

"You think Cardozo's clean?"

"I wouldn't waste time trying to prove he's not. But, you know, that slip at Clay's Marina has been rented until day after tomorrow, like the one in Mangrove. But, after what happened, nobody's coming back to South Cherokee and nobody's going to use Julia's boat. Right now I've got two people checking boat rentals."

"Another interesting thing about that BOLO," Moira said. "Tyonek got spooked when he heard about it. He jumped out of his chair and went straight down to the parking lot. From the office window I saw him heading up this way."

When they had finished their coffee and chatted a while about turf problems between the two agencies, Randa walked Moira to her car.

"I wish we could work together on this," Randa said, "but my boss doesn't want me talking to you."

"Because of what happened?"

"Tell your people we're not enemies," Randa said.

She stood near the lemon tree and watched Moira's car drive away.

CHAPTER TWENTY-SIX

"It wasn't my fault!" Abu yelled, grabbing the claw, pushing it off his leg. "Why do you blame me? Claude told her, I didn't."

"Well she can't pull out," Tyonek said. "They'll kill her. Doesn't she know who she's dealing with?"

They were in Abu's car outside a small restaurant in Cherokee City. It was raining. Great torrents were pounding the roof, streaming down the windshield. The windows were clouding up. It was hot.

"Put on the air-conditioner," Tyonek said.

Abu started the engine. Wipers slapped across the windshield. Through the cleared glass they could see people huddled on the long porch waiting for the rain to let up.

"Turn those damned things off," Tyonek said. "Why the hell did they send him down there?"

"They don't trust Claude," Abu said, shutting off the wipers. "They couldn't understand why he needed a boat." With rain pouring down the windshield, he began to feel trapped in this small space.

"So what was the moron supposed to do?"

"Not kill anybody. He was supposed to ride wherever Claude was going. But Claude was gone when he got here. He had to wait. Maybe he saw Fronzi standing in the shadows."

"And he just went in and killed him?"

"Fronzi and Claude were fighting. Believe me, Hammid didn't order it. He didn't want that to happen. He didn't know

Fronzi would be there. How would he know? I didn't know."

"Well, Claude sure as hell can't use the boat now."

"What if she doesn't change her mind?" Abu said.

"They'll change it for her. Tell her they'll cut her throat if she doesn't follow through."

"They don't know where she is."

"They can find her, believe me. You know where she is."

"I don't. She moved again."

"You've got Claude's cell-phone number. He knows where she is. You tell him to make sure she understands her situation. That thing on the boat hasn't changed anything."

"She's scared," Abu said. "She doesn't trust anyone. She even suspects I'm working for the CIA."

"She wants her five million, doesn't she?"

"I'll talk to Claude."

"If it goes sour, Abu, you're a dead man."

Abu took a deep breath, both hands trembling as they gripped the steering wheel.

"You've got three hours," Tyonek said. "Find out where the crates are. Get the diamonds—is Claude's appraiser down here?"

"He's in Seacrest."

"Then get the diamonds into the bank. Let Claude know what will happen if this goes sour: he'll go down, his lady'll go down, you'll go down, those people in Marchland will go down, and I'll be a hero."

Claude watched Paris standing at the screen door. Now that the rain had stopped he could see people out there strolling along the beach.

"They'll check every motel," he said. "But they won't look for you in a cottage on the beach."

She wasn't listening. She went back into the bedroom where she had been packing to leave. "I'll call a cab. They don't know

225

me. They're not looking for me. It's you they want. I wasn't on that boat."

"Don't kid yourself." Claude said. "They know you were in Abu's room at the motel when that detective was shot. You just can't walk away from this. It's possible every cab driver in this city has your description. We've got to go through with it. Those people aren't human. They'll track us down. They've taken too many risks."

In anger she threw what she was holding into the opened suitcase. He could see pain and fear in her drawn features as she sat on the edge of the bed. She put her face in her hands. She hadn't prepared herself for any of this. She had thought it would be a simple exchange, the crates for the diamonds.

"I didn't want anyone killed!"

Claude sat next to her and took her hand. It felt thin and cold in his fingers.

"We've come this far . . ."

"But I don't want to go to prison."

"You won't. Stop thinking negative. Think about the millions, the freedom, everything you've ever wanted."

She pulled her hand away and looked angrily at him. "You didn't tell me it would be like this."

"Nothing's going to happen."

"But if the police are looking for me?"

"They'd just want to talk to you. But that won't happen. We'll be out of here before they even know we're gone. We'll have five million dollars in diamonds that can't be traced. They'll never find us."

"What if they know everything and are just waiting? What if they know where the crates are? They must know about those people in Marchland."

"Abu said they're not under suspicion."

"How does he know?"

"He worked for the CIA. He knows." He put his arm around her and pressed his face into her hair. "They don't know anything," he said.

"They know you were on the boat."

"They don't know it was me. Even if they think it was, they don't know where to find me."

"Abu does."

Claude shrugged. "All he has is my cell-phone number. He doesn't know where we are."

"I shouldn't have asked you to use the boat. That was foolish."

"It's too late for that. But we don't need it and nothing has changed. When Abu calls, I'll meet him just as we planned. We'll get the diamonds and put them in the bank. I can take the storage key with me and give it to Hammid right there."

"What if he doesn't trust you? He'll have to go to Port Mangrove to get the crates."

"He knows if he doesn't find them, he can get back here in the morning with that goon. That's only an hour up the highway. He isn't worried."

She pulled away from him and left the room. He found her standing with her back to him at the screened door gazing out at the beach.

"There's a risk, you know," he said. "If I have to come back here to get the key—oh, and the combination to get into the enclosure—if I have to come back here, I could be followed. Look, it's the last day. I'm sure as hell not going to go get them and run off. Besides, you've got the plane tickets and the passports and everything else."

"I wish you hadn't used your real name at the bank," she said.

"I had to. I couldn't use our new identity. That would be stupid. They needed a driver's license with my picture on it and my Social Security number or I couldn't have opened an account. And without an account, I couldn't have got a security box. But that protects me."

"How?"

"I'm the only one who can go to the box in the morning. They won't let anyone else into the vault. Abu explained all that to them. They won't kill me. It's foolproof," and he gave her a playful peck on the cheek.

"The police will find out."

"How? They won't know anything about the diamonds or the bank or anything else. They're interested in solving murder cases. They don't know a thing about what we're doing. Abu's taken care of that. You're worrying about nothing."

She wasn't convinced, but she went back to the bedroom and came out carrying a small suitcase and a cardboard box. "Be careful when you take the vehicle out. It's very fragile."

"Is this the one I practiced on?"

"All the others are in storage. Of course."

"And they were shipped from Denver?" He doubted she used FedEx or UPS. She probably used some out-of-town moving company. He was quite sure she hadn't gone personally to Mangrove.

He followed her into the kitchen and watched her pour an inch of Scotch into a small glass.

"Take it easy with that stuff," he said.

"You take it easy, and be careful when you make the demonstration."

"I'm always careful," he said.

CHAPTER TWENTY-SEVEN

Bouncing the rented SUV inland on what was little more than a widened path into the Everglades, Claude became a tourist guide, explaining everything they were witnessing to his Arab passengers, Hammid Ramzi who was sitting next to him, and Abu, in back. They were men of the desert who he believed must want to learn about this semi-tropical swamp. He loved explaining things to people.

"Now that crooked tree over there with the red bark is a Gumbo Limbo," Claude said, pointing past a thicket of wax myrtle at the edge of the slough. "I think it's peculiar to this part of Florida. You won't see many in the interior because they like lots of sunshine. In fact, it's called the 'tourist tree' because it gets sunburned and peels."

"How far into this swamp do we have to go?" Hammid asked, gazing straight ahead, a fretful look on his long, bearded face, bored perhaps—another reason for Claude to keep him entertained.

"Oh, not too far," Claude said.

"Will we have to walk?"

"Only a few hundred yards. Now, there ahead," pointing as they entered low ground under a canopy of tall limbs and dangling vines, "you see the rotted trunk of a Cyprus. They're very valuable as nurseries for smaller plants and insects."

"This field we're going to," Hammid said, "it's large enough for a complete demonstration?"

"Absolutely. Once in the air, the vehicle can fly over the trees and provide pictures in great detail. Imagine how useful that will be in urban combat. It can hover outside windows and take pictures of what's going on inside. But it's main use, I would think, is to locate and assess enemy locations. Now, there is a wood stork," pointing at a large bird wading in shallow water surrounded by big-leafed plants that nearly obscured it. "It's the only stork native to the United States."

"Yes, yes," Hammid said impatiently. "Does she have more than the fifteen we're purchasing?"

"That's all Dr. Wang made. It's not like building a model airplane, you know. It takes months and months, and very expensive equipment, some of which he had to use surreptitiously."

"You say their wings are no more than six inches across. If they're that small, why three crates?"

"Because of the packaging. They're very fragile." He pointed into a shallow pool. "Storks don't look for fish, they feel for them with their legs. If they touch one, their beaks dart into the water. It's quite something to see."

"Yes, yes, very interesting, I'm sure." He grabbed at the dashboard to steady himself. They were now in the slough, maneuvering around fallen logs and Cyprus knees.

"If you look carefully," Claude said, "you'll notice that the water is moving . . ."

"Even so, it stinks," Abu said. "Do those white patches on the trees tell you where the road is?"

"They're not man made," Claude said. "I've been here many times. I don't need markers. Those patches are lichen. Sometimes they're pink. You'll notice they aren't found at the base of trees because they don't grow below the high water mark. In fact, that's how you determine where the high water mark is," he said, pleased with himself for sharing that.

"Tell me again what they call these things?" Hammid said.

"Lichen," Claude said.

"The gadgets, man. I don't give a damn about your trees and your algae and your wading birds."

"They're called micro infiltrators, MIs."

"And he's dead, and you have everyone he made? We'll get all of his notes and photographs?"

"Everything," Claude said. "And one of them, which I haven't brought with me, is only partially complete. It's what he was working on when he died." He pointed. "That rise just ahead, dry ground, is where we stop. There may be a little wading beyond it. We can't drive to the field. The growth beyond there is impenetrable."

He squeezed the SUV into a narrow space between a cabbage palm and a tall slash pine. "They call them 'slash pines,' " he explained, "because of marks on the bark made for the extraction of turpentine. Ah, what are you doing?"

"Taking my shoes off," Hammid said.

Claude thought about it, shrugged and did the same.

Carrying the control case and the small carton in which Paris had stored the sample, Claude led the two men through shallow water, sloshing over dead leaves and swamp lettuce. Hammid was complaining, Abu tiptoeing like a ballet dancer, laughing at the sport of it, delighted probably because they had reached the final stages of this long ordeal.

They finally came onto dry land and emerged into a large clearing.

"This is where the Cuban soldiers trained?" Abu asked.

"One of the places."

"Your President Kennedy abandoned them?"

"That's what was said, but he never promised them air support."

"How far will this thing fly?" Hammid asked, watching

Claude open the suitcase-size control console.

It took Claude only a few minutes to unfold the antenna and hook up the viewer—a long box-like television receiver. He showed Hammid how to hold it. "It's not to watch the flying vehicle, which will be invisible from the ground; it's to watch what the camera is transmitting back. The vehicle can fly out to any distance, at least until it runs out of fuel, but can transmit pictures no more than a mile."

With the console prepared, Claude unpacked the MI, lifting it out of the plastic cushioning material. It looked less like a model airplane than a large insect.

"Are the wings this fragile just to reduce weight?" Hammid asked.

"It's a lot more complicated than that," Claude said, searching for a level spot. "These diaphanous wings were inspired by insect wings. Earlier attempts to make these things simply miniaturized airplane wings. It didn't work. I'm sure you've heard what people used to say about bumble bees—that their weight and bulk relative to their wingspan meant they couldn't fly. That led to an analysis of the aerodynamics of insects. Air, to an insect, is not the clear gas that we experience. It's chunks and globs of molecules they have to struggle through. Unlike a soaring airplane, they have to flap their wings to keep from falling. Their flight dynamics are very different."

"Let's get this into the air," Hammid said, impatiently, looking around at distant trees and undergrowth as though for intruders.

Claude flipped on the master switch in the vehicle's belly, set the vehicle down, and went back to the console. "It leaps into the air, so watch carefully." He pressed a button and the tiny craft left the ground and was soon flying across the clearing.

"The flight is controlled pretty much as model airplanes are— the joystick, all of that. Which, of course, will help you get these past security at the airport. We'll give you a regular control console for model airplanes, clearly marked as such, which you can ship with the crates. Even if they insist upon opening a crate, these MIs will pass as toys. And you can ship this console separately with television equipment and pretend it's for that."

Hammid was holding the viewer to his eye. "Where is it?"

Claude pointed at a cluster of pines in the distance. "Beyond those trees."

He flipped a switch.

"Aah," Hammid said, the first smile of the day appearing at his lips, enchanted by what he was seeing. "Make it come down the side of that tree and hover," he said.

Claude played with a toggle on the console.

"Aah," Hammid said. "Now make it go up again."

Claude made it rise above the trees.

"Now circle it around and bring it back."

Within a few minutes the tiny craft was hovering over them. Claude told Hammid to hand the viewer to Abu. Then he showed him how to lower the craft. "Move the toggle very gently," he said. The craft dropped into Claude's hands.

"How did your Chinaman get it to hover?" Hammid asked.

Claude didn't know, but he said, "I think he learned that from watching the flight of dragonflies. I think he used a high-speed camera."

As they drove back to the highway, Claude explained that the partially completed MI can do all the maneuvering but cannot transmit pictures. "But you can use it to practice on. One of the features of Dr. Wang's model is how simple it is to operate. It takes only a brief study of the manual and a few hours' practice to become an expert."

They drove in silence for more than an hour until they reached the supermarket parking lot where Claude transferred the console and the sample to Hammid's SUV. Fakhri, the menacing hulk who had knifed Lee Fronzi, was waiting behind the driver's seat, left there to guard the diamonds. When he got out, Claude stepped away from him, intimidated by him, and stared at the briefcase he was holding.

"He will go with you," Hammid said. He told Fakhri to get into Claude's SUV. "I assume before reaching the bank, you'll have this vehicle washed."

"Washed and returned to the rental," Claude said.

"Is your car registered here in Florida?"

Claude nodded, wondering why Hammid asked.

"What I don't understand," Hammid said, "is why your government wouldn't underwrite Dr. Wang's experiments."

"They did at first, in the fledgling stages. Hundreds of scientists were trying to make these things. But several universities, including the University of Cambridge in England, carried more punch in the budgeting conferences. Most small applicants like Dr. Wang were dropped."

"And Dr. Wang continued on his own?"

"Not entirely. He disguised what he was doing to get funding from a few foundations and some commercial sources. He was a very clever man."

"And this woman worked for him?"

"In some ways she was his superior. She listened to his complaints. He apparently was a lonely man. She may have comforted him in a variety of ways. She's quite resourceful," he said, grinning, tempted to slap Hammid's knee but thinking better of it.

"And the company they worked for, they don't know these things are missing?"

"They don't know they exist. Nobody does, except us. Dr. Wang told everyone he abandoned the project when his funding stopped."

"And they believed him?"

"Apparently. But nobody in any position to hurt us knows a thing about these MIs. You can take them out of the country and nobody on any battlefield will know that you have them. An excellent miniature tactical weapon."

Chapter Twenty-Eight

Randa pulled off the highway, made a U-turn and headed south. She had just received notice from a deputy that Claude's car was spotted on South Cherokee Beach Road. She cautioned the deputy to keep him in sight but not pick him up. She couldn't hold him as a material witness because she couldn't yet prove he had been on the boat when Lee was killed. Believing he was there wasn't enough. But she could question him. Maybe he would stumble.

The deputy's cruiser was parked down the street from a beach house where he had discovered the car. The deputy was in the shadow of a live oak, leaning on the fender of his cruiser. She knew him—a cute guy with a wife and two kids. She waved him away with a thank-you smile—didn't want Claude to see him waiting there.

It was a small, framed house on stilts with a wooden staircase to a platform outside a curtained door, the kind of place that might ride out a storm surge but would collapse like cardboard in a category 3.

Randa rapped on the door, stared aimlessly down at sea oats and sand, inhaled warm odors of the gulf, rapped again and got a call, "Just a minute!"

She had to wait nearly two minutes before a harried Claude Lazard pulled the door open. "Randa!" with fake enthusiasm. "What's up?" looking worriedly past her toward the street, blocking the doorway, one hand on the frame, one hand on the partially opened door. He was barefoot and wearing only yellow shorts and a T-shirt. He needed a shave.

"Want to invite me in?" she said. "It's hot out here."

"Oh, sorry," still looking toward the street.

She stepped into the comfort of air-conditioning. He pointed at stools at a bar in a small kitchen. She saw a TV behind him down a short hallway, two chairs, and ceiling-to-floor windows in a large room that looked out on the beach. Wouldn't a man ordinarily invite her to that room rather than to a stool in the kitchen? What's down there?

"I was bare-assed in the bathroom about to shower," he said, still blocking the hallway. He didn't move until she was perched on a stool.

"Someone else here?"

He shrugged. "There was."

Whether someone was in the house he didn't want her to see, she couldn't tell. But the air was tainted with the odor of cigarettes and Claude didn't smoke. Julia smoked. Vicki Bryant smoked.

"I guess this is about Lee," he said, opening a small refrigerator, maybe to hide his face. "I've got bottled lemonade and some ponies of beer."

Randa put her bag on the counter, looking around for signs of a woman, noticed a cell phone on a counter under some cupboards. "I heard you had moved out of Julia's house," she said.

"Sure you don't want something?" He had taken a small bottle of beer from the refrigerator and was twisting the cap off.

"Lemonade sounds good. Why would I be here about Lee?"

"I don't know . . . I mean . . ." He managed a weak laugh. "Gotta be a reason, right?"

"He was murdered on Julia's boat, Claude. And you've been using the boat."

"Me . . . ?" His face went pale. "Jesus! You don't think I did it? Come on. I haven't used that boat I don't know . . . since you were out there. Julia took my key. Raphael would have me shot if I took it."

He raised the bottle to his mouth, hiding behind it, his hand trembling. She couldn't see sweat but knew it was there. She let him soak in it for a moment.

"One of Raphael's boys saw you bringing the boat back to the mooring the morning Lee was killed," she said.

"Me?"

"That's what he said."

"That son of a bitch! He said that? It's a lie! He's trying to set me up!"

"What's in Mangrove you're interested in?"

"Mangrove? Nothing. . . . Why? He said I was up there? What's he accusing me of?"

"He hasn't accused you of anything. He just told me what the kid said. So why were you making those nightly trips to Mangrove?"

"I don't know what you're talking about, Randa. What nightly trips?"

"I'm talking about you and Abu Mosul and Vicki Bryant . . . or is it Paris Courtland?"

"Oh . . ." He actually looked relieved. "That's what this is about." He took a deep breath, held it with billowing cheeks, then let it out. "Whew! Had me for a minute there. Julia—"

"This has nothing to do with Julia."

"Okay," he said. "There is a woman and her name is Vicki. I've known her for years. She came down and we got together. I guess the detective told her that."

"Isn't she Paris Courtland?"

"That's her real name, yes. 'Vicki Bryant' is what I call her motel name."

"Is she here?"

"In the house here? No. She was," he said, possibly to explain the odor of cigarettes. "She left only a few minutes ago. You probably passed her on the road."

"What kind of car does she drive?"

"I think it's a Jag, one of those low-slung jobs. Green. What do they call it, 'hunter's green'?"

The woman was visiting southwest Florida and had been for some time. And she was driving a rented Jaguar? Then why, only a few days ago, had she needed a ride from Lee?

She raised the bottle to her lips and watched worry lines deepening in his face. "I don't think you killed Lee. That's not why I'm here. But I do think you were on the boat when someone else killed him. You may not have wanted it to happen, but cleaning the boat up afterwards makes you an accessory."

"Randa, for chrissakes! I wasn't there! I had nothing to do with it! I didn't clean up anything! I haven't been on that boat—"

"We've found blood, Claude. We've found footprints and fingerprints tainted with blood. If the tests come back positive for signs of your presence . . ."

"My prints could be all over that boat. It doesn't prove anything. Randa, for God's sakes! You can't be serious."

He was squirming, he was scared, but he obviously intended to stay with his story unless she could throw proof in his face. And she didn't have any.

"I'm trying to make it easy on you," she said.

"But it's bullshit! Raphael's trying to set me up. He hates me. He's always hated me. Come on, Randa. I've been seeing another woman. That's all. He ought to be glad, for God's sakes. Julia kicked me out. I'm gone. That's what he wants. What the hell's he making up this other stuff for? Some kind of revenge?"

The color was gradually seeping back into his face. He apparently believed his story was working. She sipped from the bottle, her eyes not straying from him. The man was a practiced liar.

"How does Abu fit into this?"

"Lee didn't tell you? He knows . . . I mean, he *knew* about it. Jesus, I still can't believe he's dead."

"About what?"

"Some surplus navy material, Vicki"—he smiled—"Paris hopes to sell. Abu had hoped to connect with Julia, but she wasn't interested. It's stuff from where she worked in Virginia. Lee didn't tell you about it?"

"Ordnance?"

"That's Abu's specialty. We're not hiding anything. The FBI knows why Abu is here. It's all above board." He shook his head as though unable to understand why she was making an issue of it. "I can't imagine it has anything to do with Lee's death."

"Why was Lee on that boat?"

"I have no idea. Maybe he thought I was using it. He had a thing about . . . I mean, he didn't like the way I was treating Julia. He was very fond of her, you know."

"Claude, I know that Woodrow Barstow was following this woman you call Vicki. I know it was for what the NCIS and the FBI called 'national security'."

He made a wry face. "That was all bullshit. They accused her four years ago of screwing up a shipment to the Israelis. Lee didn't tell you about that?"

"Why did she quit her job and go out west after she cleaned out Dr. Wang's shop?"

"What do you mean 'cleaned out'?"

"I mean she took everything except the benches. I was up there. Barstow brought her back from Colorado, and it wasn't because he needed her. She's been under surveillance ever since."

He was running his tongue around his mouth, apparently working up moisture. "I guess you don't know how it works."

"How what works?"

"Turf wars in D.C."

"Let's hear it."

"You know about the screwup in Hawaii. The Israelis accused us of skimping on a shipment? Nobody screwed up. The stuff they expected to get just didn't test out. So we shipped them something else. The State Department raised hell. Rather than take the blame, the navy blamed the company where Paris worked. They put on a show to make the Israelis think they were taking their accusations seriously. Paris was in charge of the civilian end of it, so they blamed her. For the Israelis' benefit they put on a show at Pearl and assigned some dunkhead to investigate her. It was a joke. They got her fired from her job and forced Barstow to resign, all of it to satisfy the State Department. The whole thing was bureaucratic bullshit."

"And this surplus . . . ?"

"She bought some stuff and thought Julia might help her sell it. She came to me because I knew Julia."

"How does Abu Mosul fit into this?"

"When Julia turned us down, I contacted Abu. He's right now trying to make a deal with some South Africans. It's all legit, Randa. Arms dealing is big business. We're not doing anything wrong."

It sounded good—at least without thinking too hard about it. And maybe the FBI reads it Claude's way. Maybe that's why they don't appear too interested in what's going on. Maybe it explains why Tyonek isn't doing anything. But it doesn't explain Moira, and it doesn't explain three murders. And it doesn't explain dragging me to North Carolina.

She had to give herself time to think about this version of things. It sounded pretty good. But it wasn't true—too many holes in it. As she lifted her bag off the counter, she noticed that Claude appeared relaxed, no more dry mouth.

"Well, you've given me a lot to think about," she said.

"Jesus, you had me scared for a while," he said, laughing, leading her to the door, again putting himself between her and the front room. There was triumph and a renewed self-assurance on his face. He was sure she had bought his story. The confident swagger was back.

She went down the wooden steps through burning sunshine and walked to her Cherokee, got in, turned on the engine, turned on the air-conditioner, looked at herself in the rearview mirror and banged her hands in frustration on the steering wheel.

"Shit!"

"That's it!" Vicki said when Claude came into the front room. "I'm getting out of here. It's finished!"

"Settle down, for chrissakes," Claude said. "She doesn't know anything. It's not about us. She thinks I know who killed Lee. It has nothing to do with us. She's investigating a murder."

"She knows who I am. She used my name! I heard it!"

"She got it from that detective. It has nothing to do with the sale. She wouldn't be investigating that. She's a local cop. She has no idea what's going on. None of them do."

"But she knows I'm here!"

"She's gone. All she knows is you're my girlfriend from up north."

"She knows you were on the boat. I heard that."

"She doesn't know anything. She knows I used the boat before Julia kicked me out. That's all. They think I was taking women out for joyrides. You're working yourself up over nothing."

He put his arms around her. He could feel her heart racing.

"It's okay. We're in the clear. She's a local cop investigating a murder. There's nothing to worry about. Now, I'm going to shower and dress and meet Abu." He kissed her temple. It was moist. It was salty. If she were another woman he might believe she would quit; but she had gone through too much, waited too long. She was scared, but she wanted the money as much as he did.

When he came back wearing loafers and slacks and a golf shirt, she was dragging on a cigarette staring out the window at people walking along the beach.

"The key," he said.

She had been holding it in a clenched fist. "I've never been so frightened in my life."

"Why don't you give me the location of the storage locker so I won't have to call you. Is it that place across from the marina?"

"Call," she said. "I want to know the diamonds are in the bank."

"Okay." He drew her to him and kissed her. "Tomorrow when we're in Miami on a plane flying out of here . . ."

"If we ever are."

"It will happen. Believe me. And we'll be millionaires."

She handed him the key and a slip of paper with numbers on it. There was fear in her eyes. The haughtiness was there, but it was subdued. She was scared, and that pleased him. He had never before seen this degree of vulnerability in her. It was gratifying. It would help him enjoy her until they got to France.

"I will have the stones inspected. We'll put them in the bank. Nobody will be able to touch them until morning. The Arabs will be gone. I'll bring the diamonds here, and we'll head for Miami. Everything will go smoothly as planned."

He tapped her on the chin and smiled. "There's nothing to worry about. I know what I'm doing. We're in the clear. Everything's under control."

He was reasonably sure the crates were in that storage facility across from the marina, but maybe not.

At headquarters, Randa found Buckles leaning back in his swivel chair eating an apple. He was in a good mood. Derek was probably out of the building.

"Fog called in," he said. "Julia Hodges's boat was in Mangrove Harbor the night Lee was killed. They couldn't say who was aboard."

"It was Claude Lazard. I'm sure of it." She lowered herself into one of the chairs facing his desk. "I want to search the storage facilities up there."

"What brings you to that?"

She told him about her meeting with Claude.

"Not a bad story. It could tell us why the FBI aren't doing anything."

"It doesn't explain my little trip to North Carolina."

"Maybe that wasn't the FBI."

"Yeah, right," she said. "Be serious."

He laughed. "Just don't tell Claude's story to Derek."

"Why?"

"He might want to use it. About an hour ago there was a man came here in a chauffeured limousine. He went straight into Derek's office, stayed there no more than fifteen minutes. I don't know who he was or what he wanted, but Derek left with him and Mary said he was from the Attorney General's office. She said he flew down from D.C."

"It could be about anything," Randa said.

"Of course. But what else are we doing that's of interest to the federal government?"

"They can't stop us from investigating homicides."

"Don't bet on it. Derek is very ambitious."

"He'd sell us out?"

That got a dry laugh. "As you observed the other day, all three victims were probing into whatever the feds are interested in. They could put a blanket over it."

"And shut me out?"

He gave that a helpless look. "Randa, we're in a war. If what's going on here really involves 'national security,' they've got the authority to do any damned thing they want."

She couldn't believe she'd be taken off this case.

"Maybe Derek won't budge," Buckles said. "Maybe Mr. Limousine has nothing to do with any of this. But if the sheriff comes back with orders to lay off, we lay off."

"And they'll bury everything under 'classified'?"

"It could happen."

"I want to go through the storage lockers in Mangrove Harbor."

"We don't have enough to get a warrant, especially out of county. We couldn't get past the sheriff's office up there. Did Fog check in with them?"

"I'm sure he did."

"If he's still up there, bring him home."

"But not right away." For a long time she stared at the man whose orders she had to obey. Her heart was pounding. She imagined she looked anxious.

He relented.

"When I let Claude think I bought his story," she said. "I put us in the same fix the FBI is in."

"Giving them slack, you mean?"

"I don't even dare put surveillance on Lazard. I don't want him spooked. And if those rental dates mean anything, they're working their game right now, this afternoon and tonight."

"We can alert the Coast Guard."

"After what happened, I don't think they'll be using a boat."

"Is Bea having any luck finding those guys she saw with Abu?"

245

"I haven't talked with her."

Buckles nodded. "I heard from my friend in D.C."

"He learn anything?"

"The gun that killed Barstow was taken from a woman in Roanoke. He thinks it's in storage in Quantico."

"But it obviously isn't," she said.

"And . . . ?"

She shrugged. "Nothing really. Just a hunch."

CHAPTER TWENTY-NINE

Claude stepped onto the asphalt in an alley outside a Buy & Bye and stamped sand off his shoes. He quickly crossed the parking lot and got into the passenger side of Abu's two-door, his legs aching from the long trek down the beach.

"The blonde," Abu said, starting the engine.

"What blonde?"

"The one I told you about. In the pickup truck."

"What about her? You been eating something? God, it stinks in here." He rolled down the window, his gaze dwelling for a moment on the bosom of a girl lugging groceries to her car— young, dark, interesting.

"She just drove by. I'm sure she's watching us."

"Which way did she go?"

Abu pointed to the left.

"Then we go to the right," Claude said, telling himself to settle down. But his body was on fire with anticipation, every nerve jittering. Within the hour he would have diamonds in his hands. By morning he would be a multimillionaire! Within weeks he would be tooling a Ferrari down the Champs Élysées with someone other than "Vicki" in the seat beside him. He hadn't yet decided when he would dump her.

"Come on," he said. "Move!"

Cautiously skirting the fallen husk of a palm frond, Abu turned onto the beach road while Claude adjusted his side mirror. "Is she in a mini?"

"A mini . . . ?"

"The little truck, for chrissakes. They come in different sizes."

"I guess. I don't know."

In his mirror Claude saw a small black pickup eclipsed by a large SUV that pulled out of a side street in front of it. For the next twenty minutes Abu nervously followed Claude's instructions, changing lanes, little frightened squeaks leaping from his mouth as he zipped through the traffic.

When they reached the north/south freeway, Claude saw the black pickup several cars behind them. He told Abu to turn onto the inside southbound lane. He waited until the pickup turned onto the freeway, made sure it was boxed in on the outer lane, then told Abu to cross the median.

"We'll get arrested!"

"Cut across the goddamn median!" Claude bellowed.

Abu hit the brakes, skidded on deep grass but made the U-turn and climbed onto the northbound lane. Claude watched the truck, trapped in the outside lane, speeding southward unable to get to the median.

"Get off at the next exit," he said. "Go back to 41 and turn right."

After an anxious half hour, Claude decided they had lost the pickup.

As they turned into the parking lot at the supermarket, Abu said, "I've never been so frightened in my life," his expression halfway between fear and exultation.

"You did well," Claude said, searching the cars, finally spotting a white SUV edged into the grass at the rear of the lot. "Over there," he said, pointing.

Fakhri stayed at the wheel until Claude and Abu joined Hammid in the shade of a small tree. As usual, Hammid was annoyed.

"It is dangerous for us to sit here and wait," he said. "People notice things like that."

"We got caught up in traffic," Claude said, pretending to care.

Fakhri got out of the SUV holding a cloth sack. Hammid restrained him with a raised hand until he was assured that no one was watching. When he lowered his hand, Fakhri undid the drawstrings and permitted Claude to look into the sack.

"Two," Fakhri said as Claude reached hesitantly inside, moving his fingers lovingly through the hard-edged stones, his heart pounding. He removed two of the stones and showed them to Fakhri, who promptly closed the sack and lowered it to his side.

"Leave your car here," Hammid told Abu. "We'll pick it up later."

Claude had wanted to go to the appraiser's in Abu's car, but this was preferable. It would allow him to keep his eye on the sack.

It took them twenty minutes to reach the small jewelry store on Brent Street in downtown Jackson. Hammid wanted Fakhri to stay in the SUV, but Claude insisted that he come inside. Hammid relented and the four of them went into the store. The jeweler, a small man with graying red hair, led them into a back room that smelled of dust and decay. He sat at a table strewn with tools and bottles and what looked like cookie crumbs. He snapped on a lamp that hovered like an old bird over the table and held the stone under it. He fitted a loupe to his eye and hunched over the stone, turning it in small fingers. He did the same with the second stone. He put both stones on a soft square of cloth and handed them to Claude.

"As good as they get," the jeweler said. "What are you asking?"

"Nothing at the moment," Claude said. "But I'll be back."

"Then that will be twenty dollars," the jeweler said, snapping off the light, getting up, startled when Fakhri roughly snatched the stones from Claude's hand, letting the square of cloth fall to the floor.

Claude muttered an inaudible protest as he handed the jeweler two ten-dollar bills. He hadn't intended to come back, but the jeweler didn't know that.

"Now we go south," he said, getting into the SUV. He sat forward on the back seat, watching Hammid, making sure he didn't switch bags.

All four went into the vault at the bank watching the banker open a safe-deposit locker, remove the tray and hand it to Claude. When he went outside, Hammid put the sack into the long steel drawer and closed the locker. Claude locked the drawer and put the keys into his pocket. In the lobby on their way to the front exit, Claude asked the banker, "You open at nine?"

"Promptly," the banker said.

"And no one can open the vault until then?"

"Not even the manager. It's on a time lock."

Outside, while Abu waited at the SUV with Hammid and Fakhri, Claude called Vicki and assured her that everything had gone as planned. "The stones have been appraised and they are in the vault."

She gave him the address of the storage locker in Port Mangrove.

"That's where I thought it was," Claude said, suggesting that she hadn't shown much imagination: it was right across the street from the marina.

No one said a word during the long ride north on the interstate. Claude looked out the window at empty pastures and scrub pines and palmetto, his mind filled with dreams of Paris—without Paris, he laughed to himself picturing himself at a table with a beautiful woman in a sidewalk café, sipping wine, anticipating the pleasure of taking her to his bed.

"We turn off here," Claude said as they approached the exit at Gaines Street.

Fakhri drove past the exit.

"You missed it!"

"You are going with us to Port Mangrove," Hammid said.

"We'll need our car," Abu said, looking anxiously at Claude.

"It's all right," Claude said. "They'll bring us back. They just want to make sure."

"Drive slow," Hammid said. "We don't want to get there until dark."

CHAPTER THIRTY

Tyonek watched the boy with the tray of dirty dishes go into the kitchen. He glanced at the clock above the kitchen door. It was six-thirty. Only two minutes had passed since the last time he had looked.

Where the hell is Abu?

Again the waitress paused at his booth, a tall girl with droopy hound-dog eyes. "Will there be something else, sir?" she asked, less patiently than the last time, plump in the belly, maybe pregnant.

He tapped his coffee cup. "A refill," he said, and glanced past her at people waiting at the entrance to be seated—a family of five. Rednecks. Let them wait.

When the girl tilted the carafe over his cup, he raised the prosthesis from his lap and thumped it onto the table, startling her. The carafe jiggled in her hand and she spilled hot coffee on the steel claws.

"Oh, God, I'm sorry," she said, staring in awe at the prosthesis. She ran to the kitchen and came back with a cloth. He hadn't moved his arm. She held the cloth above the claws, not knowing what to do. He gave her a sour look and snatched the cloth from her hand, wiped the claws and handed the cloth back.

"I'm really very sorry, sir."

He condemned her clumsiness with a nasty glance and waved her away. He sat there ten more minutes, then asked for a check.

She watched him holding his wallet with the claw while he removed bills with his left hand. He waited for the change and left her nothing and went out to the sidewalk.

Abu should have been there an hour ago. He was to have overseen the deposit of the diamonds and driven straight to this small diner.

Where the hell is he?

In his car outside the Coast Guard office, Sparzo heard something snapping in Chief Petty Officer Daniels's knees as he crouched outside the door, looking past Sparzo at Moira Pelletier.

"We could," he said, "post a man in the marina up there, but like you said he's probably not going back there in a boat. And all my man could do is tell you he's there. He couldn't hold him. We could arrange for someone from the sheriff's office."

"No. We'll take care of it, and thanks again for your help."

"Nice seeing you again, Moira," Daniels said.

"Me too," and she gave him a little wave.

Sparzo raised the window and watched Daniels walk to the edge of the water and yell something at two men out on the wharf.

"Now, how do we get out of here?" They were on a narrow dirt road in a cluster of small buildings dwarfed by the massive underside of an arching bridge.

"You go around that building and under the bridge, turn left, and get back on Sledding Boulevard," Moira told him. "That is, unless you want to go the whole length of the Island, which I doubt you want to do."

"What I want is you to find that goddamned Indian. Why's he been lying to us? Why'd he say he's working with the Coast Guard?"

"I don't know, but I'll try to find him."

"I need more agents," Sparzo said. "What the hell do they need four agents in Marchland for?"

"They probably don't think anything's happening down here. They probably think Tyonek's enough."

"That doesn't make sense. If nothing's happening down here, why'd they drag Randa Sorel to North Carolina?"

"That wasn't very smart," Moira said. "Now she's back and they can't do much about it. They don't want to tip their hand."

"Does she know it was us?"

"She's not stupid," Moira said.

Later over coffee at a small diner, Sparzo said, "I can understand it's the Marchland group they want to bust up. They haven't met Abu and I guess they have no reason to doubt he's doing what he says—trying to get back into the arms business."

"Maybe Tyonek is following him around hoping something more is going on," Moira said.

"Did you read Barstow's reports?"

"From the famous green valise? Oh, yes, except some of the scribbles. Couldn't decipher those."

"And his memo about Dr. Henry Wang? You read that?"

"I read it."

"So if that factory in Virginia never sold anything to anyone without government approval, was Abu lying or the people Barstow talked to, were they lying?

"Maybe that's why Barstow came over here, to find out. And maybe it's why the Indian came here."

"So why hasn't he told us?"

"Like you said, he maybe wants to make a big bust single-handed, go out with flags flying. Why don't you drag him into your office and dig it out of him?"

"If he was working with us, I would. But he's operating out of D.C. It's their game he's playing. I just don't know why the hell they're not letting us in on it." And that, Moira believed, was what really worried him. Was he on somebody's shit list?

They stopped talking when the waitress took their order. He ran his finger up and down the menu, finally deciding on a tuna melt. She ordered grilled cheese.

"That woman," Moira said. "What was her name, Olivia something? After the navy dumped this on us, why'd she want to know what was at the daughter's house?"

"NCIS got pissed off we didn't tell them about Barstow's reports."

"The Indian never got them either, did he?"

"As far as I know, the valise hadn't been opened until after he was transferred down here. It's when Barstow was killed they went through his reports and, finally, those assholes decided to send all that material to us."

And that's when I got it, Moira reminded herself. "And you never told the Indian anything?"

"Haven't had a chance to," Sparzo said.

So how much does the Tyonek know and how'd he find out, she wondered. Sparzo wouldn't tell her. He and Tyonek were cat-and-mousing each other for reasons she couldn't figure out. What she did know is that Sparzo didn't want headquarters to find out Tyonek wasn't being up front with him. Tyonek, he believed, had more friends up there than he had.

"You think you can find him?"

"I have no idea where to look except he eats around the same time every evening. Two places I've seen him at. The only other place I can look is his apartment."

He thought about that a while, then asked, "Is Cardozo involved?"

"Randa Sorel doesn't think so."

"How does she explain his name on that card?"

"I didn't ask. What I know is she's convinced he has nothing to do with what's going on."

"Well, she's only a local cop." He wiped something off his lip. "I wouldn't rely on her judgment. If something of major significance is going on, she's probably unaware of it."

"She knows we want her out of the way."

"That wasn't my doing."

"I know she suspects Tyonek of more than goofing off. What she said to me is, 'if Tyonek is here just to wait out his pension, if he's neglecting his job because he doesn't care, then why'd he bother getting Woodrow Barstow over here? Why go to that trouble?' "

"That's just her interpretation. It's that captain in Beauregard who got him over here. I think Tyonek put her nose out of joint. Probably belittled her. You know how he is," sipping his coffee, gazing complacently across the room.

The condescension didn't sit well with Moira. Belittling Randa Sorel was to her another form of class discrimination. Everybody got hit with it one way or another, and she hated every form of it.

"And you think he just wants to retire with headlines?"

"I don't know what he wants. I don't really care."

But if he brings in the bad guys all by himself, it'll make you look like an idiot, she thought, watching his eyes, watching annoyance crawl over his face. Tyonek Horse was one cat he didn't like talking about. Men with connections in high places scared the hell out of him, and that thought amused her.

When he let her out of the car, he said, "If you run into Randa Sorel, keep her occupied. If something *is* going down we don't want her messing it up."

CHAPTER THIRTY-ONE

Fog lowered his portable to the passenger seat and climbed down from his truck. On Randa's instructions they were using their private cell phones. Their voices didn't go to the dispatcher. And the voices, unlike the sputtering gargle on the system phones, came out clear.

He went into the convenience store where he found Oscar—the name on the shirt—who managed Phil's Storage, which was almost directly across the street from the Port Mangrove Marina.

Fog had smelled the hot dogs when he came in. They were cooking on one of those roller grills.

"Cold beer?"

"That cabinet on the end back there," Oscar said, pointing. "What you want on the dog?"

"Onions, a little mustard," Fog said across his shoulder.

He twisted the cap off a seven-ounce bottle of lager, handed Oscar a ten-dollar bill, stuck the change in his pocket and stood at the counter munching the dog. The bun was stale and the dog tough, but he pretended to be enjoying himself eating it and lubricating his mouth with the beer.

"That string of storage lockers. You handle that?" he asked.

Oscar nodded, arms folded, leaning back on a rodeo poster on the wall. Although Fog hadn't identified himself as a deputy sheriff, there was probably something about him that made Oscar think he was more than a truck driver in off the street.

Fog asked, "You happen to know a man named Claude Lazard rented one of your lockers?"

Oscar reached under the counter, took out a book, ran his finger down a few pages. "Nobody by that name."

"A guy maybe a little shorter than me in his forties, brought a boat in across the street."

"Can't help you with that," Oscar said. "Have to ask Helen over there at the desk."

"I did, and she told me he came here inquiring about locker space. His rental over there ends tomorrow."

That kindled some interest. "You have something to do with the Coast Guard?"

Fog showed his ID. Oscar came close to the counter and studied the folder.

"Cherokee County," Oscar said. "This is Mangrove County."

"This is not official. I think you told the Coast Guard one of your lockers—"

"Number seventeen," Oscar said. "It's the only weekly due up tomorrow. It came in by mail—twenty-dollar bills and a note, no signature. Don't get many like that, unsigned, I mean." He dropped back to the wall and again folded his arms. "Could be the one you're looking for."

"No cargo in it?"

"That came a week later. I didn't see it. There's a night watchman at the marina came over when a small panel truck came in the yard here around midnight. They had trouble getting the gate unlocked—combination lock. That's what got him interested. They didn't tell him anything, but he watched them put some big boxes into seventeen. That's what I told the Coast Guard."

"You tell that to the man who came over?"

"Didn't know at that time."

"That stuff still in there?"

"Don't know. As long as it's paid for—"

"I don't suppose you could open it."

He shook his head. "Invasion of privacy."

"Your watchman, he get a tag number on that truck? Any lettering on it?"

Oscar checked his watch. "He comes on in about two hours you want to wait. Or maybe Helen could give you his number."

Fog finished the dog. "How long are you open?"

"I close at six. But the lockers are twenty-four seven."

Before going outside, Fog asked whether Oscar had kept that unsigned note.

"My wife keeps the records at home. She's probably got it."

"I'll need a copy," Fog said, handing him a card. "You do that for me?"

"Sure thing," Oscar said, reading the card.

Before driving off, Fog walked to the chain-link and located locker 17. It took him just a few minutes to position the truck in shadows down the street from where he could see the yard. He settled behind the wheel, lifted his portable and called Randa. She told him what Bea had reported.

"They may be headed your way, so stay right there. If they show, don't move in. Call me."

"The FBI—"

"No. They'd cut us out. We're just investigating a homicide—remember that. Call me, don't call them."

"What I mean is if these people carry anything north, the FBI will catch them when they approach that store in Marchland."

"I don't think they'd go there," Randa said. "They have to know it's being watched. If they get something out of that locker, or even go to it, follow them, but stay well behind. You cool with the sheriff up there?"

"They said as long as I don't shoot anyone."

"Just observe."

"Another thing," Fog said. "When Moira Pelletier told you what the Coast Guard told her boss, did she mention locker seventeen?"

"No."

"The Coast Guard must've told them about it."

"She didn't mention it."

"I suppose Horse must know it if they know it."

"You'd think so. Any sign of them or him up there?"

"Not that I've seen."

"Well, you've given me something to think about," Randa said. "You be careful up there."

"Will do," and Fog lowered the phone.

After an hour on the hard seat of the truck wondering what Rita was doing, he saw Oscar close up the store and drive off. In the next hour, a woman came to the gate, went inside and opened one of the lockers, put something in, took something out, drove outside the fence, got out of her car, closed the gate, and drove away. Two more people came, both with children in their cars. He saw a white SUV arrive just after dark. A large man got out of the driver's seat and bent over the combination lock, shining a flashlight on a piece of paper. Fog crossed the street to get a closer look. It was the man he had seen with the Arab at Clay's Marina. When the big man got back into the SUV and the interior lights came on, he saw Claude and Abu Mosul sitting in back and the Arab in the passenger seat. Feeling a warm surge of adrenalin, he watched the SUV pull up in front of 17. The big man removed three cardboard cartons from the locker and put them into the back of the SUV. Fog scooted back to his truck and called Randa.

"That could be our suspect—the man with the knife," she said. The phone went silent for several seconds. "Stay well back but follow them. Keep me informed where you are."

"Think we should notify the FBI? It could get bigger than we can handle."

"Let's just see where they go."

"If they've got the stuff, why you suppose they got Claude and Abu in the SUV?"

"I don't know, but be careful. Stay well back. We just want to know where they go. Keep me posted."

"Roger that."

The sheriff was leaning back in his squeaking chair listening to Randa. He yawned without apology and squeezed something out of his nose—made you proud to work for him. Until she had known this man, she had always thought Englishmen were more mannerly than Americans—one of her mother's observations.

"She got trapped on the wrong lane," Randa said. "By the time she crossed the median, they were gone."

"And you've reported none of this to the FBI," Chubleigh said.

"I'm just investigating a homicide," glancing for support from Buckles.

"We thought that'd be better handled by you," Buckles said. She knew he was laughing inside, though not a glimmer of amusement showed on his face.

"Well, I can't put that in my news release," the sheriff said. "You can leave Rudenski up there if you want, but be damn sure you keep Kaplan on the island."

"I don't think Raphael Cardozo has anything to do with what's going on," Randa said.

"Then you're more naïve than I thought. He's at the center of it. But the FBI knows that so he won't get away. You best stay here and finish up your report. I want to be on speed when I face those reporters. And remember," he said, glancing at

Buckles for emphasis, "it's only the homicides we're investigating."

"And you think Cardozo ordered the hit on Lee Fronzi?"

"Who the hell else would?" Chubleigh said, surprised she'd ask such a stupid question.

Earlier, Buckles had told her the sheriff had been strongly persuaded to keep the homicide investigation scrupulously separate from what the FBI was involved in, and he hadn't been told what that was.

"What he said to me was, 'Vigorously pursue the homicide investigation, but don't call those bastards in on it.' "

"The same as before," Randa had said.

"No. Before, he didn't give a damn if you stepped on their toes, now he wants to be sure you don't. He wants to explain what you're doing is within these new guidelines."

"That what the man in the limousine was all about?"

"He doesn't share those high-level secrets with me, but I'd guess so. Oh, and my friend in D.C.—remember you asked me to call him. He has nothing on the gun, but your other question. . . . He says Peenzo Industries does not sell surplus anything to anybody, for what that's worth."

"It could be huge," Randa said.

"Or it's not true. Every manufacturer has salvage, even if it's just scrap. They don't throw things away that have value."

"And they make things for the Defense Department, a lot of it classified."

"There you go," Buckles said. "Lots of reasons to lie."

"Why don't you run for sheriff next election?"

"Oh, I'm not smart enough for that job," he said, laughing.

In Cherokee City out in the parking lot, Randa called Kappy on her portable. He reported that Tyonek had left his apartment around four and was sitting in his car outside a small diner on

Cleveland Avenue.

"Just sitting there?"

"Like he's waiting for someone."

"Stay on him," she said. "Call me if he moves. If anyone asks, you're out on Boliva watching the Cardozo front gate."

"I am?"

"If anyone asks."

She had just started to leave the parking lot when Moira showed up.

"Glad I caught you," she said, a little breathless. Sometimes she came on playfully, and that's when Randa trusted her least. Not content to talk over a lowered window, Moira got out of her car and came around front of Randa's minivan and climbed inside.

"I'm running late," Randa said, not hiding her impatience. She didn't want to be seen talking with an FBI agent, especially not here in the headquarters' parking lot.

"You have any idea where the Indian is?"

"None at all. Maybe at his apartment."

"I went there."

"Well, wish I could help you, Moira. But I've got to get somewhere," clearly indicating that she wanted Moira out of her car. She had to believe that Moira knew about locker 17. She didn't mention it and if Tyonek wasn't told, what did that say? If Tyonek did know about it, why wasn't he up there?

"I heard there was someone down here from the Attorney General's office," she said.

Moira played dumb. "I don't know anything about that."

Like you don't know something's going down tonight. "I'd like to stay here and chat," Randa said, "but I really have to run."

When Moira didn't move, Randa reached across her legs and opened the passenger-side door. Moira got the message. She looked sadly at Randa, opened her mouth as though to say something, changed her mind and got out.

As Randa drove off, she looked for Moira in her rearview mirror but the brown sedan wasn't following her. Randa reached under her seat for the grip on her pistol. With a quickened heartbeat she headed toward the interstate. As she went up the ramp, she got a call from Fog.

"We're now going south on Seventy-five."

"Then they're not going to Marchland," Randa said. "Be careful."

Five minutes later Fog reported that the SUV had turned east onto a country road that would take them into the 'Glades. He gave her the mile marker. "And I'm back in our own county."

"Can you follow discreetly?"

"I can follow. But there's no way I can dim the headlights, and there's a lot of open country in there—swamps and snakes and every other goddamn thing."

"Just stay well back." She dropped the cell phone onto the passenger seat. She had never gone off the highway into that back country and had no idea what was in there except inland, off state road 571, there was a huge tract of privately owned undeveloped land.

Unless Claude and Abu were being held against their will—and she had no way of knowing that—she couldn't call for backup. She had no proof these people were doing anything wrong. Her suspicions aside, they could be dealing in surplus stuff bound for South Africa, as Abu claimed. Perfectly legal.

When she was crossing the big bridge outside of Cherokee City, she put in a call to Fog. After a delay, she got a woman's voice telling her the number she had reached was not in service. Maybe she had punched in the wrong numbers. She tried again and got the same voice and the same message.

She pressed down on the accelerator and sped north on the interstate, her heart pounding.

CHAPTER THIRTY-TWO

Fog remembered shutting off his headlights when the SUV rounded a curve in a tangle of underbrush. The lights in front of him had gone off and he had stepped out of his truck in total darkness. He remembered the soft earth under his feet, the swamp odors, the silence in the trees. But why were his arms cramped behind his back, his wrists tied? Why was he face down with prickles of grass and mud in his face?

He heard voices. A bright light shined on him, then went off. What the hell's going on?

Something scraped his shoulder. He felt tightening fingers gripping the back of his shirt and lifting him, dragging him, toes digging the ground, dropping him face down onto something flat and hard. He smelled dust and gasoline. He remembered the white SUV. He was in the SUV and there were people inside.

Through a swirling clot of pain, he felt hands bending his legs upward. Something came down on his legs, pushing him inboard, jamming his head into cardboard boxes. He cried out in anger. A voice hovered over him. He couldn't understand the words.

"Speak English, you fucking prick!" he yelled, his voice smothered in stale air, his mouth buried in filthy carpeting, a knot of pain throbbing at the back of his head.

He remembered following the white SUV. There were trees and a gravel road and a building. He remembered stopping behind some trees and getting out of his truck.

He cramped his hands upward to his right side. He felt the holster. His gun was gone.

Someone said, "He's a deputy sheriff. Are you crazy?"

"*Iskut!*" in a deep voice.

"What does that mean?"

"It means shut up." Abu Mosul's voice.

"But why are they bringing us here? And the deputy. This is stupid!"

Fog heard gravel crunching under the tires. For several minutes he heard water moving against the wheels. More gravel. Finally, the SUV stopped. The back doors were opened. His legs were lowered. He was pulled outside. Lights shined on him from windows in a small building.

"Free his ankles." It was the Arab.

Something tugged at his legs. His ankles were freed and he was lifted to his feet, the shift in position making his head ache.

"You should not have followed us, friend," the Arab said.

The big man was ripping duct tape off his knife, muttering something in anger apparently because the tape had fouled the blade. He slid the knife into a sheath at his side, then stepped behind Fog and pushed him, stumbling through an opened doorway into a low-ceilinged room where a woman in a dark dress with a scarf on her head stared at him, then looked hesitantly at the large man behind him. She was like the women he saw every night on news broadcasts of the war zone—an Arab woman.

She made guttural sounds he couldn't understand.

The Arab pointed with Fog's gun at a wooden chair. "Sit down," he said.

Fog studied the woman, the chair, the gun. He tugged at the bindings on his wrists. "Untie my hands," he said.

"I said sit down!"

"I'm a police officer! Untie my hands!"

The Arab dismissed that with disdain.

Abu and Claude had come into the room looking like children entering a slaughter house, timid school boys looking around, not familiar with the room—an ordinary small kitchen in a manufactured house.

"You know what you're in for, you goddamn fools?" Fog yelled at them. "These people are criminals! If they shoot me, they gotta shoot you!"

"No one's shooting anybody," the Arab said.

Fog was furious for having allowed himself to get sapped out there. And these two idiots cowering against the wall, he'd get no help from them. The guy in charge here, the Arab, was acting like he thought all of this was beneath his dignity. But he was capable of telling his goon to kill the three of them. Fog didn't question that.

"I said 'sit down'!" the Arab yelled, pressing the gun into Fog's chest, backing him up until his legs hit the chair.

As he dropped onto the hard seat, he yelled at Claude, "You think they're gonna let you go?"

"You're being absurd," the Arab said. "You followed us here. This is private property. What do you want?"

"Hammid, for godsakes, he's a deputy sheriff!" Claude said.

"I don't know that, and it doesn't explain why he's here. Do you have credentials?"

"Your name is Hammid?"

"Where are your papers?"

"In my truck."

Hammid said something to the big man who slid a flashlight into his hip pocket and went outside. He came back into the room carrying a stack of three long cartons. He set them on a table.

"Why have you brought us here?" Claude said. "You think we cheated you? Open the crates, you'll see everything's there." He was scared but pretending this was only an unnecessary inconvenience.

The little man, Abu, was pale with fear. A refugee from Iraq, he had to know the kind of trouble he was in.

They all watched the woman carry one of the cartons to a counter and, helped by the big man, lift out a wooden crate.

Hammid said something to the big man who again went outside.

"In the glove compartment!" Fog yelled to him.

While Hammid was prying the lid off the crate, Fog tried to get Claude's attention, but Claude was watching Hammid standing over the crate moving a pointing finger across whatever was inside. He stepped back and the woman lifted the other two crates out of the cartons. Hammid pried off the lids and checked the contents. He seemed satisfied. He wiped his hands down his legs as though to rid them of contaminants—a fastidious son of a bitch afraid to get his hands dirty.

He said something to the woman and watched her positioning the lids on the crates, pressing them into place. What was inside apparently was fragile.

Hammid rubbed his palms together as though warming them. He drew up a chair and confronted Fog, his face only inches away.

Fog smelled fish odors on his breath. The whites of his eyes were tinted gray. There were gray hairs in his mustache and beard, a small cut on his lower lip. But it was his eyes that interested Fog. They lacked soul. There was evil in them. They were heavy with hatred.

"You've got your goods," Fog said. "If, as this guy Abu told the FBI, those are legitimate packages going to South Africa, why the hell did you come after me? Holding me against my will is a felony. Assaulting me is a felony. These are serious crimes. Now why don't you get smart and free my hands before this goes any further."

"I have questions," Hammid said.

"Fuck your questions! I'm a deputy sheriff and you're in serious goddamn trouble. Now stop pointing my gun at me and untie my hands!"

Hammid sat back and regarded Fog with impatience. "If you are a police officer and you know what we're doing is legitimate, why were you following us?"

"Why don't you put the gun down? Take the bullets out if you know how. There's a little—"

The eyes sparkled with anger. "Answer my questions! Why were you following us? Is it standard practice for the police to check on every vehicle that goes down the highway? What is it you think you know?"

"Look. Just untie my hands. You've got the gun. What are you afraid of?"

"Nothing, I assure you. I'm afraid of nothing. I've committed no crime. You were following us on a private road in an ordinary unmarked vehicle. You didn't identify yourself as a policeman. We have a perfect right to defend ourselves."

"But no right to tie my hands and hold me."

"I know he's a deputy sheriff," Claude said. "I know him."

"Yes, so you say." Hammid pushed his chair back, stood up and held out his left hand, his right hand holding the gun at his side. Addressing Claude, he said, "I'll take the keys."

Claude looked puzzled. "I gave you the key. You left it there in the lock."

"Not that key. The keys to the safety deposit box."

"What are you talking about?"

Abu was cowering from all of this, looking nervously at the gun, then across the room at Fog who wanted to scream, *Grab the gun!* He jerked his head at the gun. *Do it! Do it before the goon comes back!*

Abu, white with fear, knowing better than Claude what Hammid intended to do, took a deep breath and lunged at the gun. The woman screamed a warning.

Abu gripped Hammid's wrist with both hands, clinging like a pit bull when Hammid tried to wrench his arm free. Fog leaned forward and dove across the room, his head and the back of the chair crashing into Hammid's chest. The gun went off. It fell to the floor. Fog drove Hammid against the wall. The woman scurried across the floor toward the gun. Abu stepped on her hand. He lifted the gun and stood back with shaking hands, pointing the gun at Hammid, who had fallen to the floor.

"Get a knife!" Fog yelled at Claude, who was backed against the wall, looking like he wanted to cry.

The woman had gone to the counter and was reaching into a drawer. Claude slapped her behind the head, reached across her shoulder and took a small kitchen knife from her hand. She scratched Claude's face. He batted her hand aside and grabbed cloth at her chest and threw her across the room. She tripped over Hammid and banged her head on the opened door. Fog was yelling. Abu was holding the gun on Hammid. The woman was screaming.

"Cut the tape, for chrissake!" Fog yelled. Claude was just standing there holding the knife, uncertain what to do.

"Free his hands!" Abu yelled at him.

Claude cut the tape. The chair clattered to the floor and Fog kicked it across the room. With tape sticking to his wrists he took the gun out of Abu's hands.

Abu pointed at a flash of light on the trees. "Fakhri," he said.

Fog stepped over Hammid and crouched in the opened doorway. He saw only the SUV and rectangles of light on the gravel. He moved back inside.

"Is he armed?"

"He has a knife."

"A gun?" He yanked Hammid to his feet and shoved him against a wall. The woman, like a frightened puppy, crawled over to him. "Does he have a gun?"

Hammid regarded Fog with contempt. The woman said nothing.

Abu piped up, "The man outside, Fakhri, he killed Mr. Fronzi. He's a wild man. I have nothing to do with any of this. I don't know what's going on. I thought we were dealing with—"

"Sit down," Fog said to Hammid. "You too," to the woman. In unison they slid to the floor.

He looked at Abu. "You sure which side you're on?"

"I'm not with them! I hate them!"

Fog handed him the gun. "Shoot this son of a bitch if he makes a move. And sit over there," pointing to the inside wall. "If that guy outside comes in, shoot him."

He switched on a hall light and went to the other end of the building, opened a window, and crawled outside. If all four people in that house were killed, he didn't give a shit. All he wanted was to find his way in the dark to his truck and his portable. A few feet of road behind the SUV were illuminated by light from the windows. For a while he was guided by reflections on the trees. Then he was in darkness, unable to find the road, groping his way like a blind man. He was lost. There was only darkness ahead of him. He dropped to his knees and crawled forward, crawled into a patch of palmetto. He pulled back and searched the ground for the kind of indentations the SUV might have made. It was useless. He felt only patches of grass and wet earth. He crouched there in the darkness, in the odors of the swamp, listening to strange noises coming from out in the trees. He turned and looked back at lights in the clearing. Cursing himself for getting into this mess, he realized it was foolish to stay out here. He'd have to go back.

CHAPTER THIRTY-THREE

As Randa drove north on the interstate, images and ideas she had wrestled with for days were forming a pattern.

If Peenzo Industries didn't sell Paris Courtland anything, what was stored in the locker? If Claude and Abu are in an SUV going into the woods with the two men Fog saw with Abu at Clay's Marina, what does it mean?

She raised her portable and called for backup, using the code for "No sirens, low lights, approach with caution."

If Claude was on Julia's boat when Lee was murdered, why did the murderer allow Claude to live? If he's not in league with the murderer, why didn't he go to the police?

She thought about his protestations of innocence.

He's not worried. By tomorrow morning he intends to be gone!

She turned into a road at the end of a barbed-wire fence, stopped and shut off her lights. She could see nothing ahead. She lowered her window and inhaled odors of the fields and listened to a roar of insect noises. She put on low beams and leaned into the steering wheel and drove cautiously down a rutted road toward a wall of pines and bone-white trunks of maleleuka trees. After twenty minutes in the woods, she saw Fog's truck on high ground under hanging branches of a large cyprus tree.

She stopped and shut off her lights, got a flashlight from the dash, her pistol from under her seat. Instead of pushing her car through underbrush, she locked it and waded through palmetto fronds and opened the door to the cab. Interior lights came on. No keys in the ignition. She closed the door and waited in darkness. Nothing came at her.

To avoid becoming a target, she used her flashlight only to provide glimpses of what was ahead, then walked in the dark listening to jungle sounds, smelling odors of the swamp. She waded on spongy earth through ankle-deep water almost a quarter mile before she came onto high ground. There were lights in the distance. She tucked the flashlight under her belt and had reached a clearing when she heard a woman's scream and the unmistakable sound of a gunshot. She dropped instinctively to a knee and turned to see whether she was being followed.

Where's the backup?

She ran in squishing shoes through heavy grass and dropped to her knees a hundred feet from a dark mass that shielded her from the house lights. It was the SUV. She heard something moving—noises on the gravel. She drifted back to the cover of the trees. Where was Fog? He could be hurt. She wanted to rush in with gun blazing, but her training made her wait. She had no idea what was in there. She knew only that someone in that room had a gun.

Where the hell is the backup?

Fog gripped the window frame of the back bedroom and pulled himself into the building. He moved cautiously down the hallway watching Abu and Claude in the far corner of the kitchen. Abu's hand was trembling, aiming the gun just to Fog's right inside the room where the crates were, where Hammid and the woman were. Anxiety melted off Abu's face when he saw Fog.

"Where's the big guy?" Fog yelled at him.

Abu waved the gun at the outside door. "Fakhri. His name is Fakhri. I think I hit him. I'm not sure. There's a gun."

Fog crossed the kitchen floor and snapped off the lights. "What kind of gun?"

"I don't know—a rifle, maybe shotgun. It was in the SUV."

"Give me mine," Fog said, crouching at the open door. "Come on, come on, for chrissakes, bring it over here."

"What about them? I can't see them."

Fog heard a footstep, then a knee clipped his shoulder. He grabbed legs and pushed whoever it was, probably Hammid, into the doorframe, gripped shoulders and drove a knee into the man's groin, knocked him down, stepped over him, and—*If that big bastard out there's got a shotgun and a flashlight, I'm fucking dead!*—scrambled on hands and knees to the back of the building—no gun, no flashlight, no cell phone.

Son of a bitch!

Randa was on her knees in tall grass trying to figure out what was happening—the scuffling sounds, a woman screaming in Arabic.

She was startled when lights suddenly came on inside the SUV. She watched a man lean in, then back out holding something. The lights went off. Randa moved closer. She was less than a hundred feet from the building when she heard a gunshot. A flashlight fell to the ground shining a circle of light on clapboards. She saw a blast of fire from what sounded like a shotgun. Loud yelling. Another blast. Flame streaking across the room.

She thumbed the switch on her flashlight. A man was backing out of the doorway. It wasn't Fog. She yelled "Police!"

The man turned, aimed a shotgun at her. She fired point blank at his chest. The shotgun clattered to the ground. She moved toward the man. He was on his knees, roaring in anger.

She walked around him, so intent upon him she did not see a man who suddenly lurched at her.

"I'm the police!" she yelled. A forehead hit her mouth, a body crowding into her, hands grabbing her waist.

"Get back!"

A hand struck her mouth. She pressed her pistol into the man's gut and squeezed the trigger. The man stiffened, emitted a loud sigh. She stepped back as the man collapsed, his hands sliding down her legs.

She swung the light around. The big man was staggering toward the back of the SUV. She searched for the shotgun, found it, and stepped on it.

Fog had retrieved the fallen flashlight and was shining it on his face. "Randa, it's me!"

"He's gone," he said, aiming the beam past her, past the SUV. He knelt over Hammid, felt for a pulse under the jaw.

"This one's done," he said.

Randa shined her light on the sightless face of the man she had just killed. She could feel muscles hardening in her face as she forced herself to look away, telling herself she was a trained police officer; it was a good shoot.

Fog had snapped the kitchen lights on. Abu was handing him a pistol, shaking with excitement. "I shot him! I shot Fakhri! I'm not one of them! I hate them!"

Randa was looking at the woman lying across the boxes. Half her head was gone. Blood over everything.

Claude was sitting against the refrigerator, staring down at bloody hands gripping his belly. He was crying. He looked piteously at Randa. His shoulders sagged, his hands went limp, his eyes lost focus. He slumped forward and she leaned down and felt for the neck artery. No pulse. Her fingers were on a corpse.

Fog had gone outside and Abu was whimpering about not knowing what was in the boxes. "I don't know what those things are." he said. "They forced me to come here. They were going to kill me!"

"Stay here," she told him and went outside. She ran down the gravel toward the moving beam of Fog's flashlight. He was at the edge of the trees.

"He's gotta be down here somewhere," he said.

"Claude and the woman are dead. That man outside the doorway is dead."

"Yeah, and maybe this bastard is dead. But I'm not walking down that road to find out."

"Backup's coming in. They'll have lights."

"What's that stuff in those boxes?" Fog asked.

"Have no idea. But Abu's back there crying his ass off about how innocent he is, says he never saw that stuff before."

"Let's go back and talk to him."

As they turned, the beam of his flashlight happened upon a dark mound in the grass twenty feet from them. It was Fakhri. Fog kneeled over him, felt for a pulse.

"He's gone," he said. "Abu says he's the one knifed Lee." He was pulling at the jacket. "He's got a knife."

"Don't touch it," Randa said. "There may be usable evidence on it."

She gazed at the man with the same lack of feeling she had had when looking at Claude. She felt no remorse, no hatred, no sense of closure. She felt nothing.

As she stood with Fog watching headlights coming at them from the road in the woods, she wondered what was wrong with her. Why don't I feel bad? Why don't I feel anything?

"There's nothing wrong with you," Gloria had told her a hundred times. "The feelings are there, you just don't want to deal with them. Don't worry about it. You're normal."

"Sometimes I think I'm crazy."

"Join the club."

Later in an interrogation room at headquarters, Randa leaned over Abu Mosul.

"Don't lie to me!"

Fog was sitting next to her, Abu across from them, little blisters of sweat on his face.

"I'm not lying!" he said. "She told me they were surveillance devices. I never saw them. I swear to God. She said she bought them. I'm telling the truth. I would never sell weapons to terrorists. I want to stay in this country. I love this country. Why would I jeopardize—"

"Where did she go?"

"I don't know! It was Claude. He dealt with her."

"She came directly to your motel room. Claude was not with her."

"Only that one time, I swear. She didn't want me near her. I dealt with Claude! He lied to me. He said the buyers were from South Africa. They said it. Hammid. He said it!"

"You were with Hammid and his man when he removed those boxes from a locker in Mangrove Harbor. You went to that place in the woods. You say you weren't paid. We found no money or anything else on Claude. And no money in that SUV or on the person of Hammid or his man. I can't believe you released those boxes without having been paid."

"I have received no money. Claude was supposed to pay me. Maybe his woman. Maybe she has the money."

"You're lying," she said. "You were with Claude from early afternoon. He was never out of your sight, you said."

He gave her a cautious look. "Yes."

"You would know if he had been paid. Is there a third party

involved, someone holding the money until both sides are satisfied?"

"I don't know! I swear to God! Claude and the woman were handling that. She didn't trust me with any of that information."

"Bullshit," Fog said. Throughout the questioning he had watched the little man with growing disgust. He was exhausted. Like Randa he wanted to go home. She imagined he would like right now to haul out his cannon and blast this man out of his chair.

They couldn't hold him. She'd been informed that the FBI would pick him up in the morning. They had a court order allowing them to hold him as a material witness. Once he was in their lockup she wouldn't have access to him. She went to the door and asked a deputy to bring him down to a holding cell.

"Why waste our energy?" she said to Fog. "He isn't going to tell us anything."

Walking out to their cars, Fog asked, "Where do you suppose the money is?"

"I have no idea, but I'm pretty sure Abu isn't the only one who hasn't been paid."

He didn't seem to know what she meant, but he was tired. He let it go.

A half hour later, as she pulled up next to the lemon tree outside her apartment, she got a call from Bea Kim.

"No sign of Paris Courtland in the beach house," Bea said. "Nothing of interest here except she left the TV on."

"She probably found out what had happened and took off. I understand it was on local TV, even on CNN."

"Want to put out an alert?"

"Go home, Bea. I don't think she killed anybody. Let the FBI worry about her."

"Oh, and another thing. That guy who picked Barstow's

watch. He's locked up for petty theft."

"Good." Right now all she wanted was to shower and shut off the lights and climb into bed.

CHAPTER THIRTY-FOUR

Randa was on the concrete ramp behind the headquarters building with the sheriff, Buckles, and two deputies. Although Chubleigh knew she hadn't gone to bed until early that morning, she suspected his waiting until afternoon to call her had less to do with courtesy than with an unwillingness to have her around when the FBI came to fetch Abu.

"This is wrong," she said. "I need to talk to him."

The sheriff obviously didn't give a damn what she needed. He hadn't even looked at her except once, with disapproval, when she had first climbed out of her minivan.

"You know he's going to lie," she said.

Buckles and the two deputies were watching the SUV making a turn in the yard. Abu, visibly unhappy, was looking at them from inside the cage behind the driver.

"He knows who committed those murders," she said.

Buckles put a restraining hand on her arm, telling her with a glance to stop talking.

"They'll bury him," she said. "I'll never get a chance . . ."

Chubleigh turned his back on her and walked down the ramp.

Explaining the sheriff's behavior, Buckles said, "He got a call from Washington raising hell because we interfered with their operation. I don't know what he expected—a pat on the back or a big job up there. Who knows? But they kicked his ass."

"And he blames me? We prevented those people from getting that spy equipment. That ought to—"

"Yeah, but they wanted Hammid—wanted him alive. He could give them that whole operation in Marchland."

"It was him or me," she said. "I had no choice."

"I know. It was a good shoot. And the sheriff knows that. Right now he's not thinking about you. Just make sure in your narrative you emphasize it was the murder suspect, Fakhri, Fog was chasing, not Hammid."

"I can't stay out of this."

"Are you listening to me?"

"I'm listening, but I can't stay out of this."

"You can and you will. Now be reasonable." They entered the building in silence. Upstairs, approaching his office, Buckles said, "We had to send the knife north but Al found blood on the handle and Fakhri's fingerprints."

"He got them off the corpse out in that field?"

"I guess," Buckles said. "And he says the blood on the knife is the same type as Lee Fronzi's. That won't nail it down, but it helps your argument." He opened the door, waited for her to go in ahead of him. "In your report stay strictly with the homicide part of it. Don't say anything that smells of 'national security.' You've got three days coming. Go fishing. Take a trip. You okay with the shooting?"

"I'm fine."

"Want to talk to Dr. Perkins?"

"He's an idiot. No, I'm fine."

"Look, you did a good job. It was their choice to keep us in the dark. Chubleigh knows that. Right now he's not thinking about you. He's trying to figure out how to handle the media. One way or another he'll come out of this looking good for the locals, and it's the locals who keep him in office. He might even say he personally ordered Fog to follow the SUV—like he said when you sent Skip Morrow to Georgia."

"And it could backfire."

Buckles laughed. "Yeah. That's true."

Tyonek was sitting next to Moira in front of Sparzo's desk.

"I let him think I bought that bullshit," Tyonek said, tapping the prosthesis on his knee, glancing at Moira to see how she was taking this. "I didn't know what he was trying to sell to those people. I knew it wasn't what he said. The people at Peenzo Industries told me that Wang dropped his experiments with those micro air drones, but I knew he had a shop where he lived. I couldn't find out what he did there. She beat me to it."

"Barstow knew?"

"I'm sure he did. That's why he was tracking Abu. I was hoping to work with him. I was sorry as hell he got shot."

"You don't think Hammid had him killed?"

"Not the way it was done. His guy would've used a knife like on Fronzi."

"You say Sorel got the knife?"

"That's what I was told."

"Well, at least we got those MIs. And we've got Abu," Sparzo said.

"He told you anything?"

"The same bullshit about South Africa is all."

"Next thing he'll say is I was in on it with him. What a loser."

"You did a good job, Tyonek, but I wish you had confided in us a little more."

"I was told not to," Tyonek said. "Well, not directly, but . . ."

"With the big shakeup that's going on in D.C. All that'll change. We'll all be under the same roof."

"I won't see it," Tyonek said. "But it would've made my job easier if I'd been able to consult with you." He gave Moira a quick smile. She didn't trust him, probably didn't like him, but what the hell did he care?

"Well," Sparzo said, pushing his chair back, "we didn't get

everything we wanted, but we made a big score. Strange we haven't found any money. It has to be out there somewhere."

"I agree," Tyonek said. "It's the part they were very secretive about. Abu said Claude Lazard was handling that end of it."

In the few hours since he had learned about what Sparzo called "the massacre in the woods," he had taught himself to accept that he would never get his hands on the diamonds. Only Claude Lazard could have retrieved them from the vault without a court order. And he sure as hell couldn't make a claim on them then. Now, he'd have to pretend surprise when they were discovered.

In a way, he felt relief. Getting the diamonds was crazy. He'd've spent the rest of his life scared they'd catch up with him. This way he'd take his pension and maybe go out west and live on a reservation, get back to his roots, maybe take a job at one of the casinos, maybe find himself an Indian girl. Who knows?

Was he worried about Abu? Not a bit. Abu had that Arab mentality: he wasn't going to confess to anything. He had a story and would stick to it. How he'd get anyone to believe he thought Hammid represented buyers in South Africa, Tyonek had no idea, but he sure as hell wouldn't tell anyone he knew he was selling those things to terrorists, and he knows he'd get nowhere saying he had partnered up with an FBI agent. The two excuses were incompatible. Why would he partner up with a cop if his deal was legit?

"You have any idea where the money is?" Sparzo asked, affecting a guilelessness that slid into Tyonek's defenses like a burning blade.

The bastard suspects me!

But he was prepared. Yesterday when he was staking out the bank in Seacrest he thought he had seen a brown car at the curb down the street with someone at the wheel. He had thought at the time it might be Moira. It probably was, and she had obviously reported it to this prick.

"Of course, like I said, I knew there'd be money floating around here somewhere. And I knew Lazard had opened an account at that bank here in Seacrest. In fact, I was staking out that bank just yesterday." He was tempted to give Moira a gloating smile but thought better of it.

"Was it a joint account?"

"I don't know. I just saw him sitting with a woman at a desk in the lobby. You could tell what was happening. I didn't talk to anyone."

Now he glanced at Moira, matter-of-factly, seeking agreement that he had handled things sensibly. He couldn't tell what she was thinking. She didn't look at him.

"I guess we can find out," Sparzo said.

"Think she got the money?"

"Who knows? And who knows where she is?"

"Long gone," Moira said. "I'd be on a plane to Brazil or someplace else the U.S. can't extradite me from."

"Too bad Lazard got killed. He'd know."

"You're right," Tyonek said. "A shame."

At nine o'clock the following morning Randa was drinking from a paper cup at the water cooler down the hall from Chubleigh's office. She had been at headquarters for an hour finishing up the report Mary had brought to the sheriff.

"He's still pissed off," Buckles was saying, "but if you can convince him it was necessary to your investigation, he'll at least listen. I don't know who's been talking to him or what he's been told, but he'd love to beat them to the draw."

She laughed. "You've been watching too many cowboy movies," and stood back while he opened Chubleigh's office door.

The man with the puffy nose was up there on his perch reading, probably Randa's report. When he finally looked up, he said, "Goddammit! I told you to bring Rudenski home! You disobeyed a direct order!" giving vent to anger left over from yesterday.

Dismayed by the quickening of her heartbeat—*He's only a man, for godsakes, Randa!*—she forced herself to say nothing until she was seated and had folded her hands in her lap, affecting a sedateness she had learned from her mother, who used to say, "Show them your dignity. Let them know you're a lady. It takes the starch out of them."

"The man who murdered Lee Fronzi was in that white SUV," she said. "I told Agent Rudenski to follow it."

"Fakhri," he said, looking at something on his desk. "You know it was him?"

"We have the knife. There's blood on the handle. We have his prints on the sink in the boat."

"But you didn't know that when Rudenski chased him."

"I had good reason," she said.

All of this was in her report but, even if he'd read it, he'd want to hear it from her face.

"But he's dead and the man with him is dead, and so is the only witness." He held up the report. "And says here *you only think* he was a witness."

"It's more than that, Sheriff. We have prints in blood on that boat, Lazard's prints. A presumptive test makes it Lee Fronzi's blood. When confirmed, that makes Claude Lazard a witness."

"But he's dead and of no goddamned use to us."

"If you give me a free hand, Sheriff, I'll deliver the man who killed Woodrow Barstow and Bill White."

"Cardozo? You'll give me Cardozo?"

"He didn't do it, Sheriff. He didn't have it done. It has nothing to do with him."

"Then you're not as goddammed smart as people say you are."

She glanced at Buckles, hoping he'd add something. And, to her surprise, he said, "This Abu Mosul told the FBI he was trying to work out a deal with Cardozo, but we think he was lying. He's been seen with those people from Marchland, the ones who were eliminated the other night. He's been working with the woman in that report," pointing at what Chubleigh was holding. "And the only link we can find to Cardozo is Claude Lazard. Maybe he tried to get help from Cardozo, but we believe Cardozo rejected him."

"He was using Cardozo's boat. What kind of rejection is that?"

"Not with permission."

"You don't know that. All you have is his word, and he's a goddamned liar."

"If Cardozo had had anything to do with Lee Fronzi's murder," Randa said, "or with the MI transaction, he wouldn't have let us search that boat for evidence."

Chubleigh gave that some thought, not convinced but willing to hear more.

"So who is it you think killed Woodrow Barstow?" he asked.

"The same one who killed Bill White."

"And who's that?"

"Until I—"

"Goddammit, you don't have anybody. Just more of your bullshit!"

She wouldn't give him a name because she didn't trust him to keep it out of circulation. She didn't know what kind of deal he had made with the man in the limousine.

"All three homicides have one thing in common," she said. "They were all against men who were investigating the activities of Claude Lazard and Paris Courtland."

"That doesn't tell me anything."

"I can't give you a name, Sheriff. But I know I can put one on your desk if you'll give me a free hand."

He looked at Buckles, who was looking at something on his thumb. "I'll tell you this, young lady, if you get this office into trouble, you might as well hand me your gun and your badge. You have been insubordinate. You disobeyed a direct order." He let that sink in. "Now, get the hell out of here," waving her out of his office.

"He's not angry at you," Buckles said inside his own office with the door closed. "He's angry because you've made him question his own judgment."

"About Cardozo?"

"Among other things."

"I wonder what kind of reward he was promised?"

"We'll never know, that's for damn sure. He'll never say it, but he hopes you'll deliver something he can throw back at them. I don't want to be dramatic, Randa, but what you do now could save you or sink you. If it comes down to it, he'll blame you for the whole disaster."

"Thanks. That's very comforting."

CHAPTER THIRTY-FIVE

Late the following morning as she stood over her kitchen stove scrambling yolkless eggs in the skillet her mother had brought to America from Cairo, Randa was haunted by a question she had wrestled with throughout the night.

How did Tyonek know how "fast" she had arrived at the motel where Bill White was shot? How did he know when she got there? How did he know when Bill was shot?

She hadn't seen him at the crime scene. Had he talked with Abu Mosul?

He had used Abu as bait to bring Barstow to Cherokee City. Then Barstow was killed. Bill White went to the Beach Motel to check on Abu, and Bill White was killed. Was it by someone who knew I had come to the scene but who wasn't there when I got there?

She sat for a long time at her kitchen table, staring across the room through the distant window at her minivan parked out near the lemon tree, out where Lee used to park his convertible.

She cleared the table and got her cell phone from the bedroom and called Fog.

"Check out a metal locator from property and a couple of shovels and ask Bea to join us in the parking lot of the Beach Motel. And pry Kappy out of his girlfriend's bed and get him out there."

Within a half hour Randa was in broken fronds of palmetto and

289

crumpled underbrush, inhaling odors of decaying vegetation, standing a few feet from where she had seen Bill propped against the cypress tree bleeding to death.

"I came in from down there," she said, pointing past trees to the path where she had cut her arm. "So, if he saw me or heard me coming, he could have escaped that way," pointing into the woods toward the canal.

"This still designated a crime scene?" Bea asked.

"No," Randa said. "And we're not violating anyone's Fourth Amendment rights."

"We're outside the curtilage of the dwelling," Kappy told her, showing off his law school background.

"Can't tell whether these are footprints or hoof prints—no accurate definition," Fog said. "How many nights of rain we had?"

"All we need is one clear print," Randa said.

"What size are the shoes?" Fog asked, standing behind her examining something on the detection head of the locator.

"I don't know," Randa said. "Cowboy boots, those long skinny pointed toes."

"Rodeo heels? That'd help."

"The two-inch variety," Bea said. "High heels so he'd look taller."

"So let's go. Spread out," Randa said.

They moved slowly through the woods, studying the ground, heads lowered, hands behind their backs. Fog was waving the metal detector over every space where someone might have dug a hole. He found nails and bottle caps and a crushed beer can but nothing useful. Kappy found a little dip in the sand he thought might be hiding something. Fog hovered the detecting coil over it. Nothing registered. Bea plunged the blade of her shovel into it and dug up a piece of wood—part of a baseball bat.

They prowled along the canal for more than an hour before Randa found a clear print under a fallen palm frond near a parking lot. The frond had apparently protected it from the rain.

"Here!" she yelled, crouching over it, pointing. "And the rodeo heel," she said, grinning at Fog, elated. "Son of a bitch!"

"I'll get forensics," Fog said. He handed Kappy the locator and sprinted off toward the motel.

They had to wait an hour before Al Martinez arrived in the crime-scene van. He knew the area and came directly to the lot down a narrow gravel road.

"That's probably how Horse came in," Randa said. "Parked his car right out there," pointing.

"How soon can you get me a cast?" she asked Al, who was squatting over the footprint, photographing it.

"When do you need it?"

"Before Buckles goes home."

He had it for her by mid-afternoon, with photographs and a sketch of the area. She brought it all into Buckles's office. "I've posted Bea Kim outside Tyonek's apartment. She said the boots are outside his kitchen door where he always leaves them."

"In the open?"

"In a small vestibule."

She handed Buckles the affidavit she had drawn up.

"Not much to go on, Randa."

"If those boots are a match—"

"Yeah, I know. But the footprint was more than a quarter of a mile from the crime scene. Even if he left it—"

"It proves he was there."

"It proves he was a quarter of a mile from the crime scene. And you don't know when. Maybe he was just down there fishing."

"Come on," she said.

"There's no way you can get approval to look for guns. And if you want the shoes, add 'on his person' to the location. He could be wearing them. This will alert him, you know. If he's still got those guns, he'll get rid of them."

"But I don't have enough to get inside his apartment."

He agreed. Later, when she brought the amended version to him, he said, "Mary's been trying to reach Derek. I really ought to have his okay, but she thinks he's in a chopper somewhere over the 'Glades. Can't reach him. There's going to be hell to pay over this. You know that."

She didn't say anything.

He reluctantly handed the paper back to her. "Okay, go ahead. I want that little bastard as much as you do, but—"

"I don't have to say I brought it to you."

He gave her a reflective look. "Get the hell out of here."

The sun was glowing red through distant island palm trees when she stood over the patio table at the waterfront restaurant and watched Judge Kaplan sign the search warrant.

"This the FBI agent?"

"Yes, sir."

He laughed and handed it to her. "Have fun."

She found Tyonek leaning on the roof of Bea's pickup truck. He was wearing the boots. Moira Pelletier was a few feet away sitting at the wheel of her brown Camry.

"And now you're here," Tyonek said as Randa approached him.

She handed him the warrant. He read it, read it a second time. "My boots? What the hell's this about?"

"Please take them off and hand them to me," Randa said.

"My boots," he said, looking down at them. "You want my boots. Why?"

"I'm not here to argue. Hand them to me."

A bitter hatred burned in his eyes. She stepped back, half expecting him to lunge at her. In that instant she knew this man was capable of murder. It was right there in his face—cold, brutal hatred.

She waited.

"What the hell have my boots got to do with anything?"

He glanced at Moira, watched her get out of her car.

"I told you these fucking locals . . ." He turned back to Randa. "What the hell's the matter with you people?"

"Just give me the boots," Randa said.

"Maybe it's my other pair you want."

"It's these—tooled-leather pointed toes and rodeo heels that match the print I found near a crime scene."

"What crime scene? What are you talking about?"

"I don't have to explain anything, Mr. Horse. Just give me the boots."

"You want my boots? Here." He tugged them off and stood on the bare ground in gray socks, a much shorter man. He threw them at her. One went past her. One bounced off her leg. She picked them up.

"What do you think you can prove?" he yelled as she walked away. "I go to a lot of crime scenes. It's my job, you fucking idiot!"

At nine the following morning she was in Buckles's office.

"Mary said the FBI contacted Derek. She wouldn't say what transpired, but he wasn't 'pleased,' to use her word."

"He's gone for the day?"

"He's gone. I don't know for how long. But he's with them somewhere. Don't worry about it." He smiled. "So where are the boots?"

"They went by courier to the Marchland lab," she said.

"And they match that print?"

"No question."

"Does Al think there's blood on them?"

"He's leaving that to serology up there. He didn't want to disturb anything. But they made that print in the dirt, no question. Tyonek was there, and he wasn't fishing."

"You didn't find a gun."

"All we found was that one print."

He leaned back and gave her a look she didn't like.

"What?"

"They're shutting you down. They've put Tyonek off limits. The whole thing is now in their hands."

"And the sheriff won't do anything about it?"

"His hands are tied. Tyonek and that whole thing are off limits."

"They can't do that! We've got two homicides to solve!"

"You better pray there's blood on those boots."

Around noon a few days later, Buckles found her on a bench in the shade of the headquarters building watching an egret stepping with majestic patience through tall reeds at the edge of a retention pond searching for food. She had gone out there to get away from her desk. She had been working on backlog. She had a headache.

"What's he expect from me?" Randa said. "They cut off all my leads. Even if they find Paris Courtland, they won't let me talk to her."

"He's just frustrated," Buckles said.

"He walked right by me like I'm not there."

"Count your blessings."

"What was I supposed to do? I had to send Fog in there."

"I'm sure he knows that, but he can't stand being ignored. They've tied his hands. All those people down here—the FBI, NCIS, Homeland Security. They're ignoring him."

"And giving Tyonek Horse credit for breaking up a terrorist cell."

"And he's blaming you for killing Ramzi and the goon."

"And I can't prove he's a liar."

"Step away from it."

"He killed Woodrow Barstow and Bill White! I know he did!"

"And I trust your instincts. But they're not worth a damn right now. Don't give yourself ulcers over this. You did your job. They have their reasons for locking you out of it. The country's at war, Randa. Those guys take precedence. Nothing you can do."

For the next ten days she buried herself in backlog. The story had gone off the front page of the local paper and was no longer mentioned on TV. The Marchland operation had been closed down. Moira stopped by to tell her Tyonek was going out west somewhere and wanted his boots. She also said he had received a commendation for his fine work in protecting our nation from the terrorists.

She was at her desk when Al Martinez called. He told her the report had come in from Marchland. "Negative for blood," he said. "There was no blood on the boots."

"Shit!" She slammed down the receiver and felt a stab of pain in the back of her head. She glowered at Fog who was sitting beside her.

"Bad news?"

She was too disappointed to respond. She got up to go to the john when the phone rang again.

"You answer it," she told Fog.

He picked up the receiver, listening for a second, then handed it to her.

"It's for you."

She put the receiver to her ear. "Yes . . . ?"

"What'd you cut me off for? There's more," Al said. "They didn't find blood, but they found DNA in deposits of urine in the welt on the right boot."

Adrenaline surged into her heart. "Whose DNA?"

"Woody Barstow's."

That very afternoon, the part-time waitress at the Brig identified Tyonek from a set of pictures as the man she had seen sitting with Barstow the night he was murdered. The feds caught up with him getting off a train near an Indian reservation in northern Montana.

At a press conference the next day, Chubleigh gave credit for the capture of Tyonek to the task force he had appointed. He didn't mention Randa by name.

ABOUT THE AUTHOR

Jim Ingraham is a World War II combat marine veteran and a graduate of New York University. He taught history at Bryant University in Rhode Island for thirty-five years. On the Portland waterfront in Maine, as a boy, Jim delivered newspapers where his famous character, private investigator Duff Kerrigan, lives and works. Upon retirement from Bryant Jim moved with his wife and two children to Florida where he writes everyday and loafs on the beach.